PURSUIT OF
HAPPINESS

What Reviewers Say About Carsen Taite's Work

Outside the Law

"[A] fabulous closing to the Lone Star Law Series. …Tanner and Sydney's journey back to each other is sweet, sexy and sure to keep you entertained."—*The Romantic Reader Blog*

A More Perfect Union

"[*A More Perfect Union*] is a fabulously written tightly woven political/military intrigue with a large helping of romance. I enjoyed every minute and was on the edge of my seat the whole time. This one is a great read! Carsen Taite never disappoints!"—*The Romantic Reader Blog*

Sidebar

"As always a well written novel from Carsen Taite. The two main characters are well developed, likeable, and have sizzling chemistry."—Melina Bickard, Librarian, Waterloo Library (UK)

"Sidebar is a love story with a refreshing twist. It's a mystery and a bit of a thriller, with an ethical dilemma and some subterfuge thrown in for good measure. The combination gives us a fast-paced read, which includes courtroom and personal drama, an appealing love story, and a more than satisfying ending."—*Lambda Literary Review*

Without Justice

"This is a great read, fast paced, interesting and takes a slightly different tack from the normal crime/courtroom drama. …I really enjoyed immersing myself in this rapid fire adventure. Suspend your disbelief, take the plunge, it's definitely worth the effort."—Velvet Lounger, *Lesbian Reading Room*

"Another pretty awesome lesbian mystery thriller by Carsen Taite."
—Danielle Kimerer, Librarian, Nevins Memorial Library (MA)

Reasonable Doubt

"Another Carsen Taite novel that kept me on the edge of my seat. …[A]n interesting plot with lots of mystery and a bit of thriller as well. The characters were great."—Danielle Kimerer, Librarian, Reading Public Library

"Sarah and Ellery are very likeable. Sarah's conflict between job and happiness is well portrayed. I felt so sorry for Ellery's total upheaval of her life. …I loved the chase to find the truth while they tried to keep their growing feelings for each other at bay. When they couldn't, the tale was even better."—*Prism Book Alliance*

"The story was a great ride! Mixing both dramatic moments with fast-paced action, along with heartfelt and gentle occurrences. …Carsen Taite brought all of her own history as a criminal defense lawyer to the forefront of this novel in order to help tell the story. …Bravo to the author! A wonderful story all around. I will be adding Carsen Taite to my list of authors to watch for when new novels are released." —*FarNerdy Book Blog*

"The two main characters are well written and I was into them from the first minute they appeared. It's a modern thriller which takes place in the world right now."—*Lesfic Tumblr*

"Nothing is what it seems. Carsen Taite did a great job! The two main characters are well written and I was into them from the first minute they appeared. It's a modern thriller which takes place in the world right now."—*Lesfic Tumblr*

Lay Down the Law

"Recognized for the pithy realism of her characters and settings drawn from a Texas legal milieu, Taite pays homage to the prime-time soap opera *Dallas* in pairing a cartel-busting U.S. attorney, Peyton Davis, with a charity-minded oil heiress, Lily Gantry."—*Publishers Weekly*

"This book is AMAZING!!! The setting, the scenery, the people, the plot, wow. ...I loved Peyton's tough-on-the-outside, crime fighting, intensely protective of those who are hers, badass self."—*Prism Book Alliance*

"I've enjoyed all of Carsen Taite's previous novels and this one was no different. The main characters were well-developed and intriguing, the supporting characters came across as very 'real' and the storyline was really gripping. The twists and turns had me so hooked I finished the book in one sitting."—Melina Bickard, Librarian, Waterloo Library (London)

"In typical suspense fashion, twists and turns abound as the two women collide within each other's spheres, eventually leading to the inevitable happy ending. ...This novel is recommended for general LGBT and mystery collections."—*GLBT Reviews: The ALA's Gay Lesbian Bisexual Transgender Round Table*

"Suspenseful, intriguingly tense, and with a great developing love story, this book is delightfully solid on all fronts."—*Rainbow Book Reviews*

Courtship

"[T]his is a classic page turner. ...The political drama is just top-notch. The emotional and sexual tensions are intertwined with great timing and flair."—*Rainbow Book Reviews*

"Taite (*Switchblade*) keeps the stakes high as two beautiful and brilliant women fueled by professional ambitions face daunting emotional choices. ...As backroom politics, secrets, betrayals, and threats race to be resolved without political damage to the president, the cat-and-mouse relationship game between Addison and Julia has the reader rooting for them. Taite prolongs the fever-pitch tension to the final pages. This pleasant read with intelligent heroines, snappy dialogue, and political suspense will satisfy Taite's devoted fans and new readers alike."—*Publishers Weekly*

Rush

"A simply beautiful interplay of police procedural magic, murder, FBI presence, misguided protective cover-ups, and a superheated love affair…a Gold Star from me and major encouragement for all readers to dive right in and consume this story with gusto!"—*Rainbow Book Reviews*

Battle Axe

"This second book is satisfying, substantial, and slick. Plus, it has heart and love coupled with Luca's array of weapons and a bad-ass verbal repertoire. …I cannot imagine anyone not having a great time riding shotgun through all of Luca's escapades. I recommend hopping on Luca's band wagon and having a blast."—*Rainbow Book Reviews*

Beyond Innocence

"Taite keeps you guessing with delicious delay until the very last minute. …Taite's time in the courtroom lends *Beyond Innocence*, a terrific verisimilitude someone not in the profession couldn't impart. And damned if she doesn't make practicing law interesting."—*Out in Print*

"As you would expect, sparks and legal writs fly. What I liked about this book were the shades of grey (no, not the smutty Shades of Grey)—both in the relationship as well as the cases."—*C-spot Reviews*

Slingshot

"The mean streets of lesbian literature finally have the hard boiled bounty hunter they deserve. It's a slingshot of a ride, bad guys and hot women rolled into one page turning package. I'm looking forward to Luca Bennett's next adventure."—J. M. Redmann, author of the Micky Knight mystery series

The Best Defense

"Real Life defense attorney Carsen Taite polishes her fifth work of lesbian fiction, *The Best Defense,* with the realism she daily encounters in the office and in the courts. And that polish is something that makes *The Best Defense* shine as an excellent read."—*Out & About Newspaper*

Nothing but the Truth

Author Taite is really a Dallas defense attorney herself, and it's obvious her viewpoint adds considerable realism to her story, making it especially riveting as a mystery. I give it four stars out of five." —Bob Lind, *Echo Magazine*

"As a criminal defense attorney in Dallas, Texas, Carsen Taite knows her way around the court house. ...*Nothing But the Truth* is an enjoyable mystery with some hot romance thrown in."—*Just About Write*

"Taite has written an excellent courtroom drama with two interesting women leading the cast of characters. Taite herself is a practicing defense attorney, and her courtroom scenes are clearly based on real knowledge. This should be another winner for Taite."—*Lambda Literary*

Do Not Disturb

"Taite's tale of sexual tension is entertaining in itself, but a number of secondary characters...add substantial color to romantic inevitability"—Richard Labonte, *Book Marks*

It Should be a Crime—Lammy Finalist

"Taite also practices criminal law and she weaves her insider knowledge of the criminal justice system into the love story seamlessly and with excellent timing."—*Curve Magazine*

"This [*It Should be a Crime*] is just Taite's second novel…, but it's as if she has bookshelves full of bestsellers under her belt. In fact, she manages to make the courtroom more exciting than Judge Judy bursting into flames while delivering a verdict. Like this book, that's something we'd pay to see."—*Gay List Daily*

"Taite, a criminal defense attorney herself, has given her readers a behind the scenes look at what goes on during the days before a trial. Her descriptions of lawyer/client talks, investigations, police procedures, etc. are fascinating. Taite keeps the action moving, her characters clear, and never allows her story to get bogged down in paperwork. It Should Be a Crime has a fast-moving plot and some extraordinarily hot sex."—*Just About Write*

Visit us at www.boldstrokesbooks.com

By the Author

Truelesbianlove.com
It Should be a Crime
Do Not Disturb
Nothing but the Truth
The Best Defense
Beyond Innocence
Rush
Courtship
Reasonable Doubt
Without Justice
Sidebar
A More Perfect Union
Love's Verdict
Pursuit of Happiness

The Luca Bennett Mystery Series:
Slingshot
Battle Axe
Switchblade
Bow and Arrow (novella in Girls with Guns)

Lone Star Law Series:
Lay Down the Law
Above the Law
Letter of the Law
Outside the Law

PURSUIT OF HAPPINESS

by

Carsen Taite

2018

PURSUIT OF HAPPINESS

ISBN 13: 978-1-63555-044-3

This Trade Paperback Original Is Published By
Bold Strokes Books, Inc.
P.O. Box 249
Valley Falls, NY 12185

First Edition: December 2018

CREDITS
Editor: Cindy Cresap
Production Design: Susan Ramundo
Cover Design By Jeanine Henning

Acknowledgments

I own the DVDs for all seven seasons of *West Wing* and have watched the entire series numerous times. If I happen to be flipping through channels and see the movie *The American President* on TV, I stop and watch it whether there's an hour left or only five minutes. Every. Single. Time. The reason for my obsession with these shows? Because they combine two of my favorite things: politics and happy endings. Give me a political-themed story with a happily ever after and you've made my day. Lately, we could all use a big helping of hope with our daily dose of politics, and that is what has inspired me to continue this series of romantic political-themed stories starring principled and idealistic characters that began with *Courtship* and *A More Perfect Union*. I hope you will find both an escape from today's headlines and hope for the future in the pages of this book.

Thanks to Sandy and Rad, and everyone else who works for Bold Strokes Books for all your support for my writing career. Thanks to Jeanine Henning for a terrific cover. A big shout out to my editor, Cindy Cresap, for her guidance on this, our twentieth book together—I can't imagine doing this with anyone else.

Ruth and Paula, thanks for being great pals, and always being willing to kick around legal strategy and plot points. Georgia, thanks for helping me stay on track with our daily word count check-ins.

To my wife, Lainey—thanks for all the things you do and the sacrifices you've made to make it possible for me to have this career. Your kindness and compassion inspires me to be a better person, and your keen eyes on this manuscript drove me to be a better writer.

And to you, dear readers, who have followed me on this journey—I am so very grateful for you all. Your loyal following makes it possible for me to have this career that I love. Thank you, thank you, thank you.

Dedicated to

Lainey and pursuing happiness together. Always.

CHAPTER ONE

Senator Meredith Mitchell struggled to concentrate on the witness's testimony, but the woman's long, slender neck and waves of golden blond hair generated a buzz of attraction that blocked out the captivating story told by an obviously accomplished storyteller. Despite what sometimes aired in prime time on C-SPAN, these Senate Judiciary Committee meetings were usually notoriously dull and dry, but Stevie Palmer, the public defender currently fielding questions from Meredith's fellow senators about proposed changes to the federal sentencing guidelines, was riveting.

"Leroy Johnson's only real crime was loyalty," Stevie said. "Loyalty to his older brother, the only father figure he'd ever known, and the only person who'd ever supported him or cared for him. When the police came calling, threatening to take away the only constant Leroy had ever known, he lied to protect his family. A lie that would land him in federal prison for the next ten years of his life."

"Well, isn't that a sad tale."

Meredith glanced at her colleague, Senator Connie Armstrong from Texas, who'd made the remark, and wondered if she'd missed something in Stevie's testimony that had gotten under Connie's skin. God knows she might have zoned out on the actual words Stevie was saying. But who could blame her? Stevie Palmer was breathtaking. *You should be ashamed of yourself for ogling the woman.* She should, but she wasn't. It had been way too long since she'd paused to enjoy the beauty of anything, let alone a gorgeous woman, and she couldn't help it if the sentencing commission, which was normally composed of stodgy old men, had decided to send a young, hot public defender to testify before her committee.

"Senator Mitchell?" Connie asked.

She tore her gaze away from Stevie. "Yes, Senator Armstrong?"

Connie raised an eyebrow but pressed on. "I've heard all I can take about the woes of Ms. Palmer's drug-dealing clients. It's your turn to question this witness."

Meredith cleared her throat to buy a moment of time. She'd prepared a long list of tough questions for the witness, but that was when she thought she'd be sparring with someone who didn't look like a movie star and wasn't as compelling. No way out now. "Thank you, Senator." She took a drink of water and jumped right in.

"Ms. Palmer, you argue that mandatory minimums in drug cases are inherently unfair, but isn't it true that over half of the offenders subject to these laws receive sentences below the minimum in exchange for cooperating with the government?" Stevie's eyes locked on hers, and the room was silent for several beats. When she finally spoke, Meredith realized she'd been holding her breath.

"Stats like the one you just quoted only add to the problem," Stevie said. "When you say 'over half,' most people assume something in the seventy to one hundred percent range, but the truth is that the total number of offenders who received some reprieve from mandatory minimums as a result of their cooperation was less than fifty-two percent, barely over half."

"But isn't the goal to raise that number, and doesn't doing so benefit society as a whole? The more incentive offenders have to give up other criminals, the safer we will all ultimately be?" Meredith kept her tone even and her gaze trained on Stevie, but she shifted in her chair as she asked the questions, unaccustomed to the sudden and stirring attraction Stevie roused in her.

"It makes for a nice sound bite, but it's not that simple," Stevie replied. "Basically, you're rewarding people involved in big conspiracies and slamming the door shut on solo operators or the low-level participants unlikely to have any useful information. The current system only benefits people who have a bunch of bad friends. If I have a client who was going it on their own or too incidental to the conspiracy to know much, they are sh—" Stevie grinned. "Well, let's just say they out of luck."

Meredith cocked her head, wishing Stevie had gone ahead and uttered the curse if only to see how the Republicans on the committee would react. Most of them were predisposed to think someone like Stevie, a public defender who argued for the rights of accused criminals, was de facto wrong about anything having to do with public policy. As a former assistant US attorney, she didn't necessarily agree with Stevie's arguments, but she wasn't about to dismiss them out of hand either. "Do you object to the imposition of mandatory minimum sentences or only the effect they have?"

"Both. There's no denying that the result of minimums is unfair and not just to offenders who happen to be loners, but there are other issues as well. Studies show that the very act of incarceration increases recidivism. Close to forty-five percent of offenders convicted of an offense that carries a mandatory minimum have no criminal history yet they will be detained at higher rates than many who are repeat offenders. That is not just."

Meredith admired Stevie's certainty, and brushed away the internal voice that whispered she might be letting attraction get in the way of objectivity. She sparred with Stevie a few more rounds and was surprised when Connie signaled their time was up by gaveling the session to a close. Meredith remained seated while her colleagues fled the building, everyone anxious to get out of town for the weekend. She noticed Stevie talking to another one of the committee members, Bob Lawton. She could've predicted Bob would home in on Stevie. He had a habit of sleeping with every attractive woman inside the Beltway whether they were available or not—the bonus of never aspiring to higher office. Wondering if Stevie were available and wishing she had Bob's kind of freedom, Meredith tucked her head down, organized her notes, and filed them in her briefcase so they'd be easy for her secretary to locate and type up for the file.

"That was quite the grilling."

She looked up to see Stevie standing next to her, and her heart raced. "That was nothing. I barely got warmed up."

Stevie grinned. "Duly noted." She folded her arms. "I'm not a fan of this format. It's extremely limiting when it comes to sharing information. I don't suppose you have time for a cup of coffee, or are you headed out of town with everyone else?"

Meredith silently gave thanks for her plans to stay in DC for the weekend, but still she hesitated. Coffee was harmless. Coffee was easy. There was a coffee shop right here in the building. A couple of grande somethings, some casual conversation, and then they'd go their separate ways. Anyone observing would think it was exactly what it looked like—a business meeting like the dozens she conducted every day in the Russell Building across the street from the nation's Capitol. But she wanted more and decided to be bold. "Let's have dinner. I have a table at the Old Ebbitt. Meet you there at seven?"

"The Old Ebbitt? I'm up for dinner, but I'd prefer someplace a bit more casual."

"I like casual." Meredith did her best not to sound too eager.

Stevie leaned down and plucked a pen off of the table and scrawled a note. She handed it over. "Perfect. I'll meet you there at eight."

Stevie turned and started walking toward the door before Meredith could answer, but it didn't really matter because there was only one possible response, and Stevie clearly knew she was going to say yes. That kind of confidence was intoxicating, and Meredith couldn't wait to have another drink.

❖

Stevie could barely believe her own nerve, but hell, it wasn't like she had anything to lose. She knew the hearing hadn't gone her way, but maybe if she had a chance to talk to the senator without C-SPAN filming their every word, she could convince her to see the light. It didn't hurt that Meredith Mitchell was breathtakingly beautiful.

Stevie walked out of the Russell Building and cut across Constitution Avenue to stroll by the Supreme Court building. It was already getting dark outside, and the lights on the building captured the majesty of this place in a way that daylight never did. She took a few moments to enjoy twilight before she walked to the Metro and took the Orange Line to her office. She'd welcomed the opportunity to appear before the Senate committee, but the day spent waiting to testify meant that her desk was likely piled high with work. For a brief moment, she regretted challenging the senator to meet her for dinner. What she should do is make a sandwich from whatever random fixings she could find in the fridge at the office and get caught up on her files, but it was too late now. She wasn't about to call the senator's office and cancel. The look in Meredith Mitchell's eyes told her she was intrigued, and a little intrigue could go a long way toward persuasion.

She strode through the door of her office and shoved the stack of files on her dinged up wooden desk to the side. Everything was as she'd left it that morning with the exception of one new file with a neon green Post-it prominently placed that read "See me before you do anything on this." She picked up the file and walked to her boss's office and knocked.

"Joe, what's up with this?"

"Have a seat." He waved her toward a chair. "Tell me about the hearing. How did it go?"

"Fine, I guess. I don't think we changed any minds, but I felt like they were listening at least."

"How about Mitchell? Was she as rough as I've heard?"

"She played the part of a former prosecutor to a tee, but I felt like she was actually listening." Stevie toyed with mentioning their dinner date, but date was too strong a word, and she didn't feel like giving him a play-by-play of how it had come about. "Convincing her or anyone else that offenders have rights is an uphill battle, but I remain confident everyone will eventually see the light."

"You're such a glass half full kind of gal." He pointed at the file in her hand. "Which is exactly why I wanted to talk to you. I've reassigned this case and it's yours now. Defendant refused to talk to pretrial services, so he's sitting in a cell when, based on how he looks on paper, he should be out on bond. I sent Santos to talk to him," he said, referring to another public defender in the office, "but the guy wouldn't talk to him either, and when I say wouldn't talk to him, I mean would not utter a word. Judge continued the detention hearing to Monday afternoon."

Stevie opened the file and scanned the scant information, noting the client's name was William Barkley. "It says here he works in IT for Folsom Enterprises. Shouldn't he be able to afford an attorney of his own?"

"Worked for Folsom, past tense. He was fired because of this case, and his credit report doesn't paint a pretty picture. The magistrate has appointed us for now."

"Any idea if he's just stubborn or is there some competency issue?"

Joe shrugged. "Opinions vary, but I don't think we're going to get very far on his case if we don't make a good faith effort to check it out. I know you're busy, but I need someone with experience to assess the situation. These new kids are killing me—too much energy and not enough savvy. Go see him Monday and let me know what you think."

Stevie answered quickly to keep from having to hear his usual lament about the more inexperienced attorneys at the office. "I'll look at the file this weekend, and we'll go from there."

Joe gave her a curious look. "You calling it a day already?"

"After the grilling I just had, I think I deserve to leave before ten o'clock on a Friday night for once."

"Fair enough. You want to grab a beer? Some of us are headed to Quarry House."

"Thanks, but I'm going to bow out tonight. Believe it or not I have plans." The minute she spoke the words, she was sorry. The folks who worked at the public defender's office were a tight-knit group, and her peers knew she hadn't been out on a date in forever. She could see Joe starting to form a question, and she beat him to the punch. "Not for public consumption yet. Probably never. If there's ever anything serious going on in my life, I promise you all will be the first to know."

"Sure, yeah." He play-punched her on the shoulder. "Have fun, you deserve it."

Stevie considered his words later as she walked from the Metro stop to her house in Maryland. She didn't know about the deserving part. She took time from her demanding schedule to fit in a personal life now and then, but this wasn't that. She was meeting a US senator to sway her to her side on an issue that had become politicized. A business meeting and nothing more.

Then why hadn't she just stayed in the city instead of coming home to change, and why was she exhilarated at the prospect of seeing Meredith again? And when had she started thinking about her as Meredith instead of Senator Mitchell?

She peeled off her suit and hung it back in the closet. Dressed only in boy shorts and a tank, she wandered into the kitchen and debated whether or not to have a drink before she headed out to meet Senator Hotness. Opting to keep her wits about her, she fixed a glass of ice water and did a mental inventory of everything she knew about the senator.

Meredith Mitchell was the youngest of four children, and had been born into a family full of political power players. Her father, the former governor of New York, served three consecutive terms before stepping down to run a nonprofit foundation whose stated goals were to create economic opportunities and inspire civic service. Her oldest brother was the current governor of Massachusetts, and her other siblings, Michael and Jennifer, had spent their lives working in politics, but out of all of them, Meredith was the golden child. Two thirds of the way into her freshman term as senator, rumors swirled that she might enter next year's presidential race.

Stevie didn't believe the rumors. She hated politics, but living in DC, they were impossible to avoid, and even she knew that with the primaries starting just a few months away, Meredith would have a lot of catching up to do if she entered the race now. The current slate of presidential candidates had been working for months to lay the groundwork to hit the campaign trail full-on right after the first of the year, and filing deadlines for most states were only a couple of weeks away. Besides, the Democratic party already had their darling picked out, the senior senator from Texas, the feisty Senator Connie Armstrong.

Stevie glanced at her phone and realized she'd drifted off. She'd have to rush to get ready in time. She dressed quickly in jeans, a sweater, and a pair of boots, and grabbed a leather jacket on her way out the door. The Metro ride was quick, and she spent the few minutes on the train wondering if Meredith would show up and questioning whether she should've chosen a different spot if she'd really wanted to discuss business. Of course someone like Meredith would rather meet in a more traditional venue like the Old Ebbit where power plays were discussed on the daily. She was beginning to think this entire exercise was silly and she should go back home and dive into her work, when the train lurched to a halt, and the conductor announced her stop. Stevie shrugged off her second guesses and stepped off the train.

A few minutes later, when she walked into The Saloon, she spotted Meredith, seated at the bar. She was pleasantly surprised Meredith had beaten her here, but she tried not to read too much into her early arrival. Stevie stopped in the doorway, taking a moment to take in the juxtaposition of Meredith, still dressed in her business suit, holding a beer and chatting with the usually reticent bartender. Despite her formal clothes, she looked relaxed, casual, and utterly charming, and if Stevie really was here for a date, she couldn't have asked for more.

❖

The minute she walked into The Saloon, Meredith felt a sense of relief. At the Old Ebbit, she would've been stopped at least five times on the way to her table by shout-outs ranging from attagirls to blunt requests for favors, but here the patrons were more interested in the people at their own tables than whoever else might be inhabiting the same space.

She didn't spot Stevie, so she took a seat at the bar and debated whether she should order a drink. Lord knew she needed one. She placed her cell phone on the bar, pulled out her credit card to start a tab, and smiled at the bartender who strode her way.

"You're going to need to put that away," he said in a gruff voice, pointing at a sign on the wall.

She followed the direction of his gaze. No cell phones, No TV, No standing, No martinis, No American Express. She palmed her platinum card and shoved her phone into her purse. Obviously, this place didn't cater to politicians, but that was a good thing, right? Since her usual Hendricks martini was also off the table, she decided to embrace the challenge and put her beverage fortune in this guy's hands. "Give me whatever you drink."

He grunted and stepped to the row of tabs, pulled a beer, and clunked the glass onto the bar. Meredith set a twenty-dollar bill next to the glass and took note of the bartender's slight nod. Well, she'd gotten that part right at least.

She sipped her beer while keeping watch on the front door. No matter what Stevie had said about this being a chance to discuss the pending legislation, she'd agreed to take the meeting because Stevie intrigued her. Anyone else and she would've told them to schedule an appointment with her staff. At exactly eight o'clock, the door opened and Stevie walked into the bar. She was no longer dressed in the sharp black suit she'd had on at the hearing, but the sportier look she was wearing now suited her like a second skin. Meredith envied the casual comfort—she couldn't remember the last time she'd appeared in public in anything but senator-drag.

"I see you found the place," Stevie said with a grin. She waved at the bartender and pointed to Meredith's glass. "You like?"

"The beer's amazing, but I'm a little surprised at your choice of venue."

"Is that so?"

Meredith gestured toward the wall of rules. "This speaks more prosecutor than defense attorney."

Stevie settled into the seat beside her. "Ah, that's right. You worked for the US Attorney's office once upon a time."

"Guilty as charged."

"Did you like it?" Stevie asked.

Interesting question. Meredith couldn't remember the last time someone had asked her about her time as a prosecutor. "Looking back, yes, but at the time I remember feeling boxed in. Young AUSAs don't get to exercise a lot of discretion."

"Interesting observation. I would've expected you to say something about how your time as a prosecutor gave you valuable perspective and all that."

"Oh, I can say all that," Meredith said, "but I get the impression you aren't really impressed by political bullshit."

"Would it be bullshit?"

"Not entirely, but there's not a ton of room for nuance when it comes to sound bites. Which brings me to the subject of this meeting. I get the feeling you were feeling a little boxed in with the time limits during the hearing."

"You read that right," Stevie said. "If something's important enough, it seems like you would want to hear everything there is to say on the subject."

"And you think we don't get much done now. Just wait and see how little we'd accomplish if everyone got to say their piece." As she spoke, Meredith studied Stevie's face, certain she'd seen a twinge of disappointment after she'd brought up the hearing. Maybe she wasn't the only one who'd had an ulterior motive for tonight's meeting. Before she could test the water further, Stevie smiled and said, "Are you hungry?"

Meredith's head spun at the abrupt change in subject, but she didn't let it show. "Starving. Is the food good here?"

"Basic bar food, but yes. Trust me to order?"

"Absolutely." Meredith sat back and watched Stevie negotiate with the bartender, occasionally looking over to confirm that she was okay with the selections. Meredith didn't say anything other than to nod her assent. She was used to everyone deferring to her choices, and it was nice to have someone else take control for a night.

"We can move to a table if you want," Stevie said once she'd completed their order.

Sensing that Stevie was only making the offer for her benefit, she demurred. "I'm fine here if you are."

"Good."

A moment of silence slipped between them, but instead of being uncomfortable, it felt natural, like they were old friends enjoying a night out with the knowledge there would be many more. Meredith raised her glass and took a drink, enjoying the idea of spending more time with Stevie.

"Do you really believe that mandatory minimums work?"

Again with the abrupt change in subject. Meredith took a moment to consider before shaking her head. "Not always, no."

"Then why the fuss about getting rid of them?"

"What do you suggest in their place?"

"Better treatment options for prison populations. More options for probation with treatment. Stop filling the prisons with low-level drug offenders."

"I agree with you in theory."

"I hear a but."

"But nothing is ever as simple as it seems. Treatment programs have their own issues." Meredith ticked off the points. "Cost. Recidivism. When treatment is dangled as a way to get out of prison early, people will do or say anything to get a clean bill of health. Put them back on the streets and they'll be using again in no time without ongoing treatment which most convicts do not continue once they get their get out of jail free card. Then there's the problem that many times the people you want to help avoid mandatory minimums aren't addicts at all so they don't qualify for the sentence reduction a treatment program would give them."

"You really know your stuff."

"Did you think I wouldn't?" Meredith was genuinely curious.

"I don't know. I guess I thought you were pretty far removed from your days dealing with criminal law."

"Doesn't feel like it was that long ago. Sometimes I miss being a prosecutor."

The clatter of plates interrupted their conversation, and the bartender shoved the food toward them and then strode off to wait on some new arrivals.

"Let's talk about something else," Stevie said. "No sense inducing heartburn."

"I have a feeling these onion rings will do that all on their own."

"But totally worth it," Stevie said.

Meredith nodded and tugged one of the golden rings free from the pile. She was just about to put it in her mouth, when she noticed Adam Rondell, a reporter, striding toward them.

"Hey, Senator, you slumming it with us regular folks tonight?"

She set the onion ring down and cast a quick look at Stevie who looked between them with a curious expression. Meredith smiled to signal all was well. "Hi, Adam, am I encroaching on your space? I'd say I'm sorry, but since you spend your life following me around, I think turnabout is fair play."

"Touché."

Hearing Stevie clear her throat, Meredith broke contact with Adam and turned her way.

"Adam Rondel, meet my friend Stevie Palmer. Stevie, meet my stalker, Adam. He works for the—"

"*The Metro Mash-Up.*" Stevie interrupted. "I'm familiar with your blog."

"Smart and pretty," Adam said. "She's a keeper." He turned back to Meredith. "So, I heard something interesting today. Do you have a minute to answer a couple of questions?"

If she were dining alone, she might, but Meredith had sensed Stevie tense up when Adam approached the bar. She had a reputation for allowing the press extensive access to her professional life, but no matter what she'd told herself about her reason for this meeting with Stevie, it was no longer purely professional, and she was more interested in pleasing her than satisfying the insatiable appetites of the reporters who dogged her on a daily basis. "Call my office Monday and we'll set up a time to talk."

"Sounds like a brush-off."

Meredith spotted Stevie opening her mouth to respond and she jumped in, pointing at her onion rings. "Dinner. It's a thing. You should try it sometime." She smiled to defuse her refusal. "Later, I promise."

He shook his head. "I heard a rumor today that you are jumping in the presidential race. Sure you don't want to comment?"

Meredith kept smiling, but she wanted to strangle whoever had started the rumor and Adam for spreading it. "Here's my comment and listen close because I'm not going to repeat it and I'm not answering any follow-up questions. I fully support Senator Armstrong in her bid for the Democratic nomination, and I think she'll make a wonderful president."

Adam made a show of pretending to take notes on his hand while she spoke. "Got it. Okay, ladies, have a nice evening." He tipped an imaginary hat and strode away.

Meredith watched until he walked out the door of the bar. "Sorry about that. It's a hazard of the job."

"Definitely a hazard," Stevie said. "That guy's an ass. Have you read the stuff he writes that passes for news? Of course, that's more the norm than not nowadays."

She heard the edge in Stevie's voice and noted that it sounded like Stevie had a personal bias against Adam Rondel and the press in general. She started to form a question, but Stevie beat her to it.

"Although he's not the only one speculating about you entering the race. Is it true?"

Meredith took her time chewing her food. The rumors had swirled after her speech at the Democratic convention during the last election cycle. She'd been given the speaking spot mostly because of her family connections and she knew it, but showcasing her at the convention had been part of a grand plan to put her on the path to an eventual run for the top office. "Maybe someday. Senator Armstrong is going to carry the standard this time around, and I support her all the way."

"Connie Armstrong, really?"

"What, you don't like her? She's a strong woman with a deep history of service to her country."

"Is that the party line?"

Meredith bit back a sharp retort. "If you think I walk a straight party line, you don't know me very well. Do you have a specific beef with Senator Armstrong?"

Stevie nodded as if to acknowledge Meredith was right to put her to the test. "If she's the nominee, I'll vote for her, but only because the alternatives on the other side of the aisle are positively frightening, but you have to admit she comes with a lot of baggage. Armstrong's had to walk a pretty fine line between liberals and conservatives to maintain her popularity in Texas, and she's a little too moderate for my taste."

"Sometimes moderates are the only ones who get things done."

"At what compromise to their principles? Don't get me wrong, I'm all for moderation when it comes to things like foreign affairs, but when it comes to civil rights, gun control, poverty, the environment, someone has to take a stand on the side of what's right and just."

"And you think I would be that person?"

Stevie looked taken aback by the question, and she took a moment to answer. "You come closer than Armstrong."

Not exactly a ringing endorsement. "It's not as difficult for me since my New York constituents expect me to lean left, but Connie's had to work hard to build a base in a state that has teetered back and forth between liberal and conservative. What she's managed to accomplish in the South has groomed her for this position."

"You have a point."

"I'm guessing you don't concede that very often."

Stevie grinned. "Only when necessary."

Meredith tossed a half-eaten onion ring down and pushed her plate aside. "I couldn't possibly eat another bite."

"I'm thinking you're mostly a salad girl."

"Is that so?"

Stevie blushed slightly. "Either that or you work out a lot."

"I'm going to take that as a compliment. And inspiration not to skip my morning run." Meredith noticed for the first time that she hadn't wanted to glance at her phone the entire time they'd been sitting at the bar. The relaxed vibe was refreshing, more like a date than a business meeting. She tipped her empty glass at Stevie's. "Are we having dessert or another drink? My waistline can't afford both."

"Which one will convince you to change your mind on the sentencing guidelines?"

And just like that, they were back to business, but Meredith didn't want to be. "Tell you what, let's have whichever one you want tonight and skip the shop talk. Tomorrow, send me whatever additional information you want me to review, and I'll have my staff put together a position paper. I promise to give it a full review before we vote on the amendments."

"And if you're convinced about my position, you'll sway some of the other committee members?"

"If you convince me, I'll convince them."

Stevie stuck out her hand. "You've got yourself a deal. And prepare yourself because we're having apple pie. With ice cream."

As Stevie waved a hand at the bartender to order their dessert, Meredith reflected on what a pleasant surprise this evening had turned out to be. Sometimes being prepared was overrated.

CHAPTER TWO

First thing Monday morning, Stevie filled out the prisoner request form and handed it to the warden at the DC detention center. He examined the form and pointed to a row of chairs along the wall.

"We've got a space for you at the third window."

Stevie shook her head. "I need a room."

"The notes say no contact visits for this guy."

She'd dealt with this before, increased restrictions on defendants deemed to be a threat to national security, and she was fully prepared to push back. "I'll take the room," she said, keeping her tone even but firm, and hoping her hard stare conveyed what she didn't want to have to say. A few beats passed and she was about ready to tell the warden he'd hear from the judge, but he relented before she had to go all law-and-order on him.

"Sign the sheet," he said in a curt voice.

She complied. She didn't blame the guards for having a little bit of attitude. Working in the prison every day had to be a drain, but ultimately her allegiance was to her client not their keepers. Once she was in the attorney room, she selected the best two of the three chairs and positioned them on either side of the rickety table in the center of the room. The file wasn't very thick, and she spread it out in front of her, counting on the fact the guards would likely take their time getting the client to her to allow her time to prepare.

She'd skimmed the file the night before, but she'd been distracted and she knew why. She'd been completely unprepared for Meredith Mitchell in real life. She was even better looking than she was on camera, and her charm was palpable. Stevie had half expected Meredith to be uncomfortable in the casual bar with its restrictive rules, but by the end of the evening, she had the surly owner eating out of her hand, and a casual observer would think she was a regular. Except for the encounter with Adam Rondel, the entire evening had been easy and comfortable, and Stevie couldn't remember the last time she'd enjoyed herself as much. So why did she feel unsettled?

Maybe it was because now that Meredith had agreed to take a second look at the committee's report, she no longer had an excuse to see Meredith again.

The door opened and jarred her from her reverie. Three guards escorted a tall, skinny guy who looked to be in his late twenties into the room, and she shoved aside all thoughts of Meredith Mitchell and focused on assessing her new client.

He slid into the chair across from her and tucked the extra folds of his orange jumpsuit under his legs while she motioned to the guards that she wanted to be alone with him. The one in the lead shrugged and motioned for the others to follow him out. She waited until the door was firmly shut behind them, and then turned to her client. "Are you William Barkley?" She felt silly asking the question, but when she was a young lawyer, she'd had a very confusing new client conference until she realized the guards had brought out the wrong inmate.

He nodded.

"How old are you, Mr. Barkley?" She knew what the file said, but this was a softball question designed to get him to start talking.

He wasn't falling for it. Barkley jabbed a finger at the file, and Stevie pulled out the page that listed his personal data. William Barkley, age twenty-five, six two, one hundred sixty pounds. Resident of Maryland and employee of Folsom Enterprises, an IT company whose primary work was as a subcontractor for government agencies. He was accused of violating the Espionage Act for sending classified documents to an online news outlet. She vaguely remembered the information having to do with the FBI having a lead on Russian hackers infiltrating social media and failing to act on the intel. She didn't get why the government was still trying to keep a lid on that since these kinds of stories were popping up all over the place now.

She decided to start with the basics. She slid the paper with his personal data across the table. "Is this information correct?" She watched him scan the paper and then look up to meet her gaze. He nodded again. Good. So far he didn't seem crazy, just really reluctant to say words out loud. "I don't suppose you'd like to talk to me about the charges against you?" A slight shake of his head was his only response.

Stevie mentally reviewed the prior attorney's report and recommendation for a competency screening. He'd listed only a couple of factors as a basis for the recommendation, relying heavily on Barkley's failure to communicate. She decided to dive right in. "Your last attorney believes you need to be evaluated for competency. Do you know what that means and why he would make that kind of recommendation?"

Barkley hunched down in his seat and placed a finger over his lips. Stevie braced for whatever he was about to say, certain this was the crazy she'd been warned about. He pointed at her pen. She hesitated for a just a second to consider how dangerous a pen could be in the wrong hands and decided to risk it. She shoved her legal pad and pen across the table and watched him form big block letters. He tore the paper from the pad, folded it in half, and slid it back toward her. She lifted the edge and peeked at the secret note.

NOT SAFE TO TALK HERE.

And there was her first glimpse at crazy, but it was only borderline. She wrote back. *This room is secure. The guards aren't listening. You can talk to me.* And slid the note back to him.

He scanned her writing several times before reaching for the pen, scrawling words in a firm press, and sending it back her way.

YOU DON'T KNOW THAT.

Okay, this was the real deal, but she'd need more specifics to file a motion with the judge and this back and forth note thing was getting old fast. "Talk to me about what you've experienced. I can't help you unless you tell me what's going on."

He shook his head and crossed his hands on the table as if to signal he was done. She gave it one more try. "Mr. Barkley, this afternoon, we're going to be back in court for your detention hearing. You haven't provided any information to pretrial services, and without their report, the judge will have no choice but to keep you in custody while we either prepare for trial or work out a deal, neither of which can I do if you do not communicate with me. In addition, if I have reason to suspect that you may not be competent to stand trial, it is my duty to ask the court to have you examined by a mental health practitioner, which sounds like an easy process, but it isn't. You might be shipped off to another facility for an undetermined amount of time while the process is taking place. If you are indeed competent, the examination will only delay your court procedure, and delay is not always to your benefit, especially since you will remain in custody while your competency is being assessed. Ultimately, you will wind up right back here with me asking you to provide information so that I can assist you with your case, a lot like what I'm doing right now. Do you understand what I'm saying?"

Barkley frowned as she spoke and shifted in his chair. When she was done, he reached for the note and pen again and drew heavy black lines beneath the words *NOT SAFE TO TALK HERE*, and then shoved the paper across the table with enough force to send it flying onto the floor. Stevie leaned down to pick it up and placed it in her bag. If she chose to file a motion to have him examined for competency, this would be exhibit A.

Back at the office, Stevie tossed the file on her desk and stretched her arms over her head. Joe poked his head in. "What's the verdict? Cray or no cray?"

"Anyone ever tell you you're not the most sensitive person in the office?"

"I'm okay with that assessment."

"Good. The guy is paranoid, for sure, but incompetent? I'm not convinced. Besides, isn't there a saying, 'Just because you're paranoid doesn't mean they aren't after you'?"

"Maybe he spent too much time working on top secret projects for Folsom. The real question is whether he's nuts, er, I mean mentally challenged, and whether you think he'll respond to you."

She considered his question carefully. As unsure as she was about her interaction with William Barkley, she did feel like they'd made a connection. At the very least, he seemed to want to confide in her even if he was leery about doing so at the jail. "I'll stay on it. Maybe once he gets hauled in front of the judge again, he'll agree to talk to me."

"Fair enough." He handed her an envelope. "This came for you. Hand-delivered. Hannah asked me to give it to you. She wouldn't let me open it."

"Maybe because it says 'personal and confidential' on the outside of the envelope."

"We're a law office—almost everything says that." He jabbed a finger at the envelope. "You going to open it or what? It's from Senator Mitchell's office."

Meredith's name in the upper left corner had been the first thing she'd noticed when Joe waved the envelope her way, but she didn't want him to know that. She tucked it under Barkley's file. "If there's anything in it that affects you, you'll be the first to know."

He scrunched his face at her, but she wasn't deterred and waved him off. "Now go. I've got work to do."

He wandered off to bother someone else in the office, and she slowly slid Meredith's envelope out from under the pile on her desk. It was thick and heavy, and curiosity quickly took over. She grabbed a letter opener and sliced her way in, quickly shaking the contents out onto her desk. On top was a note card in heavy linen stock engraved with Meredith's name. In flowing script it said: *I followed your suggestion (that's twice now) and found the enclosed articles. I made copies for the rest of the committee members and thought you might like to have a set for yourself. Thanks for the nudge. Yours, Meredith.*

Stevie read the card three times before setting it aside to look at the stack of paper—articles from a cross-section of legal journals arguing the exact points she'd been trying to make when she'd appeared before the committee and with Meredith at the bar. Had it really been that easy to convince Meredith to be swayed toward her side or was there more to this message than a simple, you were right, I was wrong? Stevie picked up the card and read it again. *Thanks for the nudge.* What exactly had nudged the senator: her arguments or the evening they'd shared?

Stevie set the stack of paper to the side of her desk and tried to focus on the rest of her work, but it kept calling out to her. After a completely unproductive hour, she picked up her phone and dialed. A woman's voice answered before she could talk herself out of it.

"Senator Mitchell's office, how may I help you?"

How indeed.

❖

Meredith raised her glass and motioned for Addison to do the same. "Here's to your last lunch as a single woman."

"You make it sound like I'll never have a meal again. Is that what married life is like?"

"How should I know?" Meredith delivered the casual words with a carefree tone, but the truth was she'd begun to grow tired of personal relationships taking a back seat to everything else in her life. Addison Riley, the chief justice of the United States, was the last of her close group of friends to head to the altar, and the realization she was now the only single member of the group came with its own set of baggage.

"You might want to consider joining the club you know?"

Meredith nearly choked on her drink. "Of married couples? Not in the cards, for a while anyway."

"Why? Because of a presidential run you may or may not make in the future? Seriously, Mere, you don't have to choose between ambition and happiness, and if you think you do, then it's probably best to let the ambition part go." Addison dropped her voice to a whisper. "But if you want to get the professional piece out of the way, there's still time to get in the race this go-round."

Echoes of Friday night's dinner conversation about the same subject rang in Meredith's head. She hadn't been able to get Stevie out of her mind since they'd parted. She couldn't remember the last time she'd been on a date with someone who had been utterly unimpressed with her position, and it had been refreshing. That Stevie was not only good-looking, but smart and articulate was a bonus, but she told Addison the same thing she'd told Stevie. "It's not my time. Connie's worked hard for this and she's earned her spot. It's always like this in the primaries—everyone jockeying for position and wanting to challenge the old guard. If Garrett had the chance to run again, he'd be facing the same kind of opposition as Connie, and he's got the highest favorables of any second term president in history."

"Then you might as well go ahead and start a family so when it is your turn to run, you can check those boxes."

What Addison said made sense on paper, but after surviving several grueling statewide elections, Meredith knew firsthand the toll running for office took on every aspect of a candidate's life, and she had no desire to impose the rigors of campaigning on anyone else, especially not a new love interest. Besides, she was absolutely committed to achieving her career goals before focusing her interests elsewhere. "I'm in no hurry."

"Well, neither was I, obviously, but here I am, a week away from being married to the most powerful woman in the country." Addison raised her glass.

"I think a lot of people would argue that in a race between you and Julia for most powerful woman in the country, you'd finish in a dead heat. Frankly, I don't know how you do it."

"It's not easy. I'd love to come home after work and discuss my day, but the president's chief of staff isn't a viable sounding board for Supreme Court gossip. We've learned to dance around certain topics at the dinner table. It's not always easy, but I love her so much it's totally worth it. This Saturday, when we say our I dos in front of all our friends and family, nothing will stand between us."

Meredith pointed at Addison's dreamy smile. "I'm going to get me some of that someday. But not right now. Now, I'm going to keeping working for a better future, which means campaigning for Connie to win the election. I'll be sitting in the front row when you swear in the first female president."

"Here's to that." Addison took a drink and set her glass on the table. "The wedding planner said you RSVP'd for one, but Julia told me to tell you that she had an extra spot held. You know, in case you want to bring someone. It doesn't have to be a big deal. It might be nice to have a wing woman."

"Are you scared I'm going to get drunk and sappy about my lack of a love life and ruin your special day?"

"Not hardly." Addison reached a hand across the table and squeezed Meredith's arm. "I just want you to be happy. I'm the last person in the world who thinks you need another person to make you happy, but let me be the first to admit that it's pretty fabulous when you do find someone." She pulled her hand back and smiled. "Bring someone, don't bring someone. You're always welcome with us."

An hour later, Meredith was back at her office trying to keep her mind on her briefing, but Addison's words kept cropping up and with them images of Stevie, dressed for a wedding. Would she wear a dress or a tux? Did she even own formalwear? Meredith was so used to black tie affairs being part of her job that she rarely considered whether it was optional. As soon as her briefing was over, she buzzed her secretary. "Do you happen to have a copy of the invite for Justice Riley's wedding?"

A quick knock on the door and Kate stuck her head in, waving the invite in her hand. "I loaded all the info to your phone. Pretty sure you're not going to need the actual invite to get in."

Meredith took the folded card stock. "I know, but I wanted to check the dress code," she said distractedly.

"Your schedule's pretty tight for the rest of the week. Do you need me to have Neiman's send over some dresses?"

"What? Oh no, I'm good." Meredith stared hard at the invite until she finally located the note: black tie optional. She doubted many would deviate from the norm of long dresses and tuxes for the occasion, but the word optional gave her some flexibility. She handed the invite back to Kate. Kate had been with her since she'd run for the New York state legislature many years ago, and she trusted her implicitly, but she wasn't ready to share the plan brewing in the back of her brain. "Did you send that packet over to Ms. Palmer this morning?"

"I did. Delivered by courier, like you asked. She called earlier to say she received it."

Meredith paused as she considered whether to go with her gut or abandon this half-baked plan. "Thanks. Could you get me her office number?"

"I'll get her on the line, but you have to be at the Hartford Building at four, so you have ten minutes tops," Kate said, already on her way back to her desk directly outside of Meredith's office.

Meredith waited impatiently for Kate to connect the call. She probably should've just texted Stevie or phoned on her cell instead of making a personal call under the guise of a professional one. She hadn't fully committed to what she was about to do, but she'd lead with the packet and go from there.

Her indecision was interrupted by Kate's voice. "Please hold for Senator Mitchell."

Meredith waited until she heard Kate click off the line. "Stevie?"

"I guess I have to call you Senator now."

She heard a tiniest bit of an edge behind the otherwise friendly voice. "Sorry about that. Kate has a habit of being formal."

"I get it. You probably have to do something to keep people at a distance or everyone would be beating down your doors asking for favors."

"Maybe." She considered asking Stevie what kind of favors would top her list, but stopped short. "Did you review the packet I sent you?"

"I did, and thank you. I can see you had your staff delve into the issue. I appreciate the effort."

Meredith noted, with pleasure, a warmer tone to Stevie's voice. "I did the research myself. And I provided a copy of my findings to the rest of the committee. We've put a vote on hold until we have more time to fully investigate the issues you raised."

"Thank you. I had no idea apple pie could provide such efficient results."

"Well, it was really good pie. And there was ice cream."

"You think that was good, then I've got a chocolate, chocolate cake I'd like you to meet."

There was absolutely no mistaking it—this was flirtatious banter, and Meredith was surprised again at Stevie's down-to-earth, easy manner which was not at all what she would've expected after Stevie's aggressive testimony during the confirmation hearing. Caught up in the fun, Meredith dropped her normal reticence and blurted out, "What are you doing Saturday night?"

"This Saturday?"

She heard the pause and rushed to fill the silence. "I'm sorry. I hate when people ask me questions like that. My mother does it and it's always a trap because if we say nothing then she's ready to pounce, and by then it's too late to come up with an excuse for why we can't attend whatever boring benefit she has planned."

"It's okay. I'm going to be brave and say I don't have any plans, but I'm holding my breath that you're not about to ask me to repay you by attending some fancy benefit where everyone is dressed in tuxes and gowns and there's a silent auction where we're all supposed to bid on a trip to Bali to save the children."

"Well," Meredith drew out the word. "I can promise no one will ask you for money, but the fancy outfits, they might be happening."

"I'm a little intrigued."

"It's a wedding. The brides put me down for a plus-one, and now they're hassling me about paying for the extra meal. You'd be saving me."

"Brides?"

Meredith waited for Stevie to figure it out, and it didn't take long. The newspapers had been featuring the story for weeks.

"Wait a minute. You're going to Justice Riley and Julia Scott's wedding?" Stevie laughed. "Of course you are. It's the event of the season or so the *Post* says."

"I didn't peg you for a social section reader."

"I'm not, but our secretary is up to date on all things having to do with Beltway gossip, and she makes a habit of keeping me informed."

"Then you understand how important it is for the brides not to have an empty seat. Such a travesty might make the front page and doom their wedded bliss."

"Well, if I'd truly be doing you a favor."

"You would. I promise." Meredith hesitated for a second. "It's a tiny bit formal."

"You think? Hell, those two are the closest thing to gay royalty we get around here. I'm surprised they'd let you bring just anyone."

"I won't be bringing just anyone. I'll be bringing you. That is, if you accept." Meredith resisted tacking on a "say yes." She'd lobbed the ball firmly into Stevie's court now and it was up to her to play ball. Two seconds that felt like ten ticked by before she had her answer.

"I'd love to."

Meredith grinned, surprised at how much she wanted Stevie to say yes and how relieved she was when she did. Maybe this wedding would be fun after all.

❖

Stevie walked the few blocks to the courthouse thankful for the temperate fall weather. When she reached the steps of the Prettyman Courthouse, home of the US District Court for the District of

Columbia, she took a moment to scan the area, conscious of how lucky she was to do the work she loved in a part of the country steeped in rich history. The Capitol Building loomed in the distance, and she wondered if Meredith was there today or if she'd spent the day working at her office in the Russell Building. Either way, Meredith was likely only a few blocks away, and Stevie let her mind stray to their phone conversation and their date for the Riley-Scott wedding.

"You don't know for sure it's a date," she muttered as she pushed through the doors to the building.

"What's not a date?"

Crap. Stevie looked to her right to find AUSA Emily Watkins walking next to her. "Don't mind me. Just sorting out a particularly hairy fact pattern."

"Sounds like. Hey, I heard you're the new attorney on the Barkley case. That's mine."

Stevie breathed a sigh of relief. She and Emily had started working in the District around the same time, and even though they were always on opposite sides, she'd developed a healthy respect for her as a prosecutor. "Are you seeking to detain him?"

"Yes, pending the report from pretrial services. I heard he refused to give an interview. Is that still true?"

Any hope her client had reached out to pretrial services since she'd met with him this morning vanished. Without the interview, there would be no report detailing family history, ties to the community, prior offenses, etc., for the judge to consider in his decision about whether to set bond conditions so Barkley could be free pending trial. "Unfortunately, yes, but I'm hoping Judge Solomon can scare him a bit and maybe he'll come around. Would you be agreeable to holding over the hearing another day if I can get the interview scheduled?"

Emily frowned. "Personally, I don't have a problem with it, but Stine is making us take a hard line on these cases. In fact, I'll tell you now that the only way we're going to work anything out at all is for him to roll over on someone. Someone big."

Stevie had heard that Stine, the US Attorney for DC, had instituted some tough new rules for his staff, but this was the first time she'd run up against them. "Yeah, well, considering he won't even tell pretrial his name and whether or not he's married, I think you'll have to get your big fish from someone else's line. Can you at least get me early discovery? Maybe I can use what you've got to nudge him into talking to me."

"I'll do what I can. I'm waiting on some forensics from the computer guys that I'll need for grand jury. As soon as I've had a look at it, I'll give you a shout."

"Deal." It was the best Stevie could hope for. She wasn't entitled to see anything other than what was contained in the arrest affidavit yet since the case hadn't been indicted, but without something definitive, she wasn't sure how she was going to get Barkley to talk to her.

Judge Solomon's courtroom was milling with attorneys when she walked in. Most of them were crowded around the jury box where their clients in orange jumpsuits were leaning forward, giving their best pitch for why they should be allowed to change back into street clothes and get back to their lives. The attorneys whispered details about how the hearing would go and took notes on all the reasons why their clients were upstanding citizens unfairly trapped in the oversized net of government overreach. She spotted Barkley seated apart from the rest, looking curiously nonchalant, like he was waiting for a table in a restaurant instead of waiting on a judge to decide his fate. She slid into the seat next to him.

"I heard you still haven't talked to pretrial services."

He nodded.

"Without a report from them, the judge is going to keep you in custody, and since you refuse to talk to me while you're in custody, I can't help you with your case. Plus, if you don't complete a financial affidavit, the judge is going to make you hire an attorney. See how this works?"

"It doesn't."

Pleased she'd gotten something more than a nod, Stevie pressed on. "You're right about that." She leaned in closer. "Everyone in this room is focused on their own problems. No one is listening to us. Now would be a perfect time for you to tell me what you weren't comfortable saying back at the jail."

He shook his head. "There is no safe place."

"There has to be." She uttered the words more forcefully than she'd planned, but she was growing tired of his games. "Look, if you really did send classified information to the news, you don't strike me as the kind of guy who has a problem spilling his guts. We can talk about the case later. All I want to know now is enough information to get you released on bail."

His look was sympathetic, but his reply was still vague. "Be careful what you wish for."

Before she could respond, the bailiff entered the room and called for them to rise as the Honorable August Solomon took the bench. As judges went, Solomon was fair and even-tempered. Stevie hoped he would remain so when he found out her client had snubbed pretrial services. When Solomon called her case, she approached the podium with Emily while the bailiff directed Barkley to a seat at counsel table.

"Good afternoon, Ms. Palmer," said Solomon. "I understand your client opted not to be interviewed by pretrial services."

Stevie shot a look at Barkley who sat staring straight ahead. "That's correct, Your Honor."

"Does the government have a position on this matter?" Solomon asked Emily.

"It's our position that the defendant should be held pending trial. He shared classified information from his employer with news outlets in flagrant disregard to whether doing so might compromise the safety of law enforcement personnel or government security. And because he has refused to consent to an interview with pretrial services, we do not have sufficient information to evaluate whether bail would be adequate to ensure his appearance." Emily finished her spiel and glanced over at Stevie with a semi-apologetic look, but the damage was done. Stevie didn't blame her for doing her job, but she wished she'd drawn a less qualified opponent.

"Defense counsel, please approach," Solomon said. He waited until Stevie was standing right in front of the bench and lowered his voice. "Ms. Palmer, your predecessor on this case mentioned to me he might be filing a motion to have Mr. Barkley examined for competency. Do you plan to file such a motion?"

Stevie looked back at Barkley who continued to stare straight ahead as if nothing happening in this room really concerned him. Her gut told her something was off, but nothing he'd done so far was a clear sign of incompetence. "Judge, I just met with Mr. Barkley this morning. I have no immediate plans to file such a motion, but I'd like to keep my options open until such time as I've had a chance to spend more time with him."

"I understand, but I don't want to be in the position of continuing trial dates because we're shipping him off for an evaluation, especially since I have no plans to release him on bond pending trial. Please do whatever you have to do to speed up your decision and let me know what you decide within the next two weeks."

"About that, Your Honor."

"Yes?"

"Mr. Barkley hasn't filled out a financial affidavit, which I imagine stems from the same reluctance he has to talking to pretrial services. For all I know, he might be considering retaining other counsel."

"Go ahead and step back, and I'll handle this."

Stevie was barely back to counsel table before Solomon started admonishing her client.

"Mr. Barkley, I understand you have not spoken to pretrial services, nor have you completed the paperwork necessary for me to continue the appointment of the public defender's office to your case. Do you plan to hire an attorney on your own?"

Barkley shifted in place, but he didn't answer.

"You have every right not to speak to pretrial services, but I can't use taxpayer dollars to fund your defense until you do the minimum required of you to show you can't afford to hire counsel." Solomon leaned across the bench and fixed Barkley with a hard stare. "Ms. Palmer is a fine attorney. If you want to keep her, complete the paperwork before you leave here today."

"Yes, sir."

Stevie watched the exchange with mixed feelings, but she didn't have long to wonder what Barkley would decide. The rest of the proceeding went like clockwork. The judge set a date for trial in the spring and entered an order denying bail. The minute he gaveled the hearing to a close, Barkley held out his hand and said, "I need the form."

She waited and watched while he filled it out, which didn't take long considering he had very few assets. His job had paid well, but it was gone, and she imagined he'd lived like a lot of twenty-five-year-olds, thinking they'd save when they were much older. He handed the form to her without another word, and merely nodded her way when the bailiff herded him into the holdover. Stevie watched him go wondering how the hell she was going to get him to open up to her. Frustrated, she gathered her things and walked out of the courtroom with Emily following close behind.

"Was Solomon asking you about a motion for a competency examination?"

"Maybe."

"The guy's not incompetent, you know."

"Maybe he is, maybe he isn't."

"Are you going to file?"

Stevie hunched her shoulders. "I haven't decided. Are you going to get me that early discovery?"

"I'll try."

"In the meantime, maybe you could tone down the rhetoric. 'Flagrant disregard'? If you talk like that to the press, they'll skewer this guy before he has a chance in court."

"That's my job." Emily jabbed her shoulder. "Besides, you've said much worse about my witnesses in the past." She waved. "I've got to get back to the office for a meeting. I'll talk to you later."

Stevie watched Emily go, reflecting on her words. She had said bad things about government witnesses in the past when she needed to in order to make her case. She liked to think she never stretched the truth too far out of recognition, but they all did what they had to do to advocate for their clients. She supposed it was a little like politics, which led her back to thoughts of Meredith Mitchell. Despite having lived most of her life in DC, Stevie had never in a million years thought she'd be dating a politician, having written most of them off as fake and power hungry, but Meredith struck her as uniquely genuine.

You barely even know her. Her internal voice spoke the truth, but with it came another revelation, equally true. *But I'd like to.*

CHAPTER THREE

Stevie swatted away Hannah's hand and reached for the zipper on her pants. She'd asked Hannah, the case coordinator for the PD's office, to help her figure out what to wear to the wedding, and Hannah had taken on dressing her as her personal mission. "When I asked for your help, I meant big picture. I have the mechanics down."

"Right. Sorry. I might be a bit of a micro manager."

Stevie smiled. "I probably should've gotten a clue by the way you boss us all around at the office." She started to turn toward the mirror, but Hannah held her in place.

"Give me one more minute." Hannah fiddled with her lapel and then placed a hand on each shoulder and turned her around. "Take a deep breath and then tell me I'm the master of fashion."

Stevie stared at her reflection, hardly able to believe the transformation. She was no stranger to suits, but this midnight blue, vintage cut was next level. "Who am I and what have you done with the real Stevie Palmer?"

"Oh, she's still there," Hannah said with a huge smile. "We just brought out your inner movie star. Those stodgy politicians are going to die when you walk in the room. Just you wait. You'll have every woman in the room trying to take you home."

"Sounds great except for the fact..." Stevie let her voice trail off. She was about to bring up the fact she was attending the wedding with a date, but was she, or was escorting Meredith Mitchell merely a matter of convenience? She hadn't spoken to Meredith since their brief phone conversation earlier in the week followed up by a text to say she'd send a car to pick her up at five p.m. today. For all she knew, she was meeting Meredith at the wedding. What would Meredith tell people about who she was? An acquaintance? One of the many people who testified in front of the Senate Judiciary Committee? Stevie stared into the mirror. This wasn't her. Why was she pretending to be something she wasn't just because a pretty, accomplished woman had coaxed her into it?

"I don't think I should go," she said, but her mumbled declaration was drowned out by the sound of her doorbell.

"Sounds like your chariot is here, and just in time." Hannah brushed a lock of hair off her forehead. "Any longer and you'd probably get wrinkled or spill something on yourself."

"Thanks for the vote of confidence." Stevie took a deep breath and braced for the evening ahead. She'd said she would go, and she always kept her word. Besides, there was no way she was going to disappoint Hannah by tugging off the outfit she'd so thoughtfully put together after consulting all the current fashion mags. "I promise not to spill anything on my clothes. At least not until everyone is too drunk to notice."

"That's my girl. Now go get the door before your carriage turns into a pumpkin. I'll lock up."

Stevie squared her shoulders and strode to the door determined to be confident. She swung the door open and was shocked to see Meredith standing on her front porch, dressed in a deep burgundy A-line, one shoulder gown. "Wow."

Meredith grinned. "Wow is right. That suit is stunning." She reached out and touched the sleeve of Stevie's jacket. "This looks like Dior?"

"It is. Vintage."

Stevie turned at the sound of Hannah's voice and recognized her attempt to keep from grinning with pride, but she was failing miserably. "Senator Mitchell, meet my colleague and fashion consultant, Hannah Bennett."

Hannah took Meredith's extended hand. "I merely played a small role in dressing your date." She waved her hand to indicate Stevie's outfit. "The charm is all her."

Stevie watched Meredith's face for a reaction to the word date, but Meredith's expression didn't change. She crooked her elbow and said, "Ready to go?"

The drive to the wedding venue was a delicate dance between wanting to talk to Meredith, but being ever conscious her driver could hear their every word. Stevie settled on shoptalk. "Thanks again for agreeing to take up the sentencing issue. You have a new fan base at the office."

"I'm guessing my reputation for championing the underdog was a bit lackluster before?"

"Not exactly, but your background comes with a natural bias toward the accused."

A frown flashed across Meredith's face, but it faded quickly into a lazy smile. She reached her hand across the seat and squeezed Stevie's. "Sometimes it's easy to get lost in the bureaucracy. Thanks for reminding me there are real people affected by the decisions we make. Now, enough about work. I think we're in for quite the party tonight."

Stevie embraced the opportunity to learn a bit more about Meredith's personal life. "Which bride invited you to the wedding?"

"I'm friends with both, but it was definitely Addison. We met when she was at the solicitor general's office and I worked for DOJ, years ago. And I was a guest lecturer at Jefferson College when she was dean of the law school. She's a good friend even if our schedules make it hard to connect in person. And of course everyone knows Julia Scott."

"Well, I know of her, that's for sure."

"Sorry, I forget we run in different circles."

Nothing about Meredith's friendly manner had changed, but the comment stung. "Not everyone can be one of the cool kids, I suppose."

"Whoa there, that's not at all what I meant. What I should've said was if you have to run in circles here in DC, then Julia's someone you have to know. Her campaign work is legendary, and if you're a Democrat elected to office, you have her to thank—directly or indirectly. And of course, now that she's President Garrett's chief of staff, she's the gatekeeper for all things politics."

"Got it. Sorry about that. I might be a tad sensitive." Stevie looked out the window as the car pulled to a stop in front of the massive National Buildings Museum. "And I might be a little out of my depth. Is this where the wedding is being held?"

"This is the place." Meredith squeezed her hand again and leaned forward to speak to her driver. "Erica, we might be pretty late." She handed Erica a slip of paper. "They've arranged quarters for all the drivers, but feel free to take off if you want. I'll text you when we're ready to go."

"Thank you, Senator. I'll be waiting when you're ready to go." Erica was out of the car opening Meredith's door within seconds, but by the time she'd walked around to the other side, Stevie was already standing on the sidewalk. Erica winked and tipped her hat. "See you both later. Have a wonderful evening."

"Are you ready to go in?" Meredith asked, appearing at her side.

Stevie watched the crowd of well-dressed guests making their way into the building. Half curious, half trepidatious, she put on her best courtroom game face. "Absolutely."

They'd barely made it halfway up the steps of the building before a small crowd of reporters swooped down on them, and Stevie stiffened as they shouted questions. "Senator Mitchell, any comments about the upcoming primaries?" "Will your father be attending the wedding?" "Senator Mitchell, who's your date?"

Meredith smiled and waved, but didn't otherwise respond. Stevie thought she'd done a good job of hiding her discomfort, but Meredith's whispered words told her otherwise.

"Not a fan of the press, are you?"

"Not really."

"Bad personal experience or just general disregard?"

Stevie was impressed at the insight, but this wasn't the place to have this conversation. "A story for another day."

"Then I'll hope that we have another day in our future," Meredith said, her eyes full of promise. "Rest assured there will be no reporters inside."

A moment later, they checked their coats at the door and walked into the main entry. Stevie craned her head, gazing at the tall columns in the center of the room basked in glowing light.

"Pretty amazing, right?"

"Amazing doesn't do it justice," Stevie replied. She started to say more, but a booming voice from behind startled her.

"Meredith Mitchell, didn't I teach you to show up earlier than this for important events?"

The man speaking was tall and handsome in an older gentleman kind of way, and he looked vaguely familiar, yet it wasn't until he scooped Meredith into a hug that Stevie recognized him as Meredith's father, James Mitchell, the former governor of New York and the beautiful older woman next to him must be Meredith's mother. Stevie watched their affectionate exchange with a trace of envy.

"Stevie, these are my parents, James and Anna Mitchell. Mom and Dad, this is my friend, Stevie Palmer."

Stevie shook their hands. "Nice to meet you both." It was. Kind of. But mostly it was strange to meet Meredith's parents so soon into their dating lifespan. To add to the strangeness, a male version of Meredith appeared at their side.

"Hey, sis, did you bring a date? We only saved you one seat. Jen's watching them for us."

Stevie watched Meredith's face twitch slightly, but she covered it fast with an introduction. "Stevie, meet my brother, Michael. He runs a data analytics company because he lacks the social skills to run for public office." She play-jabbed her brother in the side. "Isn't that right, Mikey?" Before he could reply, Meredith said "Actually, we already have seats reserved. We'll catch up with you all at the reception." She grabbed Stevie's arm and steered her in the opposite direction. "Sorry about that."

"No need. Did you know your family was coming?"

"Yes, but I really didn't think it through. They're all so connected with this crowd, I'm used to seeing them pretty much everywhere I go."

Stevie started to ask Meredith what the "it" was that she hadn't thought through, but before she could come up with a way to form the question that didn't sound confrontational, Meredith gestured toward a row of tables covered in white cloth and lined with glass flutes. "Glass of champagne before we find our seats?"

"Drinking before nuptials. Brilliant idea." Stevie filed away her question and followed Meredith to the table, grateful not to talk about anything too serious in the festive crowd. Although the champagne bar was fairly close, it took forever to get there since Meredith was stopped every few feet by someone she knew. She was gracious to everyone even when it was apparent she barely knew the person who'd approached her. They were steps from the table, when a handsome woman in a tux pulled her into a hug. "They just let anyone in this place don't they?"

"I guess so, if *you're* here."

"Somebody has to keep the crowd in line."

Stevie watched the exchange and noticed another woman standing beside the tuxedoed woman wearing an Army dress uniform. The colonel leaned close and whispered. "Let me guess, you're not in politics."

"Not even close."

She stuck out a hand. "Zoey Granger, nice to meet you."

Stevie returned the firm grip. "Stevie Palmer. Since you seem to know your way around, care to give me a play-by-play?"

Zoey grinned. "I'll do what I can, but I'm constantly playing catch-up." She motioned to the woman in the tux who had buttonholed Meredith. "That's my girlfriend, Rook Daniels. Former fixer, she's now—"

"The White House communications director." Stevie shook her head. "I thought she looked familiar."

Zoey nodded. "She went to law school with Julia Scott, and Julia's the one who coaxed her out of her private practice into government life." She cocked her head. "And you're here with Senator Mitchell. But you're clearly not in politics, so I'm guessing lawyer."

"You'd be right."

"You could swing a cat in this room and hit a lawyer every time."

Stevie glanced around at the formally dressed crowd and figured most of the lawyers in this room probably made more in a month than she made in a year. "True, but I'm afraid this isn't my usual crowd. I'm a federal public defender."

"I knew we had something in common. If you decide to hang around with this crowd, I predict we're going to be good friends."

"Who's hanging around with what crowd?" Rook approached with Meredith, and they passed around glasses of champagne. Zoey took the glass Rook handed to her and inclined her head for Rook's kiss. Stevie watched them intently, wondering how they'd met and if their love was still new. Lost in thought, she started at the soft hint of Meredith's breath near her ear.

"I see you're making friends with the gang."

Stevie grinned. "There's a gang?"

"There is. Rook is not just a good person to know, she's good people. I haven't had much time to get to know Zoey, but if Rook loves her, then she's top-notch."

"Are all your friends politicians?"

"You're not."

"Evasive answer." Stevie wondered again if Meredith considered her only a friend, but she didn't want to press the point. Not here. Besides, this wasn't her crowd and it never would be. Rook and Zoey and Addison and Julia might be solid people, but no way could she ever fit in here. Too much money, too much power and concern about appearances. She resolved to enjoy this evening and then go back to her life in the trenches where her version of champagne was a ten-dollar a bottle Prosecco served not in fancy crystal glasses, but from whatever wasn't already in the dishwasher.

❖

During the ceremony, Meredith glanced over at Stevie who was watching Addison and Julia at the front of the room with rapt attention. What was Stevie thinking? Was she dreaming of a romantic wedding of her own or was she merely being polite and biding her time until the reception started? Bringing a date to a wedding had been a stupid idea. First off, the entire first part of the evening involved sitting in a room and being quiet. It was like going to a movie without the snacks. No time for interaction, getting to know each other. Second, and most important, the entire romantic wedding experience gave the wrong impression. Who wouldn't end up dreamy and romantic after an entire evening spent celebrating happily ever after?

Happily ever afters were fine for people like Addison and Julia who'd already reached the pinnacle of their careers. Addison had a lifetime appointment to the bench, and Julia could write her ticket on the speaking circuit after her stint as White House chief of staff was over. Meredith sighed. Her career was only just starting to take flight. Two years ago, she'd captured the national spotlight with her rousing speech at the Democratic National Convention, and since then the murmurs had started, asking when she planned her presidential run. All of these events had been carefully planned; in fact almost every action in her life had been carefully plotted to maximize her chances at success.

"They look so happy."

She turned toward Stevie. Was that a tear she spotted in the corner of Stevie's eye? She wouldn't have pegged Stevie to be so sentimental, not after the fierce delivery of her testimony before the judiciary committee, but then again Stevie had managed to personalize sentencing guidelines—not an easy feat. The realization left Meredith torn between fondness that her date had a heart and fear that she might expect more than she had to give. "They do," she whispered. "It's a pretty grand affair."

"It is, but I was talking about the way they look at each other, like no one else is in the room. Like none of this," Stevie gestured at the room, "matters. The president of the United States is in the room, but it's like they could be standing in the middle of a condemned building with dirt floors and still be just as happy because they'd found each other."

Whoa. Stevie's statement packed a ton of emotion, and Meredith shifted in her seat. Was that the kind of relationship Stevie wanted? One that ended in dreamy looks and I dos exchanged in front of all the people in your life? Hell, they were only on their second date. She stared at Stevie who was refocused back on the front of the room, and took a breath. No, she was just blowing things out of proportion. Weddings brought out the sentimental in people, which was probably why Addison had pushed her to bring a date so she'd have someone to focus all her gushy feelings on after she witnessed their outpouring of emotion. Well, gushy wasn't in the cards. She resolved to spend the evening having a great time and not get bogged down in any greater meaning. In a minute, Addison and Julia would be hitched and they could get to the fun part of the date. She hoped Stevie liked to dance.

An hour later, the party was in full swing and she and Stevie were on the dance floor with Rook, Zoey, Addison, and Julia. "I can't believe I'm dancing to an 80s cover band, three feet from the chief justice of the United States," Stevie said. "No one at the office is going to believe me when I tell them about this."

"Especially not when you tell them the president was doing the electric slide at the very same party." Meredith inclined her head to where Garrett and Julia were doing a decent job with the steps of the line dance.

"They look like great friends."

"They are as much as any politicians can be."

"Are you saying politicians can't be friends?"

Meredith heard the edge beneath Stevie's question. "Not at all, but this life can get complicated. Fast."

As if on cue, Julia's deputy chief of staff tapped her on the shoulder, and she and Garrett stepped to the side of the dance floor to huddle. Addison and her brother, who'd been dancing before, glided over to Meredith and Stevie.

"Is something up?" Meredith asked.

Addison shrugged. "Life as usual at our house. I don't know what Julia's going to do with herself in two years when social interruptions and late night wake-up calls are no longer par for the course. In the meantime, I'm not working, so let's have some fun. I happen to know where there's an expensive bottle of Scotch squirreled away if any of you are interested."

Meredith turned to Stevie and raised her eyebrows.

"Oh, you had me at Scotch. The expensive part—that's just icing on the cake. Count me in."

Meredith smiled and took Stevie's arm and followed Addison and her brother Jack to a room off the side of the main ballroom. On the way, Addison waved Rook and Zoey over and insisted they join in. "What is this?" Meredith asked as they pushed their way in.

"This is Bride Number One's private suite," Addison said, pointing at her chest. "Meet Bride One."

"Nice."

"Thanks. This whole affair is a little over-the-top, but you only get married once. Right?"

"I wouldn't know since most of my family is wedded to their careers." Meredith raised her glass. "But if throwing a fantastic party is any indication, you and Julia are destined to be together forever."

Addison smiled. "My wife is conducting a business meeting at our wedding. I think we've gone beyond what's proper. Besides, if you love someone, there's nothing that can keep you apart."

Meredith caught Stevie watching her as Addison spoke, but she couldn't get a read on her expression. Wistful? Maybe a trace of pain? Definitely not longing, and the realization robbed some of her joy, which made absolutely no sense considering her resolution to treat this entire evening as a casual outing. Deciding not to dwell on it, she turned to Addison. "Okay, Bride One, where's this Scotch you were bragging about?"

"Jack, grab that bottle from the cabinet, please."

He did as his sister asked and read the label before setting it on the table. "Twenty-five-year-old Balvenie single malt. Nice."

"It doesn't hurt when your wife sits at the right hand of the president. President Garrett had a bottle delivered to each of our suites. When we finish mine, we can go plunder Bride Two's supply. Zoey, can you grab some glasses from that shelf over there?"

Zoey handed them each a glass and then stuck hers out toward Jack. Rook stepped up and placed an arm around Zoey's waist. "Hey, babe, I didn't think you were big on Scotch."

"Not normally, but I'm not about to pass up drinking pure gold. Since this is probably the only time in my life I'll ever drink anything this expensive, count me in."

Stevie stepped up. "I'll drink to that. Public servants lining up for a sip of fancy liquor."

Meredith laughed and joined them. Jack had just begun pouring when Julia burst through the door with Jennifer by her side.

"There are five hundred wedding guests waiting for us to cut a cake and you clowns are in here drinking."

Meredith raised her glass. "You make it sound like we're having a kegger. We're having fancy drinks. When we're done here, we're going to your suite and drinking your bottle."

"You're going to want to be sober for what I'm about to tell you." Julia glanced back at the closed door. "This can't leave the room for the next hour. Understood?"

Meredith didn't have to look to know that most of the people in the room were looking Stevie's way since she was the only one not part of the group. "We get it. State secrets and all that. Pretty sure you're safe in this crowd of attorneys and soldiers."

"Connie Armstrong is about to announce she's pulling out of the race."

Rook let out a low whistle and Addison shook her head. Meredith froze with the glass of Scotch halfway to her lips. She set it on the table, needing to be perfectly sober for this conversation. "What happened?"

"Information is still coming in, but it appears that the network at her Dallas headquarters was hacked and emails have been leaked. I haven't seen them yet, but word is they are pretty damaging. There's a meeting scheduled at Connie's office in an hour."

Addison moved to Julia's side. "Tell me you don't have to go."

"You couldn't make me. But, Rook, I'm afraid that means—"

Rook set her glass down. "On it. Zoey, you should stick around. I hear the cake's fantastic."

Meredith watched Rook dash off, and she reached into her bag, itching to make a call. Surely someone she knew had some inside info on what was about to come out. Whatever it was, it had to be big to take someone like Connie Armstrong down.

"Do you need to go too?"

She looked up into Stevie's eyes. What she needed and what she wanted were tangled up in the way she felt about this woman. She couldn't let that happen. Torn between wanting to go and wanting to stay, she searched her gut for answers, but Jen appeared at her side before she could settle on a plan.

"Mere, we should go."

Jen was right. Whatever news was breaking could have huge ramifications for their entire party, and everyone who valued their political future would be wise to stay on top of it. She trusted Jen to vet the news, but if this news was big enough to interrupt a bride at her wedding, then she wanted to hear the developments firsthand.

"It's okay. Duty calls. I get it." Stevie smiled. "Trust me. I've left plenty of dates in the lurch for an emergency client call."

Meredith ignored her sister's urgent press on her arm. "Are you sure? I'll ride with Jen, and Erica can take you home."

"Nonsense. I can find my way. Go, take care of business."

Meredith leaned forward and kissed Stevie lightly on the cheek. "Erica will drive you. It's the least I can do for bailing on you. Have a great time. I'll talk to you later." She motioned to Jen who dutifully handed Stevie a business card with Erica's number on the back, and with one last glance at Stevie, made her way to the door.

Another reason not to get serious about anyone: having to bail on dates midway through because one of your Senate colleagues can't run a tight ship. She dared not look back because she knew if Stevie were still watching her, all the reasons would dissolve in a puddle of regret.

❖

"You feel like stalking the cake table with me?" Zoey asked.

"I'm guessing you're used to this," Stevie said.

"I don't know that I'll ever get used to Rook being on call twenty-four seven, but since I used to be married to a job that sent me places on a moment's notice without ever asking how I felt about it, I know what it's like from both sides."

Zoey's words were an echo of the assurances she'd offered Meredith only moments ago, and she wondered if Zoey meant them any more than she had. The truth was, unless someone's life was in jeopardy, she wasn't certain she'd rush off to deal with a crisis in the middle of a date on a Saturday night, but politics had its own set of rules. Rules that thankfully she didn't have to live by. "I should probably go."

"Nope. I'm overruling you," Zoey said. "I could use help edging out these DC insiders who are already circling the cake table. Besides, cake is the very best reason to come to a wedding. I think it might be illegal to leave before you've gotten your share."

"Oh, you do, huh?" Stevie glanced across the room and saw Julia and Addison standing by the gorgeous, many-tiered cake. Thinking Hannah would never forgive her if she didn't provide her with a detailed report on the tasting, she reluctantly agreed. "Okay, I'm in. But you have to stick with me. I recognize a ton of faces in this room, but only from TV."

"Deal." Zoey led them over to a cocktail table on the edge of the dance floor, close to the head table where a photographer was shooting pictures of Addison and Julia cutting the cake. "How long have you been with the PD's office?"

"I started right out of law school, after an internship with the office before graduation."

"Dedicated."

"Or crazy. It's not exactly the golden ladder of legal professions."

"Consider your audience. I get consulting offers all the time, but leaving the service has never been an option for me."

"Where are you stationed now?"

"I have a tenured position at McNair, which makes it easy, but I spent most of my military career jumping from base to base, mostly overseas. It's been an adjustment staying in one place, but being close to Rook makes it worth the effort. The only land mines I'm in danger of now are the ones that are buried in campus politics. Not my favorite, but definitely not life-threatening."

Stevie got it. Her career wasn't without its fair share of politics. The federal public defender—head of her office—was usually a political appointee, and the philosophies of the office often shifted with a change at the top. But for the most part, she'd managed to steer clear of bureaucratic squabbles and focus on her cases. Until last week when she'd appeared before the committee to talk about sentencing guidelines, but even that came with the bonus of meeting Meredith Mitchell.

"Have you known Meredith long?" Zoey asked like a mind reader.

"Not hardly. We met last week. A work thing."

"That bodes well. Rook and I met at a work thing. It wasn't the most fortuitous start, but it worked out well for us."

Stevie returned Zoey's smile but not her enthusiasm. Tonight had been fun, but she could have fun with her coworkers on a night out at happy hour. Besides, fleeting fun, full of interruptions wasn't what she was looking for, if she was looking for anything at all.

Later that night, reclining on her couch with a beer, Stevie flipped through the channels looking for something mindless when MSNBC showed up on her scroll. She hesitated for just a second before stopping her search and tuned in to hear the anchor recapping the stories of the evening.

"While many of Washington's elite were gathered at the National Buildings Museum for the wedding of Chief Justice Addison Riley to President Garrett's chief of staff, Julia Scott, Democratic presidential hopeful Senator Connie Armstrong was hunkered down at her DC campaign headquarters bracing for the fallout from tonight's leading story. Earlier this evening, Justice United, the website notorious for breaking scandalous stories, published dozens of damaging emails from the Armstrong campaign on their website with promises of more to come. We're still analyzing the information that's been released, and I'm turning now to our DC correspondent to detail what we know so far."

Unable to resist now that she felt like she was part of the story, Stevie leaned back and watched the show.

"Thanks, Brian. We're only going to discuss what we've managed to authenticate so far, but even with this little bit, it's a dark day for Armstrong." He pointed to the screen beside him, and an image appeared of an email exchange between Connie Armstrong and one of her high level staffers. He spent a few minutes outlining the issue, but Stevie could clearly see that Connie had authorized firing a female staff member who'd threatened to report alleged sexual abuse from Connie's chief of staff, Dan Nealy.

The correspondent flashed a few more slides and then kicked it back to the anchor who introduced a panel. She didn't need to hear their back and forth to know that Connie Armstrong's campaign was in trouble. Her own words came back to haunt her. Connie wasn't her first choice for the Democratic nomination, but she was probably the strongest candidate in the race. Maybe she could make a comeback.

Wondering what Meredith thought about the breaking news, Stevie started to reach for her phone to text her but stopped short. Meredith was busy, and this little dalliance was over. She'd seen enough tonight to know that no matter how much they connected one-on-one, she and Meredith would never run in the same circles, and Meredith's life was all about running in circles. Tomorrow, she'd have brunch with Hannah and dish about her night of being Cinderella at the ball, and then she'd tuck away the memory as a once in a lifetime experience.

CHAPTER FOUR

Meredith sipped the cold coffee and held back a shudder. Any caffeine was better than no caffeine considering how many more briefing papers she had left to read, and she didn't have the energy to get up and make a fresh cup.

"Go home," Jen said. "I'll read the rest of those. You could use a good night's sleep. Or better yet, get laid, but be discreet. Hey, what about that woman you brought to the wedding last weekend? She looked like she'd be fun in bed."

Meredith picked up a pencil and threw it across the table with deadly aim. "You know that line you walk between sister and staffer? You just crossed it in about a dozen different ways."

Jen raised her hands in protest. "What? I was merely making an observation. You've been going ninety to nothing all week. If you don't get some rest or," she paused to offer a meaningful grin, "relaxation, you're going to implode. Besides, I set up a meeting for tomorrow morning with the DNC, and you're going to want to be fresh for what they have to say."

Meredith set her mug down hard. "No, Jen. I told you, we're not wading into this."

"They requested the meeting. Are you really going to deny them the opportunity to make their pitch?"

Rumors had been swirling around the capital since Connie had bowed out of the race about who would be the best person to take up the party banner, but the pundits were lukewarm about the rest of the candidates left in the field. The twenty-four-hour news cycle meant they'd quickly run out of things to say about the remaining players, so cable news had turned to the topic of new blood and just who could enter the race and turn the primary on its head. Meredith's name was topping every list.

"I wouldn't mind hearing what they have to say, but under very different circumstances. Whoever leaps to the front of the line is going to have a lot of catching up to do. Considering we haven't been in the race at all, there's no way we can get up to speed."

Jen tossed a file on her desk. "Not entirely true." She pointed at the file. "Take that home and read it. Michael's been hard at work over the last year gathering data, and all his projections have you ahead in the polls within a week of entering the race."

Meredith didn't open the folder containing their brother's handiwork. "Those numbers are just fluff. People like the bright, shiny new candidate. Does he have polls showing projections closer to the New Hampshire primary?"

"Matter of fact, he does." Jennifer picked up the folder and shoved it in Meredith's briefcase. "Erica's waiting for you out back. The numbers don't lie. Go home, sleep on it, and we'll talk in the morning before the meeting. If you're really not interested, I won't push you, but all the planning in the world won't create this perfect storm of opportunity. Don't waste this chance. The motto for the day is fresh face wins the race. There might be something to this."

Meredith slid into the back seat of the car and stared out the window as Erica drove to her apartment near the Capitol while Jen's words played over and over in her mind. As aggravating as it was, Jen was right. Politics was fifty percent planning and fifty percent chance. Her long-term plan consisted of finishing out her current Senate term before considering a presidential run, and if Armstrong were to have won, then waiting another four to eight years before mounting her own campaign. Stepping in now seemed incredibly risky and chaotic. But what if this was her best chance to secure the Democratic nomination?

"Will you be needing me later, Senator?"

Meredith looked up and saw they were parked outside her townhouse. She met Erica's eyes in the rearview mirror. "No, I plan to stay in for the night." She started to open the door, but paused. "Erica, may I ask you a personal question?"

"Sure."

She plunged ahead before she could change her mind. "What are the characteristics you're looking for in a president?"

Erica laughed. "Not exactly personal. I suppose I look for things like drive and intelligence. The ability to play well with others without abandoning core values."

"You've given this some thought."

"Something tells me you have too." Erica grinned. "You mind if I ask you a question?"

"Go for it."

"Are you going to run?"

Meredith chuckled. "Something tells me you've been playing talk radio while you're waiting for me." She shook her head. "If I ever run, you'll be one of the first to know." She exited the car before Erica could ask another question. As she walked up the steps, she made a mental note to have Jen prepare some scripted answers for questions like Erica's until she knew exactly what she planned to do.

Once inside, she shucked off her suit jacket and tossed it on the armchair just inside the foyer and kicked her shoes to the side of the chair. One of the joys of living alone was the ability to make small messes without consequence. She wandered her way to the kitchen and poured a glass of wine from the bottle she'd opened the night before. It was an earthy red, and her first thought was how well it would go with a burger, and her second thought was she was starving. She reached for her phone to order a delivery, and as she scrolled through the options on the app, she thought about Stevie and the burger they'd shared at The Saloon.

She'd sent a box of chocolates to Stevie's office with a note apologizing for ducking out of the wedding, but the better part of a week had passed with no acknowledgement. She knew it had been a jerk move to abandon her date, but Stevie's silence was a clear message she wasn't interested in forgiving the slight, and Meredith really didn't have any business dating someone who had a problem with her chaotic schedule. So why was it so hard for her to stop thinking about Stevie?

She knew the answer. Stevie was the first woman she'd met in who knew how long who was willing to speak truth to power. Most of the single women Meredith crossed paths with were either jockeying for favors or her money. Stevie was different. Outspoken, opinionated, and intelligent—Stevie challenged her and she liked it.

Her phone buzzed in her hand, and she nearly jumped out of her skin at the sound. She glanced at the display and smiled at the text, taking it as a sign that her fondness for Stevie wasn't entirely one-sided.

❖

Stevie walked in the door to her office and sighed at the pile of work on her desk that had grown in the three days she'd been away. The NACDL seminar in Chicago had been chock full of great information, but when it came down to it, she and the other public defenders were so busy trying to keep up with the load they had, it was hard to think about adding new skills.

She sank into her chair and tried not to let the stack of files overwhelm her when she spotted a box from Harper Macaw, well-known DC chocolatier. She shoved the files aside and pulled the box toward her, spotting a card with her name penned in lavish script.

She was still staring at the box when Joe poked his head in the door, and she crossed her arms over it, unsure why she was bothering to hide it from him.

"What are you doing?" he asked.

She jerked her chin at the files. "Getting a head start on tomorrow. I see you didn't do all my work while I was away."

He waved a hand. "Forget all that and come out with us. Hannah's holding a spot at Quarry House and she won't be able to fend people off for long."

"I can't. I've got a hearing on Friday, and I've got to play catch-up with all these files."

"Who's the boss?"

"Depends. Are you going to tell the judge why I don't have a solid argument to suppress this evidence?"

"Tell you what. You come out with us tonight and I'll carve out some time tomorrow to go through the case file with you. Deal?"

She shouldn't, but maybe a reset was what she needed to bridge from inspiring conference to back to the grind. "Okay. I'll meet you there." She noted his dubious expression and she crossed her heart. "I swear I'll be there. I just need to take care of one thing."

Stevie waited until the door was shut and his footfalls faded away before slitting open the card. Unlike her first delivery from Meredith Mitchell, this one was on personal, rather than official stationary. The note was simple and short. *A woman should never leave a date at a party, no matter what the reason. Please accept my apologies and assurance it won't ever happen again. Oh, and here's a little something to sweeten your day.*

She read the card three times before reaching for the box and surveying the contents. Her favorite chocolates. How could Meredith know she had a weakness for these bars? Before she could second-guess the action, Stevie reached for her phone and typed a quick text. *You made my day.*

She'd barely set the phone back down when it buzzed. *My goal entirely. I hope you've had a good week so far.*

Pleased that Meredith was keeping the conversation going, Stevie thumbed a quick response. *Been away at a conference and glad to be home. Ignoring the mountain of work on my desk in favor of a night out.* She hit send and immediately questioned why she had shared that little tidbit.

On a school night? Sounds intriguing.

There it was. A perfect opening. Stevie stared at the phone in her hand wavering between the safe zone of a night with her coworkers and flirting with the danger that was Meredith Mitchell. Her thumbs hovered over the phone, waiting for her to choose, but she knew before she started typing that the choice had been made the moment she'd read Meredith's apology. She was irresistibly drawn to Meredith, and the reasons why outweighed any warnings of caution her mind could conjure. Before her brain could overrule the rest of her body, she typed, *Join me? Quarry House at seven.*

Seconds passed. Long, slow, excruciating seconds, shredding the easy confidence that had driven her to issue the invitation. She considered turning off her phone to avoid further embarrassment and even moved to do so, but before she could slip the offending instrument away, it buzzed again.

Make it seven thirty and I'll be there.

This time Stevie was the one to wait, not out of payback but out of sheer wonder at what she'd just done. She'd invited Meredith to join her on a lark, but now that she'd accepted Stevie had to face the reality of Meredith showing up at a bar with a bunch of public defenders, most of whom would be teasing Stevie unmercifully the next day about her surprise guest. She didn't care as long as she got to see Meredith again.

Sounds perfect.

❖

Meredith changed into jeans, loafers, and a sweater. She took out her contacts and put on her glasses, relieved to relax her eyes and change her appearance ever so slightly. She shoved a credit card and some cash into her wallet and grabbed her phone and headed for the door, instinctively looking for her car before she remembered she'd told Erica she was in for the night. It was for the best. The Quarry House wasn't the type of place you showed up with a town car and a driver.

When she stepped outside, she hugged her arms around her chest and walked briskly to generate heat. The Metro stop was only a block away. She had to buy a card from the machine, and it took a second to dig up the muscle memory to accomplish the task, but within a few moments, she pushed through the turnstile and boarded the train bound for Silver Spring, Maryland.

Dressed as she was, she blended in with the rest of the people on the train, which was a rarity. After giving the opening speech at the last Democratic National Convention, her face had been plastered on the national news, and she'd been tagged to serve as spokesperson for numerous other candidates in her party. Things had died down a bit since then, but she rarely made it across town without being recognized and spoken to by either a colleague or a curious onlooker.

When she reached the bar, she paused at the top of the steep stairs that led to the basement destination and took a moment to experience each of the emotions churning through her. Excitement about seeing Stevie again. Apprehension about how she would be received after having abandoned her at the wedding. And nostalgia. She'd come here many times when she was just another face in the crowd, eager to escape the trappings that came with the expectations of her family dynasty.

She'd barely stepped off the last stair when she heard Stevie call her name. She turned slightly and was relieved to see Stevie wearing a broad smile, warm and welcoming. Meredith wanted to slip into the warmth of it and stay there for the rest of the evening, far away from the growing buzz of whether or not she would enter the presidential race.

"Glad you could make it," Stevie said. She stepped back and swept her gaze over Meredith. "This is a nice look."

"Thanks. I call it Metro chic."

"You took the rail? What, no Erica?"

Pleasantly surprised that Stevie remembered her driver's name, Meredith grinned. "Everyone needs a night off once in a while, don't you think?"

"I do."

Stevie reached to grab her hand and Meredith followed her across the room, noting that it felt nice to be led around instead of leading. As they approached a table of rowdy patrons, Stevie let her grasp slip. The absence of her touch was distinct, and Meredith went on alert. Did Stevie know these people?

She didn't have to wait long for an answer. Stevie turned back with an apologetic look and whispered. "I'm feeling a little guilty now that I didn't mention this was a group activity. You ready to meet my coworkers?"

Meredith wasn't, but from an early age she'd been trained to do things she didn't want to do. She plastered a smile on her face and prepared for the worst, thinking this was likely payback for the wedding stunt.

"Hey, gang," Stevie said. "I'd like you to meet a new friend of mine. Senator Meredith Mitchell, this is the gang."

While Stevie introduced her to each of her coworkers, Meredith made mental notes. The stylish office manager. The scruffy-looking but affable boss. The just-graduated from law school intern with her harried, but still enthusiastic glow. She shook all their hands and filed their names away for future use.

"Senator Mitchell, nice to meet you in person," Boss guy, Joe, said. "Although I have to say this isn't the type of place I'd expect to run into you."

"It's a basement bar with a great spread of beer. Where else would I be?" Before he could answer, she pressed on. "Believe it or not, I used to come here when I was in law school. Best post study group sessions ever. We solved all the problems of the world. I'm glad to see the restoration kept so much of the original charm."

Meredith caught Stevie's grin and Joe nodded his approval.

"Stevie tells me you are reconsidering some of the mandatory minimums in the sentencing guidelines," said Joe.

"She made some good arguments during the committee hearing. The least I could do was look into it a little further. And it's Meredith, please."

"Meredith it is, although I hear there might be a new title in your future."

She knew where this was going and sought to deflect it fast. "I'm happy with where I am for now, but as for your question about the sentencing guidelines, I think Stevie made some excellent points and I like to keep an open mind." Her words echoed in light of her upcoming meeting with the DNC, and the choices she would have to make in the coming weeks threatened to overwhelm the laid-back nature of this evening. She pushed back. "But I get the feeling you're here to decompress, not talk shop."

"Talk shop is all these lawyers know how to do," the fashionable one, Hannah, said. "Can I get you a drink?"

"That would be great." Meredith pulled out her credit card. "And a round for the group?"

Hannah waved away her card. "Your money's no good here. Any friend of Stevie is a friend of ours."

Meredith watched her walk to the bar, and she felt a tug on her arm. She followed Stevie a few feet away. "Hannah seems nice."

"You haven't seen her try to wrangle us at the office." Stevie ducked her head. "I suppose I should've warned you I wasn't going to be alone."

"Like I warned you I might ditch you at a wedding? I'm sure that I'm way ahead of you in the jerk moves column." Meredith replayed the words in her head and scrambled to recover. "Not that this was a jerk move by any means. Everyone seems nice, and it's fun to see you in your natural environment."

Stevie's face flushed slightly. "Speaking of natural environment. I don't think I've ever seen you photographed in anything but a sharply-tailored suit." She waved a hand up and down. "I like this look. You seem relaxed, approachable."

Meredith felt her own cheeks warm. "And here I was going for the I can't pick her out in a crowd look."

"Seriously, I like it. It's a side of you I wouldn't have predicted."

"I might be full of surprises." Had she really just said that? What a corny line.

"You might be."

"And how about you?" Meredith paused for effect. "Is the Stevie Palmer you see the one you get?"

"Depends on who's doing the getting."

Before their flirtatious banter could continue, Hannah returned with their drinks. "Come on, you two, let's get back to the table before someone tries to steal our seats."

Meredith dutifully followed as Hannah led her away, and next thing she knew, she was caught up in lively conversation with Stevie's coworkers. Everyone was nice and ostensibly treated her like one of them, but she couldn't help but notice the raised eyebrows and curious stares when they thought she wasn't looking. It was obvious these people were like family to Stevie, and Meredith wondered what had motivated Stevie to invite her to meet them. Was it so she could see firsthand some of the impact her work as a senator had on the lives of the people who had to work with the laws she passed or was it something more personal? Whatever it was, she was glad to be here.

They'd just finished the tie-breaking game, when Stevie appeared at her shoulder. "Come with me for a sec?"

"Sure."

They walked toward the bar. "I invited you tonight because I wanted to see you, but I also wanted you to meet these people. They work hard in the trenches every day, and everything you do—"

"Affects them. I get it." Meredith forced a smile, disappointed to hear Stevie's motivation for the invitation wasn't more personal.

"I appreciate the way you put a face on the things you're passionate about. It's one of the reasons I was drawn to you in the first place."

"And I appreciate that you were willing to hear me out."

Meredith reached a hand over to Stevie's arm. "And I really was sorry to leave you at the wedding. I may have been a jerk, but I'm a dedicated one."

Stevie waved her off. "Forgiven. Completely. But I have a question that's been bugging me ever since you asked me to the wedding."

"Fire away."

Stevie opened her mouth, but she was interrupted by a shout from her boss. Everyone's phone started dinging with alerts, and Meredith felt the buzz of her own phone in her pocket. She resisted the urge to check it for as long as she could, but as all eyes in the bar started to look her way, her resistance started to wear.

"Go ahead," Stevie said.

Meredith paused, curious if this was a test. She wanted to pass, more than she wanted to know the breaking news, but before she could test her resolve, a shout from Joe sealed her fate.

"Drudge says you're running for president. Is it true?"

Meredith met Stevie's eyes and held her gaze, willing the world to stop for just a moment so she could figure out what came next, but chimes were dinging and the air crackled with anticipation. She would have to answer the question sooner or later, but now all she wanted was to lose herself in Stevie's eyes.

❖

"Sorry about the mob scene back there," Stevie said, watching Meredith's expression for any sign she was annoyed. They'd walked across the street to where the Uber driver was slated to pick Meredith up, and Stevie felt the evening begin to slip away every time Meredith's phone refreshed with new info on how far away he was. "It was a bit of a catch-22. I was worried that if I warned them you were coming, they would've acted goofy, but I'm thinking they were pretty goofy anyway."

Meredith's smile was warm. "It's okay. Really."

"Are you sure you wouldn't rather call Erica to come get you?" Stevie glanced at Meredith, but the shadows from the streetlight hid her expression, and Stevie wondered if Meredith could read her true intent.

Meredith shook her head. "I told her I was staying in for the night."

Stevie rolled the words over in her mind, examining all the angles before asking what she really wanted to know. "I'm guessing you thought this would be a secret rendezvous? The outfit, no driver—I get it now. I suppose I spoiled that by dropping you in the middle of a batch of my coworkers who can't seem to help but make a very public scene." She struggled to keep her tone from being wistful but wasn't certain of her success.

Meredith reached for her hand. "Not even. It's true, I did slip away and was hoping not to be noticed for what I do rather than who I am. When you live your entire life in the spotlight, you learn to seize moments of anonymity."

"Why do you do it? Live in the spotlight, I mean. Do you like it?" The questions were out before Stevie could censor them into something more subtle, but she waited impatiently for the answer.

"It's not a matter of like or dislike. Public service is a calling. Surely you know that or you wouldn't work the job you do."

"I don't think there's a lot of comparison."

"Why? Because my job requires me to win the approval of crowds of people I don't know? Does it make it less worthy because it requires majority vote?"

"That's not fair, but you do raise a good point. There are dozens of ways you could serve the public without having to put a public face on it." Stevie smiled. "Not that it's not a very nice face."

"You think so?"

"I do."

"Maybe you could move to New York and tell the citizens about your endorsement of my face."

"Maybe I could just tell them here if you're going to run for president."

Meredith's face clouded. "I have no idea if that's going to happen, at least not this term."

"If you do, you'd have to hit the road soon. The New Hampshire primary is right around the corner."

"But between now and then there's Thanksgiving and Christmas and at least a dozen Senate votes that need my attention."

"And here I was hoping there might be other things that need your attention." Stevie looked down, wishing she hadn't spoken her desire, but Meredith reached out and tilted her chin back up so they were eye-to-eye.

"Only one person has my attention right now." She squeezed Stevie's hand and almost imperceptibly started to lean in. Stevie held her breath, her heart thudding in her chest, but just when she thought Meredith was going to kiss her, Meredith merely leaned close and whispered. "I think we should schedule a proper date. May I take you to dinner this weekend? Someplace public and not in a basement?"

There were all kinds of reasons to say no, but the question she wanted to ask earlier no longer mattered. If she hadn't been sure the wedding was a date, she was certain now of Meredith's intentions, but it wouldn't be easy. The swell of anticipation around Meredith's candidacy would make any dinner out a press magnet, but Stevie was powerless to resist the pull of her presence. "That would be perfect."

Chapter Five

Meredith followed Jen into the crowded conference room at the Democratic National Committee headquarters and feigned patience as she shook the hands of the power brokers who all rose to greet her, but she didn't offer any comments about the latest developments in the race. She'd instructed Jen to handle the preliminaries to keep things from going off the rails.

"I'm sorry we had to postpone this meeting," Jen said while everyone took their seats. "but the rumors from Drudge don't dictate Senator Mitchell's schedule—the citizens of New York do."

"We're wondering if the senator might be interested in expanding her voter base."

The comment came from Jeremy Peregrine, deputy director of the DNC. His smile seemed genuine, but Meredith read a level of apprehension beneath his friendly visage, which told her exactly why they were here. The party had been scrambling since Connie Armstrong pulled her name from contention. None of the other challengers had sufficient national name recognition to pull off a win against the Republican front-runner, Christopher Bosley, and the clock was ticking for anyone new to enter the race. It was already almost too late, which was likely why Jeremy had nearly had a stroke when Jen had called yesterday to reschedule the meeting to today.

The reason for the postponement was pure strategy. Meredith didn't want to be seen taking a meeting with the DNC hours after Drudge reporting she was running, as if the news was driving the facts instead of the other way around. She'd left Stevie outside the Quarry House and gone back to her apartment to think hard about the road ahead, and she still wasn't sure where she stood or the true source of her hesitancy. Several times the day before she'd come close to picking up the phone and calling Stevie, but she'd stopped before she dialed. What would she have said? Hey, I know we barely know each other, but I'm thinking seriously about this presidential run. Any thoughts?

Ridiculous, but maybe her desire to reach out to someone who might be objective was a factor of feeling like everyone around her viewed her candidacy as a foregone conclusion. And it was—someday. But now, the party was rocked by the scandal of what happened to Armstrong, and some of that animus would no doubt bleed over onto her, never mind the fact she hadn't been remotely involved with anything to do with Armstrong's campaign.

"It's a matter of honor and duty."

Meredith's head snapped to the right. The words had come from Cecily Landau, the finance chair of the DNC, and she wished she'd been paying attention so she didn't have to ask her to repeat them. "What did you just say?"

"It's time for us to have a woman president. Connie was on track to bring that trophy home, but now it's up to you."

She'd never liked Cecily and she liked her less now. "Really? My gender is my number one asset? I always thought it was my brain." She felt Jen press lightly against her arm, and she tempered the tone of her next words but not the content. "No one, I repeat no one, wants to see a woman in the White House more than me. I've worked my entire adult life as an advocate for equality of all kinds, but I'll be damned if you are going to push me into running by using the gender card. Not going to happen. If I choose to run, it'll be because I'm a qualified candidate, just like everyone else in the race. Understood?"

Cecily nodded slowly, but her lips twitched slightly, and Meredith could tell she was itching to say more. She didn't give her the chance. "I'm not convinced that this is the right time. It's no secret that I plan to run someday, but until now I didn't think that would happen until after Connie Armstrong entered her second term. Accelerating my plan by six years is not an ideal approach."

"And that's why it's important for you to know that your party will rally around you," Jeremy said.

"What about the other candidates in the primary?"

"Stroud and Denst are only running to promote their key issues, energy and choice. Neither one of them expect to win, and they'll rally behind the front-runner as soon as we get through Super Tuesday if not before. Lankin wants to win, but it's not his time and he knows it. They'll start dropping like flies after New Hampshire."

Meredith let that one go. The DNC couldn't be seen as forcing anyone from the race, but they would have their ways of showing who their favorites were and making sure the right funding and press bolstered their choice. Politics wasn't always pretty, but was definitely effective. "Okay, but there's one thing we haven't discussed, and you can bet it's going to be the first thing that Bosley or the PACS that support him will feature in ads."

The room became silent, and Meredith knew they all knew what she was talking about even if none of them wanted to broach the subject on their own. She looked at Jen who raised her shoulders as if to say she wasn't sure how to approach it either. "Really? Is no one willing to talk about the fact that not only would I be the first woman president, but I'd also be an out lesbian holding the highest office in the land? Someone needs to start talking about it because you can bet the other side will."

More silence. After a few uncomfortable moments, Cecily spoke first. "It's an issue, certainly, but I'm not sure we need to be the ones bringing it up. Like you pointed out, the focus should be on your qualifications, not personal matters that have nothing to do with your ability to do the job."

"Are you really that naive?" Meredith said. "Whoever brings it up first gets to craft the language used to frame the 'issue.'" She shuddered. "We really need to find another word for my sexuality." She glanced around the room. "And you all need to stop flinching at words like sexuality. I refuse to let my sexual orientation become the central issue in this case, and the way we do that is to normalize it right out of the gate. I want to see some ideas about strategy right away." She looked over at Jen who was grinning broadly. "What?"

"You sound like someone who's decided to run for president."

Meredith grinned back. "Maybe I am."

The rest of the morning was spent making plans. There were teams to assemble and messages to craft, but as everyone in the room started discussing the details, Meredith felt like she was in two places at once—completely engaged in this new adventure and hovering above the table watching her future play out, enthralled with the idea and terrified at the same time. Either way, she wanted to reach out and tell someone her good news, and Stevie's name was the first one that came to mind.

❖

Stevie looked up at the sound of her office door opening, ready to snap at whoever was disturbing her concentration, but when she saw it was Hannah she motioned her in. "Please shut the door behind you. The closer I get to the deadline on this motion, the more I get distracted with interruptions."

"Sorry, but I've got one more. Alice is out sick and needs someone to cover a detention hearing at one."

"Can't you get anyone else? Seriously, Hannah, I need to finish this."

"I promise I asked at least three other people first, but everyone's got a setting in some other court this afternoon. Alice said you owed her one."

Stevie sighed. She did owe Alice a favor for handling a motions hearing for her last month, one that was supposed to be simple, but had turned into an all-day affair. "Give me the ten-second rundown."

"It's a drug case. The usual, conspiracy. He's not the first person listed in the indictment, but he's not the last either."

"Gotcha." The first person listed in a typical indictment was viewed as the head of the conspiracy, and the culpability trickled down from there. "Did he take the interview with pretrial services?"

"He did, but I think that his answers might be questionable at best. On top of that, Alice is worried he'll fail a drug test."

"Judge won't hold it over for a day?"

"It's Reinhardt."

Stevie nodded. Judge Reinhardt ran a tight ship, and if you didn't follow his deadlines, you would be cast off the side to drown. "You tell Alice this makes us even. Reinhardt's going to detain this guy, so it shouldn't take too long." She reached out a hand for the file and started studying the sparse contents while Hannah ducked out of her office. After a few minutes, she determined there wasn't much she could do except make an impassioned argument. Not exactly what she'd geared up to do today, but putting on a game face was the nature of the job.

Reinhardt's courtroom was milling with attorneys when she walked in. She scanned the defendants in the jury box and matched one of the faces to the booking photo in her file, but when she started to walk over, she was distracted at the sound of someone calling her name from the other side of the courtroom. She turned to see Emily Watkins, the prosecutor from the Barkley case.

"Hey, Em, I'm just here for Alice on the Ortiz case. She and a bunch of others are out with the flu. You have a rec about detention?"

Emily looked confused for a minute and then shook her head. "Not mine. That's Simon's case. Actually, I went to your office looking for you and Hannah said you were down here. Do you have a minute? I need to talk to you." She glanced around the room. "In private."

At that moment, the bailiff entered the room and commanded everyone to rise as he announced the judge who dashed to the bench, slid into his seat, and gazed out expectantly over the crowd. Reinhardt was a seasoned judge who didn't waste time. He called the first case and tapped his finger on the bench impatiently, making Stevie wish yet again that she'd told Hannah no since she hadn't had a second to talk to the client. When the attorney for the first case walked to counsel table, Stevie walked with them and took a seat in the first row of the gallery next to a pretrial services officer she recognized.

"I'm here for Alice Luther. Do you have the report on Manuel Ortiz?" she whispered, barely getting the question in before the judge started his usual recitation from the bench. The officer handed her a sheaf of papers, and Stevie skimmed the information quickly. Any positive thoughts she'd had about getting bond for Ortiz faded as she read the report. No local family ties, lots of priors, and he'd conclusively failed the drug test administered after his arrest. Those things combined with the fact the crime he was charged with carried an overwhelming presumption against granting bail to the defendant, meant this entire exercise was an uphill battle.

When Reinhardt called her case, she hurried to counsel table, while the bailiff led Ortiz to the chair next to hers. "Judge, I'm standing in for Alice Luther, who is ill," Stevie said, deciding to risk his anger. "May I have a brief moment to confer with Mr. Ortiz?"

He glared at her, but she stared back at him, knowing from experience that showing weakness would only make him mad. She had a reputation for fighting hard for her clients, and she knew Reinhardt respected her tenacity even when she threatened to throw his tight schedule off the rails.

"Very well," Reinhardt said, waving a hand impatiently.

Stevie turned to Ortiz and shoved a copy of the PSR toward him. "I assume you know you failed the drug test," she whispered.

"Yes."

She flipped through the pages of the report until she got to the part about his criminal history. She pointed at the extensive list. "Is any of this not true?"

He scanned the list and shook his head. "I'm not getting out, am I?"

"No. I can stand up and make some arguments, but the crime you're charged with carries a presumption that you should be kept in custody until trial. There are a few exceptions, but you don't qualify for any of them. The best thing to do is to set a trial date, get discovery from the prosecutor, and see if you have a viable defense or if you can work out a deal."

"Okay. Let's do all that. I can handle myself inside."

How refreshing to have a client who actually communicated with her. Too bad he wasn't hers for the long run. For a second she considered offering to trade the Barkley case for this one, but something about William Barkley intrigued her, and she wasn't ready to give up on him just yet.

After Ortiz was squared away, Stevie walked out of the courtroom and scanned the hall, almost grateful Emily was nowhere in sight. She wanted to know what she had to say about Barkley's case, but she could find out later—after she'd finished working on her motion. She headed for the elevator, eager to get back to the office, but Emily was waiting by the elevator bank.

"We need to talk," she said, her tone ominous. "Do you have a minute to come by my office?"

Stevie hesitated for a second before giving in. She'd be working late this evening, but if she could get this meeting out of the way, maybe it would clear a path for her to focus on everything else she had to do. "Sure."

The prosecutors' suite of offices was a lot like theirs. Lots of young attorneys, bustling around, but the vibe was a little more tense, like they were scared to show any signs of humanity lest it affect their ability to put people behind bars. She followed Emily past the cubicles to Emily's office, one of the few that had a door, befitting her standing as a veteran AUSA. She purposely didn't sit, hoping Emily would take the hint that she was in a hurry.

"That box is yours." Emily pointed to a small box sitting on a table by her desk. "Don't be fooled by the size. There's a hard drive in there, a mirror image of the one we got from Folsom in response to our subpoena. It's pretty extensive."

Great. Stevie managed a fake smile as she mentally factored a large document review into her already overblown schedule. "Thanks. What's up with the early discovery? You have another couple of weeks before you have to produce this stuff."

Emily sighed heavily and steepled her fingers, pressing them to her lips like she was conflicted about whether to respond. Stevie's inner voice whispered that she should just go and get back to work on her motion, but curiosity rooted her in place. They'd known each other a long time, and while almost all of their interaction had been in the role of adversaries, she respected Emily as an opponent and a person. Stevie finally sat down in the chair across from her desk. "Spill."

"The case agents asked me not to tell you yet, but it's my decision, not theirs."

"You're right about that," Stevie said, hoping to urge her along.

"What your guy did was bad, and he's looking at going away for a while." Emily tapped her fingers on the desk for a few seconds and then crossed her arms. "But we have reason to think that there's a bigger problem with Folsom Enterprises."

Stevie instantly perked up. "Like what?"

"I wish I could tell you specifics, but I can't. At least not right now. Let's just say we believe there are other leaks, but the company is stonewalling us."

"I thought Folsom was fully cooperating with your investigation of my client."

"They were, which makes their lack of assistance now pretty glaring," Emily said.

"And you want to find out if Barkley knows anything about these other leaks?"

"Yes. It could be very beneficial for him to talk to us."

Stevie heard the unspoken promise. If Barkley ratted out his employer, the bigger fish, he could cut a deal for a better sentence. And if he didn't happen to know anything, well then, he was an unlucky bastard. Exactly the conundrum she'd described to Meredith on their unofficial first date. "You're going to have to give me something to work with here. I'm not going to ask him to start spilling company secrets without an idea of what you're looking for and some specific guarantees about what you're willing to do if he helps you."

"What's your general feel for him?"

Stevie spent a moment contemplating the question, and longer wondering how much she should share about the fact her client barely communicated with her, making the idea of him outing an entire conspiracy perpetrated by his former employer ludicrous at best. She skated the question. "He seems like a nice guy. Pretty young to be caught up in any of this."

"Youth. I remember when idealism spurred us to action that actually helped people instead of flipping off the establishment."

"Now you sound like a little old woman yelling at people to get off her lawn."

Emily laughed. "You know, you're right." She glanced at the door and back at Stevie. "I need to talk to some people before I can share specifics, but I promise you that, as much as it pains me, I will absolutely go to bat for your guy if he comes through." She stood. "Go ahead and look through the discovery and I'll get back to you soon."

Saying she had another court appearance that afternoon, Emily walked her out of the suite. As they waited for the elevator, Emily said, "*Fishbowl* had some nice pics of you at Addison Riley's wedding."

Stevie feigned a smile. "It was a beautiful evening."

"Have you and Senator Mitchell been dating long?"

"Who said we're dating? Maybe we both just happened to be invited."

"Maybe."

The elevator dinged. Stevie willed the door to open quickly. She didn't want to stick around to hear Emily gossip about her and Meredith. She stepped into the car, but before the doors could close, Emily said, "Did you know the Mitchell Foundation is a client of Folsom Enterprises?"

Stevie stuck her hand in the doors to stop them from closing. "Half of Washington is a client of Folsom. What are you implying?"

Emily shrugged. "Nothing."

"Seriously, Em, if you have something to say, spit it out."

Emily sighed. "Really, it's nothing. Just a weird coincidence."

"Don't you have enough on your plate without trying to stir things up?"

"I guess. How about you get your client to talk to us and then I'll be too occupied to get in your other business?"

Emily laughed, but Stevie scanned her face carefully for any sign she'd been serious about implying the Mitchell Foundation might have anything to do with the investigation into Folsom Enterprises. Emily didn't give off vibes either way. The offhand mention of Meredith struck Stevie as odd, but for all she knew Emily was as much of a DC gossip hound as Hannah was. Finally deciding she was making too much of it, she got back on the elevator, determined to spend the rest of the day focused on her work. If only Emily hadn't brought up Meredith, because now that she had, Meredith's deep brown eyes and extra kissable lips were all she could think about.

CHAPTER SIX

The car had barely stopped when Meredith opened the door. Erica whipped her head around, but Meredith waved her off with a grin. "I got this. You just make sure you don't get any parking tickets that will haunt my future."

Unlike the night of the wedding, when she'd been in a hurry, Meredith took her time observing her surroundings. Stevie's neighborhood was decidedly different from her own, but in a pleasant way. Instead of crowded, bustling city streets, the lanes were lined with sprawling lawns and giant trees. Stevie's house was a quaint craftsman with a wraparound porch complete with a swing, and as Meredith walked to the front door, she imagined sipping lemonade while rocking back and forth on a leisurely Sunday morning.

As if. She couldn't remember the last time she'd had a day off, and even her social engagements were usually tailored around some chance to make a new connection or be seen. But not tonight. Tonight she planned to have a quiet, private evening with Stevie without interference from her twenty-four seven career.

Stevie answered on the first knock, and Meredith's pulse quickened at the sight of her.

"Come in." She stood back and held open the door, and then peered out and waved at Erica. "Can I get you something to drink? I'm sorry. I'm running a few minutes behind."

She shook her head when Stevie pointed at a bottle of wine on the kitchen counter. "I'm good. Would it be easier if I waited in the car?"

"Maybe for you, but I don't mind the company if you don't mind waiting." She motioned for Meredith to follow her, and a moment later they were in what had to be Stevie's bedroom. "You didn't mention where we were headed tonight. Do I look okay? I have a jacket that goes with this."

Meredith took in the sleeveless, royal blue sheath dress and fought back the urge to tell Stevie it would be a shame to cover her shoulders. "You look fantastic, but you'll need a jacket for outside. It's pretty brisk."

Stevie grinned at the compliment. "Thanks. I get so tired of wearing lawyer drag. It's nice to be able to dress up for someone who isn't wearing an orange jumpsuit."

"I remember those days."

"I keep forgetting you were an AUSA."

"It seems like a long time ago."

"Do you ever miss it?"

"Sometimes, but I think it's like how sometimes you think you miss things because all you remember are the good parts. I felt like I was helping people then, but I feel like what I do now has a much bigger impact. Does that make sense?"

"It does." Stevie slipped an arm into her jacket, and Meredith impulsively reached for the other arm to help her slip it on. For a second, they were standing crazy close, and Meredith flashed back on their walk after the night at the Quarry House. The impulse to kiss Stevie was even stronger now. Did Stevie feel the same way? She looked into her eyes.

"How long does Erica wait before she decides your plans have changed?" Stevie's voice was husky with desire.

"She's never left me stranded."

"She must be a very patient woman."

"She may be, but I don't think I am." Meredith stepped closer until she could feel the heat rising from Stevie's body and the whisper of arousal swirling around her head. She was used to taking what she wanted, but she didn't want to take this; she wanted it to be offered. Stevie didn't disappoint. She reached out and curved her fingers around Meredith's neck and pulled her close until their lips met. Soft touches gave way to a firm press, and Meredith lingered in the warmth of her, not wanting the moment to end.

When they finally broke, her thoughts blurred, and everything about her carefully planned evening faded into the wonder of Stevie's touch. "That was amazing," she murmured.

"Yes, yes, it was."

"I'd like to do it again."

"If you think I'm going to protest, you'll get no argument from me."

Meredith hesitated. She could send Erica away and spend the evening here, tucked away from the world and any worries her handlers might have about whether Stevie was a worthy date. The idea was tempting, but she was determined not to let the voices of Jen and the rest of her newly formed Mitchell for President committee get in her head. There would be plenty of time for that once she officially entered the race. She held out her hand. "Then let's make a plan to come back here after dinner."

A flicker of disappointment crossed Stevie's expression, but she reached for Meredith's hand and squeezed. "It's a deal."

When they climbed into the car, Stevie made a point of saying hi to Erica and asking her how her evening was going. Meredith noted the exchange and filed it away under things she liked about Stevie. The list was growing.

When Erica pulled away from the curb, Stevie asked. "What's the plan?"

"Dinner at one of my favorite places."

"Chili Bowl?"

Meredith laughed. "Okay, second favorite."

"And you're not going to tell me until we get there?"

"We'll be there soon. I swear." A few minutes later, they pulled up in front of their destination. Erica slowed to bypass the valet, drove around the corner, and idled in front of a side door. "We're here."

"Really?" Stevie pointed at the door. "Is this one of those places where you need a secret knock to get in?"

"No, but you do need to know people to use this entrance. Sometimes the day job comes in handy." Meredith sent a quick text, climbed out of the car, and held the door for Stevie.

An elderly woman greeted them on the other side of the door and pulled Meredith into a hug. "It's been too long."

"I know," Meredith replied, stepping back to introduce Stevie. "Ellie, meet Stevie Palmer. I promised her a quiet evening and the best dinner in DC."

Ellie grabbed both of Stevie's hands and smiled. "I've got you covered on both fronts." She led them both down a darkened hallway. "I hope you like ribs," she tossed over her shoulder, continuing ahead at a brisk pace without waiting for an answer.

"This seems very *House of Cards*," Stevie said.

Meredith laughed. "I know. Trust me, I've been enjoying the barbecue here for longer than that show's been streaming, but I swear every time I watched it, I wind up craving a plate of ribs. Ellie's got the best barbecue in the country."

"And you've sampled all of it?"

"A good portion." Meredith patted her stomach. "And sometimes way too much at once."

"You don't look like a woman who indulges herself all that often."

Meredith heard the playful tease in Stevie's tone, and she felt a flush of attraction. Conscious that Ellie was getting farther and farther ahead of them and would hunt them down if they lingered too long, she merely said, "Let's just say that I save my indulgences for special occasions."

Stevie reached for her hand. "I'll keep an eye out for one of those then."

Stevie's lips curled into a flirty smile, and for a second, Meredith forgot all about Ellie and barbecue and anything that wasn't Stevie, but before she could come up with some teasing banter of her own, a loud voice interrupted the moment.

"Are you girls interested in eating or only making eyes at one another?"

Meredith spotted a slight wince from Stevie and steered her toward the table Ellie had picked out for them in a secluded corner of the restaurant, far from the main dining room.

Ellie grabbed the menus off the table and tucked them under her arm. "Neither one of you look like you're eating enough to survive. I'll bring some of everything," Ellie announced, scurrying off before Meredith could protest.

"She's bossy, but I like her," Stevie said.

"She's a DC institution."

"Oh, I'm aware, but I've only ever been in the front room of this place, and I've never met her. They say she never leaves the kitchen." Stevie motioned to the walls of the cubby where they were seated. "So, what's with all the secrecy? Now that you're all over the news, you don't want to be seen with me in public?"

Meredith thought she read some hurt beneath the lightly delivered question. "Actually, I figured you would prefer it this way. You mentioned something before about not caring for the press, and I've had a hard time shaking them lately. Besides, I wanted to talk to you about something and I wasn't keen on having the whole world listening in."

Stevie nodded. "Thanks. I appreciate the gesture. I'm a firm believer in the First Amendment, but I did have a pretty bad run-in with a reporter once who thought getting a scoop was way more important than getting the truth. Unfortunately, the damage had already been done before the actual facts were printed."

"The Wallace case. I remember reading about it. You know that reporter is now part of the White House press corps?"

Stevie cocked her head. "Either you have a truly excellent memory or you've done some research."

Meredith met Stevie's gaze and didn't look away. No use hiding the truth. "I do have an excellent memory, but I'd be lying if I said I remember much about the case, but Jen is a stickler for making sure—"

"You gals better eat up." Ellie reappeared with a tray stacked with food and a pitcher of tea. "It's going to be a brutal winter, and in my experience, skinny people are the first to catch colds." She arranged their plates and pointed out the various dishes before smoothing her hands on her apron and backing away. "No one will disturb you over here, but if you need something, knock on that wall and I'll be here in a flash."

Meredith looked up from the food to find Stevie staring at her with a frown. "What's wrong? You don't like barbecue?"

"You were saying that Jen is a stickler for…but you didn't finish your sentence."

Meredith waved her fork. "Oh, nothing."

"I'm thinking it wasn't nothing. In fact, I'm thinking you were about to say that Jen is a stickler for running background checks on the people you...*see* on a regular basis."

Meredith set the fork down and crossed her hands on the table. Obviously, they were going to need to clear the air before they could move on to dinner or anything else. "Yes, Jen insists on running background checks on anyone I'm dating. Especially if I happen to like the person and plan on seeing them more."

Stevie's frown receded slightly. "I'm not really happy about the background check, but I am interested in this plan you have to see more of this person you like."

"Me too. But first I need to tell her something. Something I hope doesn't send her running for the hills."

"Why don't you test it out on me and see how it goes."

"Great plan." Meredith paused for a moment. She'd been so anxious to tell Stevie about her plans to enter the race, but now that she was on the verge of doing so, she was apprehensive about how her announcement would be received. She supposed the answer was caught up in why she wanted to tell her in the first place. Was it about testing the waters with someone outside her close-knit circle of family, friends, and colleagues, or was it that she wanted to see how Stevie would react as a potential girlfriend to the circus her life was about to become? And as for that circus, was it a smart decision to bring someone else into it? Wouldn't it be better just to shrug off any personal connections and enter the race unencumbered by personal obligations that might fracture her focus?

Oh, for God's sake, it wasn't like she was asking Stevie to marry her. They'd barely started dating, and once she started her run, they'd hardly ever see each other. *Just tell her and let life happen.*

"I'm filing the paperwork on Monday." She blurted out the words. "I'm running for president."

❖

Stevie fixed a smile on her face because she assumed that was the reaction Meredith expected, but a flood of emotions coursed through her at the announcement: surprise, excitement, disappointment. Hell, she might at this very moment be sitting across the table from the next president of the United States with only a platter of barbecue ribs between them.

But there was a lot more between them than that. Meredith Mitchell was from a completely different world. Meredith had a family who loved and supported her, loads of money, and power and influence to change the world. She, on the other hand, had left what family she had far behind after they'd rejected who she was. Everything she had, she'd had to claw out of circumstance, and any power or influence she had was negligible at best. Meredith Mitchell was about to be in the spotlight, every minute detail of her life examined under a microscope, and those details would necessarily include everyone she knew.

Stevie stared at the plate of food and her gut churned. She'd worked hard since leaving the house she grew up in to surround herself with chosen family who loved and respected her for who she was, not who they wanted her to be. Was her comfort all about to come tumbling down?

"Are you going to say something or just leave me hanging?"

"I'm not sure what to say."

"Hmm. Not a good sign. You're the first person I've told outside of my family, and it's not going real well. Maybe I should rethink this whole running for the highest office in the land thing."

Stevie heard the levity in Meredith's voice and she wanted to join in to stave off the feeling of dread that was threatening to consume her. She forced a laugh. "Sorry, I think you took me by surprise."

"No doubt. I'll have to work on that." Meredith pointed at the food. "How about we eat first, and then talk?"

"Sure," Stevie answered. She reached for a rib and then set her fork down. "Nope. Can't do it. Have to talk first."

Meredith sat back in her chair. "Okay, let's hear it. I've got a thick skin, so don't hold back. Tell me all the reasons why you think I'm not qualified."

"Oh, you're plenty qualified. That's not even an issue."

"Okay." Meredith drew out the word. "Personally, I have reservations about getting involved so late in the race, but my statistician brother pointed out that Ronald Reagan got into his first presidential race with less than a year to go, and Bill Clinton didn't have much more than that."

Stevie shook her head. "Look, it's not about whether you're qualified or the timing. You've got people to figure all that stuff out for you, and I'm sure they know what they're doing."

"Then what is it?"

What was it? Stevie grasped at the onslaught of thoughts flooding her brain, looking for just the right words to convey exactly what she was feeling, but blindsided was all she could come up with and that didn't seem fair to say out loud. Meredith was excited—as she should be. She was about to step into the national arena in an attempt to become the first female president. If she won, she'd make history. Stevie had no desire to throw cold water on her aspirations, but the last thing she wanted to do was be caught up in the glare of public attention that would surround Meredith's candidacy, and there was no way around it if she kept seeing her.

"I'm so happy for you. This is a big step, and I have no doubt you'll make an amazing candidate. You're smart, articulate, and savvy. The party, hell, the country would be lucky to have you."

"Thanks, yet I hear a big 'but.'"

"Maybe this is a little presumptive on my part, but did you happen to see any of the press after Addison and Julia's wedding?"

Meredith looked puzzled. "Yes. Anything in particular?"

"Hannah has a penchant for reading the local gossip columns, and she pointed out the ton of speculation about who the stranger was on Senator Mitchell's arm at the wedding, down to what brand I was wearing."

"That's pretty normal."

"Maybe in your world, but not in mine." Stevie waved her hand. "Also not normal, having a driver pick me up for dates, getting in the back door at restaurants, and attending weddings of famous people."

"Oh, come on. A driver is necessary for me or I'd never get anything done. I work while Erica drives. As for tonight, I've known Ellie most of my life, and while they may be famous to other people, Addison and Julia are old friends."

"You're missing the point."

"Which is?"

"Normal is relative."

Stevie took a breath while she gathered her thoughts. Her gut reaction to Meredith's announcement was visceral, but she did have valid reasons for not wanting to be part of the circus, and she felt like she owed it to Meredith to share where she was coming from. "It might be normal for you to have all these things, know all these people. I like to think I could get used to all that, but everything about your life is about to be scrutinized. You're already the subject of half the stories above the fold, and it's only going to get worse."

"I've been preparing for this my entire life. I have nothing to hide and I can handle the scrutiny."

"Well, I can't." There. She'd said it, and though she was certain it was true, she felt a twinge of regret the moment she'd spoken the words out loud because they could only mean one thing.

"Do you have something to hide?"

"What?" Stevie shook her head. "No, not at all. I guess I should've said I don't want to handle the scrutiny. I've seen, up close and personal, the damage that comes from too much focus from the media and their insatiable desire to fill a twenty-four-hour news cycle. I have a quiet life, but it's a life I've worked hard to earn and it's my own. Your life is about to be owned by everyone but you. I wish you well, but I can't be a part of it."

"We've barely gotten to know each other," Meredith protested.

"Perfect timing then." Stevie smiled to soften the harshness of her words. "Let's enjoy this meal before your world tilts on its axis." She raised her glass. "Friends?"

"Do you mean that? I do enjoy talking to you. Not many people in my sphere challenge me like you do."

Stevie considered. She'd tossed out the word as a way of putting some closure on whatever this was between them, but as she rolled the concept of friendship around in her head, she couldn't see the downside. "Yes, I mean it."

Meredith hesitated for a moment, but then lifted her drink. "To friendship."

They spent the next hour stuffing themselves with barbecue and the banana cream pie that Ellie insisted they try. Caught up in conversation, Stevie experienced moments where she forgot she was supposed to maintain distance, and questioned the boundaries between friendship and something more, but when it was finally time to leave, she drew a hard line and insisted on finding her own way home.

"This is silly," Meredith said as they walked back down the hall Ellie had led them through when they'd arrived. "Erica can drop you off just as easily as a cab."

"I'm perfectly capable of getting home on my own. Besides, I'm heading the opposite direction."

Meredith looked like she was going to protest further, and Stevie placed a finger across her lips, which she instantly realized was a very bad idea. Just the touch of Meredith's lips against her skin sent a surge of heat through her and she quickly drew away. "Sorry. I should go."

"You don't have to." Meredith's eyes telegraphed desire.

"I would eventually, and it's best if I just do it now." She paused for a moment to gather her resolve. "You know I'm right." Stevie pushed through the door before Meredith could say another word. She spotted Erica in the town car a few feet away, but kept walking, not paying attention to where she was headed. Down the street. Turn. Down another block. Turn. Every step a feeble attempt to put some distance between her and a life that wasn't meant for her. The farther away she got the easier it was to acknowledge that she'd made the right decision. So why did she feel so empty inside?

Chapter Seven

Two weeks later. New York City.

"And you have my word I will never forget the promises I made when I first entered public office. To be accountable. To be honest. To put the needs of you and our country above my own personal gain. I want to take the ideals that fueled my very first campaign—prosperity and well-being for all—to the entire nation, and to that end I ask you to support me in my efforts, because today I am announcing my candidacy for president of the United States of America."

Meredith looked out on the crowd, fixing on a few familiar faces, but careful to also connect with the few strangers in the mix and offer them what she hoped was a friendly, winning smile. It was difficult to muster any emotion at all since she was exhausted. The past couple of weeks had been a whirlwind of decision-making. Once she'd elected to enter the race, there were a thousand choices to make and arrangements to put in place. Who would be her campaign manager? Where would she announce? She'd written the speech herself, a task she'd always assumed, but she knew she would have to start handing over duties now as competing factions pulled at her time, energy, and attention.

"Are you ready?" Jen glanced at her watch. "You need to leave in about five minutes to make it to the next stop. I need to have a quick one-on-one with the mayor's chief of staff, and then I'll meet you there."

Meredith sighed, wishing she had a bit more time to let the gravity of what she'd just done sink in, but Jen was right, they had to move quickly to build on the momentum of today's announcement. They had a full slate of appearances today before she flew to Maryland in the morning for Thanksgiving dinner with their parents, but she had something else in mind first. "I'm ready, but I scheduled a quick meeting and I want you to take it with me."

"Now?"

"Yes. It won't take long." Meredith could sense Jen's resistance, so she pushed on. "I promise. Oh, and after lunch tomorrow, I'm taking the rest of the day off. You can have me back on Friday. Deal?"

Jen looked puzzled, like she wasn't sure if she was joking around. "I mean it. I need a day, make that half a day, just for me time before we dive into this race full force. And it's Thanksgiving for crying out loud." She injected a pleading tone. "After the holiday's over, you and I both know I'll have absolutely no control over my schedule."

Jen's expression softened. "Okay, I guess one day isn't going to do any harm this early on. Now, what's this important meeting you scheduled all on your own?"

"Come on." Meredith led the way to a small conference room connected to the ballroom where she'd just given her speech. She'd wanted to make her official announcement outside, but a heavy thunderstorm had caused them to shift everything inside at the last minute. She paused at the door.

"What is it?" Jen asked.

"Just promise me you'll keep an open mind."

Jen cocked her head, but before she could respond, Meredith opened the door and led them both inside where a well-dressed, lanky man stood to greet them.

Meredith shook his hand and motioned to Jen. "Jen, I'd like you to meet Gordon Hewitt. He and I have been talking about having his team join the campaign." She braced for Jen's reaction. Gordon Hewitt was a former associate of Julia Scott and had worked with Julia to get President Garrett elected twice. When Julia had taken the job as Garrett's chief of Staff, Gordon had taken over her firm and now was the go-to campaign manager for the most successful politicians.

Jen paused before offering her hand. "Everyone knows who Gordon Hewitt is, but I don't believe we've ever crossed paths. Nice to meet you."

"And you," he said. "Looks like we'll be working together plenty over the next year."

Meredith winced, knowing Jen would quickly realize she and Gordon had passed the talking about it stage. Deciding to go all in, she said, "Gordon and I still have a few details to work out, but I'd like him to start working with us right after the holiday."

"Really? We've barely had time to establish a strategy," Jen said. "Wouldn't his team be more effective if we've already decided on a direction and best use of resources?"

"Actually," Gordon said, "I've been developing some information on that front." He pulled a folder out of his briefcase. "My numbers say we should go with a targeted geographical demographic rather than a fifty-state strategy."

"We have numbers too," Jen said, her tone icy. "You may not be aware, but our brother Michael runs one of the top analytics firms in the country."

"Great. Always good to have more than one angle for good perspective."

Meredith watched the back-and-forth, pleased to see Gordon wasn't backing down. He'd need to keep his cool and stand his ground if he was going to work with Jen, and she was determined to add him to the team. Julia had made the introduction a week ago, and after several meetings with Gordon, Meredith was convinced his national experience was vital to her success. After watching a few more rounds of them sparring, Meredith pointed at her watch. "We better get going."

Jen barely waited until they were out the door before she started in. "You've already hired him, haven't you?"

"Pending a few details that need to be ironed out. I'll leave those to you. Unless you think you can't work together." Meredith left silent which of them she would choose if Jen refused to accept Gordon onto the team, but she could tell Jen got the message.

"Can we at least revisit the decision to hire Hewitt's firm? We have the resources to handle your campaign on our own."

Meredith heard the unspoken "without bringing in outsiders" because Jen and Michael had pointed out numerous times over the past two weeks that they and the rest of the family circle could handle the work on their own. "I'm done talking about it. I'm going to need you for many things. No one is a better taskmaster, no one is more loyal, and there is no one I trust more than you. But I need someone completely objective to make the tough calls and tell me the raw facts when it comes to where things stand in this campaign. Let someone else get down and dirty with the campaign politics. Trust me, when we get to the White House, you'll be much more effective as my chief of staff if you don't have a ton of political fallout to have to make up for. And Gordon promised me they would consult with Michael for analytical data."

"I know, but—"

"You have to trust me on this." Meredith had made up her mind and she wasn't changing it. "I love you and I think you can do anything, but I need you to be my chief of staff and my sister more than I need you to run this circus. Got it?"

"Okay," Jen said. "But Gordon's going to want direct access."

"And he'll get it, but you'll be included in all the big decisions. I promise." Meredith stared her down until she was satisfied she'd made her point. She knew juggling Jen's well-intentioned bossiness combined with Gordon Hewitt's reputation for being a control freak was going to be a challenge, but she was convinced it was necessary to balance her family's political dominance with a fresh voice, someone who would be objective. Gordon had a reputation for speaking truth to power, and he wasn't one to take on a race he didn't think he could win. This would be his first solo presidential campaign, and Meredith figured she'd hear an earful from her father at dinner tomorrow about how if she was going to go outside the family, she should at least pick someone with a higher national profile. She was prepared to tell her family that, bottom line, she was the boss, and if Julia Scott thought Gordon was the guy, she was convinced he was the right choice for her.

On the way to the next stop, Meredith skimmed the newspapers the driver had left in the back seat, enjoying the tactile feel of the paper in her hands, and the sound of the paper crinkling as she folded pages to access the rest of the headline stories—a refreshing break from endlessly scrolling with her thumbs to get to the end. She set aside the *New York Times* and picked up the *Washington Post*. Yesterday's vote on the immigration bill was one of the featured stories, and she devoured the paragraphs above the fold and then turned to the back pages to catch the rest, but before she could dive back into the immigration story, something else distracted her.

A trial date has been set for William Barkley, the IT consultant with Folsom Enterprises who gave top secret information to several news outlets. Protestors in support of Barkley gathered outside the Prettyman Courthouse today, chanting about the First Amendment and oppressive government. Barkley's attorney, public defender Stevie Palmer, declined to discuss the case, but did say that her client appreciated all the people who'd gathered to support him. She said that she expected the public to be surprised by what they learned once Mr. Barkley received his day in court.

Meredith read the paragraph several times. She'd heard about the case when Barkley was arrested—everyone had. Espionage was a hot button issue right now, and her colleagues had all discussed how much they'd like to see Barkley be made an example. Meredith pulled up the calendar app on her phone and counted backward. Stevie must've drawn this case right around the time she testified before the Senate committee. Right around the time they'd met. Was this why Stevie seemed so leery of the press?

No, that didn't make sense. Most of the press celebrated Barkley's actions as patriotic and fully supported by the First Amendment. No, it had been a run-in with a reporter on a different case—the Wallace case—that had made such a negative impression on Stevie. Meredith had seen the reference on the report Jen had prepared on Stevie's background, but she hadn't dwelled on the details.

Meredith reached for her phone and Googled Stevie's name along with the name Wallace, completely unprepared for the flood of references that loaded onto the screen.

Assassin Donald Wallace and his sixteen-year-old son were arraigned yesterday in Federal District Judge Reinhardt's court. The case is reminiscent of the 2002 DC sniper case, and tensions in the community have run high. Wallace's son's attorney, public defender Stevie Palmer, vows that evidence will show he was a victim of his father's abuse as well as a developmental disability, and not at all culpable in the deaths of the seven coordinated sniper attacks that have terrorized the Maryland area for the past six months.

Meredith clicked on another link a bit farther down and read more about Stevie's young client. Phrases like "awkward in school," "slow," and "viewed as weird by his classmates and teachers alike." Ten clicks later, Meredith finally reached the article that told the end of Stevie's client's story.

Marshall Wallace was found dead in his cell at the juvenile detention center in Silver Spring, MD. Officials believed he hanged himself, but homicide had not been ruled out as of this publication. The public defender's office issued no statement, but Wallace's attorney Stevie Palmer said, "The system had failed my client. I sincerely regret that he will never have the opportunity to be vindicated." She went on to say that the spectacle of coverage surrounding this case was directly responsible for his death.

Meredith reread the quote from Stevie several times, and realization dawned. She remembered the press coverage well. Both the father and son were vilified in the press, and horrible things were said across all media about the son. Instinctively, Meredith reached for her phone and started punching numbers, but she stopped before the call could go through. She hadn't spoken to Stevie since dinner at Ellie's two weeks ago, and she feared their promise to be friends had been nothing more than a nicety, one of those things people say when they are parting because the truth—that they never plan to see each other again—is too harsh. She set the phone down and tapped her fingers on the papers in her lap.

"Oh, to hell with it," she muttered and grabbed the phone again, dialing before she could change her mind.

"Hello?"

The voice was female, but she was fairly sure it wasn't Stevie. Meredith checked the number on the screen to be sure. "I'm trying to reach Stevie Palmer."

"Senator Mitchell?"

Definitely not Stevie. Meredith cleared her throat and plunged ahead. "It's Meredith. Who's this?"

"Hannah. Hannah Bennett. We met at Stevie's place and again at Quarry House."

"I remember."

"Great speech today. You've got my vote."

"Thanks." Meredith waited a couple of beats hoping for some intel about why Hannah was answering Stevie's cell phone, but there was only silence. "Speaking of Stevie, I was trying to reach her. You wouldn't happen to know where she is, would you?"

"Uh…hang on a sec."

Meredith heard the sound of Hannah speaking to someone else, but the words were too muffled to make out. She was about to give up on this impromptu mission when Hannah's voice came back on the line.

"Sorry about that. We're having lunch or trying to at least. I'm guarding the last open table in this joint, and she's at the counter getting our food, but when I saw your name show up on the screen, well, I just had to answer."

Meredith spent a few seconds trying to unravel what Hannah had just said and came to only one conclusion. "I get it—she's busy. No worries and no need to tell her I called. I'll give her a ring later." Give her a ring? Damn, she sounded stupid. "Bye."

"Wait!"

Meredith held the phone with her forefinger poised to disconnect the call. She should hang up. Calling was a bad idea and it had accomplished nothing. She needed to focus, and everything about Stevie Palmer was a distraction. Yet, she'd already called, so what was the harm in staying on the line? "Yes?"

"My husband and I host an orphan Thanksgiving dinner every year. You know, a bunch of us who have no extended family in town get together and everyone brings something. I know you probably have plans for the day, but I can text you the address if you'd like to come by. We meet up around noon."

Suddenly very aware she and Stevie had never discussed Stevie's family, Meredith wondered if they were still alive, and why Stevie wasn't spending the holiday with them. Meredith enjoyed having her own very supportive family nearby, but she did wonder if there was a certain freedom in having no familial obligations. Her parents expected her to show up at their palatial house tomorrow, dressed in formal attire, so they could all sit around the formal dining table while the chef sent out platters of gourmet food for them to politely enjoy. A potluck sounded like a much cozier and inviting experience. "It sounds lovely, but I can't make it. Family dinner."

"Well, if your plans change, come on by. It's only for a few hours, and then it devolves into a football frenzy and Stevie always takes off early to do a shift at Bridgeway, the homeless shelter. Hey, I should get back in there or she's going to wonder what I'm up to. You sure you don't want to talk to her?"

"I'm sure," Meredith responded quickly. "I'll catch up with her later. Enjoy your lunch."

Meredith hung up the line for real this time and set the phone on the seat beside her. She should've just talked to Stevie, but something about Hannah's evasiveness told her Stevie would be as reluctant to talk to her. Which only made her wonder what Stevie had confided in Hannah about their last date.

The next day as she sat around her parents' dinner table enjoying course after course of decadent food and fielding questions about the campaign, all she could think about was Stevie dishing up plates of food for homeless people, quietly and not seeking any limelight for her efforts. How very different their lives were right now, and how she wished she could be by Stevie's side even if only for the afternoon.

CHAPTER EIGHT

Stevie pushed her plate aside and groaned. "When am I ever going to learn not to go back for seconds? That sweet potato marshmallow thing is going to be the death of me."

Hannah laughed. "If you're going to start counting calories at Thanksgiving dinner, you're going to be banned from coming back. Seriously, cut yourself some slack."

"Guilt is not good for my digestion," Stevie replied. "In an hour I'll be serving dinner to people who barely ever get a decent meal, and after stuffing my face for the past two hours, I can barely stand the sight of food. What an upside-down world we live in."

"Speaking of upside-down, I read in the paper you set a trial date in the Barkley case," Hannah's husband, Dave, said. "Do you really think it's going to trial?"

"Frankly, I have no idea. The prosecutor is Emily Watkins, and she's hot to work something out, but we're not there yet." Stevie was being deliberately cagey. She trusted Hannah and Dave, but she didn't know everyone else around the table well enough to disclose that her client still hadn't given her anything to work with in his defense. "We've still got some time."

"I think what he did was heroic," Hannah said. "The FBI is supposed to be working to protect our interests, and if they're not doing their job, the public has a right to know. If people like William Barkley didn't disclose what's going on, then we'd be blindly acquiescing to hackers, who are probably working on behalf of hostile foreign governments, infiltrating our daily lives. Frankly, I expected more from Garrett's administration."

"I'm not sure Garrett even knows that the FBI dropped the ball on the hacking case or that they were even working on it to begin with," Stevie said. "As much as they've tried to coordinate all their efforts since nine-eleven, there's still a lot of interagency power grabbing going on, and secrets are at the heart of it. As long as that's the case, we the people are going to be left in the dark with our rights at risk."

"Hopefully, Senator Mitchell will be more on top of things when she's elected," Hannah replied.

Stevie let the comment go. Hannah had made no secret of her opinion that Stevie had called it quits with Meredith too soon, and this wasn't the first time today Hannah had tossed Meredith's name into the conversation, but she refused to be baited. Unfortunately, that didn't stop everyone else at the table from jumping in with their opinions.

Jewel, Hannah's next-door neighbor, grunted and folded her arms across her chest. "I'm as liberal as the next person, and Meredith Mitchell is going to get my vote, but when it comes to national security I think anyone who gives classified information to anyone, especially the press, should be convicted of treason and left to rot in prison. We can't possibly know the full ramifications of the information he disclosed. There may be undercover operatives whose identities are now exposed whose lives are in danger. People don't take time anymore to consider the true consequences of their actions. There's a right way to do things and a wrong way."

Stevie wanted to tell Jewel that the information Barkley had disclosed to the press hadn't contained any particulars about spies, and that overall, it was pretty boring stuff, but she had to walk a fine line because the documents were still deemed classified, and further disclosure of the contents could have her running afoul of the Espionage Act. Besides, she doubted Jewel would believe her since the popular talk radio shows had been spinning the whole lives in danger theory for days. But what Jewel said was important because there would be jurors who'd feel the same way, and she was going to have to figure out how to convince them that the good accomplished by Barkley's action outweighed any associated harm. For now she nodded and smiled, grateful when Jewel and several of the others started clearing the table.

When everyone else was in the kitchen, Hannah picked up her empty plate and stacked it with her own. "You seem melancholy today."

Stevie ignored the comment and reached for the plates. "Let me help you with that."

"Nope. I got this. Take a breather."

Stevie started to protest again, but Hannah waved her away and headed off to the kitchen where the rest of their dinner companions were washing dishes and bagging up leftovers. Stevie leaned back in her chair and shut her eyes for a few minutes. She was a little melancholy. She always felt this way around the holidays—a small part of her longing for the family she'd left behind so many years ago, but she knew her longing was misplaced. The good friends and good time she'd had today was a fairy tale compared to the angst-ridden holidays of her youth where her father had always started dinner with a prayer asking the Lord to love the sinner, but remove the sin before shooting a pointed look in her direction so there was no mistaking exactly which sinner he was talking about. Her sexuality wasn't the only source of contention; she'd never been able to bite back protests whenever he or the rest of her family talked about what they perceived as society's injustices: welfare, aid to the homeless, subsidized healthcare. In their view, you earned your own way in the world and people who accepted assistance were less-than.

She'd left home when she was seventeen and never looked back. It hadn't been easy, but she'd studied her ass off while she couch-surfed with friends until she graduated from high school. She'd worked through college and law school, graduating with honors, and when her education was done, she never thought twice about entering government service where she'd have the opportunity to give back.

"Are you ready for pie?"

Stevie looked up to see Hannah and the others strolling into the room carrying three pies between them. She grabbed her stomach. "Not a chance. Besides, I need to get going." In spite of their protests, she said her good-byes and headed out.

Bridgeway Homeless Shelter was only a few miles away from Hannah's place, and Stevie spent the drive trying to shake off her own malaise. She knew part of her problem was the abrupt end to whatever had been brewing between her and Meredith. Seeing Meredith on TV making the announcement about her presidential bid yesterday hadn't helped, and she'd spent the time since wondering how things would be different if she hadn't walked away. Would she have taken off work so she could stand in the crowd and cheer on Meredith's announcement? Or would she have waited backstage to enjoy a private moment with her before she took the stage?

Her musings were silly. Even if she could've stood the media frenzy, Stevie knew there was no room for her in Meredith's life now. Meredith's path to the White House would be focused and solitary, with no time for drinking beer at Quarry House or sneaking barbecue dinners at Ellie's. She'd chosen to walk away, but she missed the idea of being with Meredith more than she'd imagined she would.

She pulled into the parking lot of the shelter and struggled to clear her head. Neither the people who worked at the shelter nor the homeless they'd be serving today needed to be subjected to her sour mood, and by the time she parked her car, she'd managed to put on a friendly face.

"Hi, Stevie," one of the regulars called out when she walked through the door. "Joanie's in the back with your friend."

"What?" she asked, but he'd already moved on to start setting tables. She glanced around the room. She'd been volunteering here for the past ten years, and they usually got around a hundred people through the doors on Thanksgiving. No doubt he'd been referring to one of the other volunteers slated to work the holiday. She strode to the back of the dining hall and pushed through the kitchen doors. "Joanie, I'm here and I'm ready to peel all the potatoes in the land," she called out.

Joanie was nowhere in sight, but a familiar voice came from the back of the kitchen. "I think I may have already done that."

"Meredith?"

Meredith stepped out from behind the tall kitchen rack wearing an oversized white apron and brandishing a knife. Stevie laughed out loud.

"What?" Meredith said, looking down at her apron. "You don't think this look suits me?"

Stevie pointed at the knife. "You might want to lose the weapon unless you plan to adopt it as part of your campaign slogan. 'I'm Meredith Mitchell and I'll cut inflation, taxes, and crime.'"

Meredith returned the smile. "I like it. Remind me when we're done here, and I'll let my campaign manager know he's been replaced."

At the mention of a campaign manager, Stevie sobered. For a brief second, she'd believed Meredith might actually be here to see her, but that was crazy. Meredith had just launched a presidential campaign, and her presence at a homeless shelter on Thanksgiving was likely nothing more than a typical photo op designed to make her like a regular person, caring about the needs of her fellow citizens. Stevie glanced around.

"Hey, what are you looking for?" Meredith asked.

Stevie did her best to ignore that Meredith had come closer and they were now standing inches apart. She lowered her voice to a whisper. "Where's the press? I don't mean to be rude, but you should really have them get their coverage before the guests start arriving. The people who come here to eat may be homeless, but they have a right not to have their pictures splashed through the news."

Meredith frowned. "Is that what you think of me?" She didn't wait for an answer. "This isn't a media bit. In fact, I wore a scarf around my head and oversized sunglasses, Jackie-O style, so I could sneak in here. Being here, doing something worthwhile, is my way of escaping from the roller coaster my life is about to become." She paused for a few beats. "Plus, I wanted to see you, and Hannah told me you'd be here."

Stevie wanted to say she was glad, but all she could manage in the moment was, "Really?"

"Yes, really." Meredith set the knife on the counter. "Look, I don't know what the future holds, but I do know it's going to be crazy. I just jumped off a cliff of sorts and I may fall flat on my face, but I'm going for this. All the way. I know this isn't your thing, but all I'm asking for is to get to know you better and maybe some companionship along the way. No big promises other than respect, fun, and when it comes to the press, a big fat no comment. What do you say?"

Stevie let Meredith's speech wash over her. Like any good politician, Meredith had the gift of persuasion, but it wasn't hard to convince someone to feel a certain way when they were already predisposed to do so, and Stevie was more than halfway there. "You can't control the press."

"You're right for the most part, and I know why you're so averse to them, but I can control the narrative." She waggled a finger back and forth between them. "How's this: we've been on a couple of dates and we enjoy each other's company. It's new and nice, but we both have busy lives that take most of our focus. We'd appreciate the same privacy any other two people would at the beginning of a new adventure."

"Are you telling me or the press?"

"I'm telling anyone who wants to know." Meredith reached for Stevie's hand. "I promise not to lead a herd of media to your door, and if we want to continue to see each other it might involve some decoy cars and other sneaky maneuvers, but I'd like to give it a try if you would."

Stevie didn't hesitate this time. Meredith showing up here today, without the cameras and the entourage, was a unique offering, a second chance. Whatever was about to happen was going to be special, and she wasn't about to let the opportunity to get to know her better pass by. "I would." She picked up the knife. "Now, let's go peel some potatoes."

CHAPTER NINE

Christmas Day

Meredith walked into her parents' living room and scanned the picture-perfect holiday scene. Two large Douglas firs flanked the massive stone fireplace, each decked out in yards of white chiffon and sparkling lights, while the rest of the room looked like a holiday window display at Neiman Marcus.

"It's the perfect photo op," Jen said from behind.

"Don't start," Meredith replied. "I meant what I said about today being off limits."

"All day?"

"What's left of it. I wore the silly Santa hat and passed out toys at the children's hospital this morning, and then read about seven hundred briefing papers, so I think I've earned a break. Even Gordon agreed I should have the rest of the day off. Every moment from now until tomorrow morning is campaign-free."

Jen let out a heavy sigh. "Fine, we don't have to let any press in, but I'd love to get a few pictures we can release later. Kind of a how the senator spent her holidays piece. It's great public interest."

Meredith knew Jen was right. The more she could humanize her campaign, the better she'd be able to connect to voters, but she wasn't convinced photos taken at her parents' opulent estate would convince regular people she could relate to their lives. Besides, none of these decorations were her taste; she preferred a much simpler style. She glanced at her watch, noting she still had a little time before Stevie was supposed to arrive, and then pointed to the French doors that led to the back deck which was decorated in a more rustic theme. "You have fifteen minutes to get whatever pictures you want and then put away the cameras, the social media, everything. Deal?"

"Deal. I'll go get the camera."

Meredith walked out to the deck. She shivered at the cold, but didn't bother going back inside for her coat. She'd learned a long time ago, on her first campaign, that candidates should never show weakness in any form, and that included bundling up on a cold day or perspiring on a hot one. God forbid anyone would want a human being representing their interests.

God, she sounded bitter, but she really wasn't. Mostly she was tired. If she'd stuck with her plan to run in the next cycle, or even the one after that, she would've had plenty of time to ease into the campaign routine, but her last-minute entry into the race meant she had to do four times the work in less than half the time. She'd spent the last two weeks working with Gordon to assemble the rest of her team and making sure she didn't miss any filing deadlines—on top of her duties in the Senate. She needed the few hours' break she'd be getting today, but mostly she needed to see Stevie.

They'd talked or texted daily, but there hadn't been time to get together in person since she'd seen her at the shelter on Thanksgiving. She'd arranged for Erica to pick Stevie up today, not in the town car that she'd used to transport her here earlier, but a more nondescript vehicle to respect Stevie's desire for privacy, and they should be arriving soon. The prospect of seeing Stevie again filled her with excitement. The only thing that would make it better would be if they didn't have to have their reunion surrounded by family.

Jen walked outside carrying a camera and wearing a frown. "What's the matter?" Meredith asked.

"I hate this thing. Too many buttons."

"You have exactly five minutes to figure it out before I bail on you," Meredith said.

"Who's bailing? I just got here."

Meredith looked up to see Stevie standing in the doorway with Nelson, her parents' butler, standing directly behind her. "You asked me to bring Ms. Palmer directly to you when she arrived," he said.

"Thanks, Nelson. Please tell Erica to do what we talked about earlier, and then she's free for the rest of the day. Please let her know I really appreciate this favor." Meredith spoke the words on her way to Stevie's side, and when she reached her, she grabbed her hands, desperate to connect with someone who had absolutely nothing to do with politics. "I'm so glad you're here," she said, and, not caring if Jen was watching, she leaned in for a quick kiss.

"Me too," Stevie said, "Although when you said your parents had a 'nice' place, you were kind of underplaying it."

"Well, it is nice, even if it's not my style."

"I'll have to trust you on that since I have no idea what your style is."

"A fact I intend to rectify. Soon." Meredith hoped her plan for the evening would work, but for now the sound of Jen clearing her throat reminded her they weren't alone. "Stevie, you remember my taskmaster, uh, sister, Jen?"

"Of course." Stevie extended a hand, and Jen set the camera down and returned the handshake. "Having a little holiday photo session?"

"We would be," Jen said, "if I could get the camera to work. I was going to get a few holiday PR shots for the website, but I'm having trouble adjusting the focus."

Stevie reached for the camera. "Mind if I give it a try?" Jen handed it over, and Meredith watched while Stevie confidently pushed buttons on the screen, pausing a few times to gaze through the lens.

"I think I've got it. Let me try a few test shots. What did you have in mind?"

Meredith looked to Jen who gestured for her to stand near the railing laced with boughs of juniper. She placed a hand on the rail and turned toward the camera. "Like this?"

"Too posed. All you need are a few hay bales in the background and you'd have the perfect Olan Mills circa 1980," Stevie replied. "Go back where you were and walk toward the rail. When you get there look toward the camera, but pretend like you're seeing someone you haven't seen for a while and you're happy to see them."

Meredith did exactly as Stevie suggested, acutely conscious Stevie was watching her every move through the lens of the camera, but instead of apprehension, she felt exhilarated. She didn't need to pretend. For the past two weeks, the glare of the national spotlight had been trained squarely on her and it had been exciting, but nothing compared to the welcome intensity of Stevie's gaze. She wanted to tell Stevie to forget the pictures, tell Jen to scatter, and whisk Stevie back to her place where they would put this intense focus to better use.

"Perfect. I think I've got what you need."

Stevie's voice broke the trance, but when she dropped the camera to her side, Meredith caught her still staring, and she smiled at the recognition.

"Let me see," Jen said, taking the camera from Stevie's hand.

Meredith kept her eyes on Stevie as Jen thumbed through the photos, not caring if there was one usable one in the bunch.

"Mere, look at these. They're amazing."

"What?" Meredith broke her focus on Stevie and looked at the camera Jen was shoving her way.

"The pictures. Look."

Jen knew her aversion to looking at pictures of herself, but her insistence made Meredith take the camera and start flipping through the images, at first fast, but then slowing down to take in the full effect of how Stevie saw her. "Wow."

"You like them?" Stevie asked, a hint of trepidation in her voice.

"Like them? I love them. I thought you were a lawyer, but clearly you are a professional photographer." She handed the camera to Jen and asked, "How come no one else makes me look like this?"

"I didn't make you look a certain way," Stevie said. "I just managed to capture what's already there. Photography is a hobby."

"I think you should have her take all of your photos," Jen said, edging her way back into the house, camera in hand. "I'm going to go upload these. Dinner's in half an hour. See you there."

Meredith waited until Jen shut the door and then she pulled Stevie into her arms and whispered, "You're pretty amazing."

"Because I can use a camera?"

"Because you see me for something other than the public persona. Those photos feel personal, like they were taken by someone who's known me for a long time."

"You wanted something different?"

"I thought so, but I was wrong." Meredith let the comment linger, certain if she added to it she would ruin the magic of this moment. Stevie was an accomplished photographer, and the photos she'd taken would help voters connect with her, but Stevie's skill with the camera was not what Meredith was interested in right now. Later, when they weren't standing yards from the perfectly set holiday dinner table and surrounded by relatives, Meredith would tell Stevie exactly what skills she wanted to explore.

❖

Dinner had been going so well, Stevie should've known a road bump lay ahead. They'd just finished a to-die-for red velvet cake, and Nelson was directing a second coffee service, when James Mitchell launched into campaign mode.

"Gordon Hewitt isn't the most experienced guy on the circuit. I'm sure he's got some good ideas, but how about we reach out to Rupert Glazer? He's worked both sides and will be invaluable in the general."

Stevie could feel Meredith tense up beside her, and she surreptitiously reached a hand under the table to squeeze Meredith's thigh, a small show of solidarity.

"Thanks, Dad," Meredith said. "But I don't want someone who's worked both sides. I want someone who is an ideological fit as well as a practical one."

"That makes sense for some things, but not a national election." James stirred his coffee, then pointed his spoon at Stevie. "Stevie understands the importance of being able to argue both sides, don't you?"

Stevie took a breath while she pondered whether the question was rhetorical, but Meredith beat her to the punch.

"Dad, no fair picking on the guests."

"It's okay. I don't mind answering," Stevie said, surprised to hear her voice calm and even. "I think there's a fundamental difference between seeing both sides and being willing to argue either one. I have an obligation to consider all the arguments my opponent will bring to bear, but that doesn't mean I would step into his or her shoes and make those same points myself."

"Are you trying to tell me you always believe your clients are innocent?"

Stevie heard the disbelief in his tone, but she didn't rise to the bait. "No, absolutely not. In fact, many times I know they have committed the crime for which they are accused, but my duty is to make sure they get a vigorous defense within the law. The prosecutor's duty is to make sure they are convicted, and sometimes that means seeing only black and white. My job is to shed light on the shades of gray."

"And a courtroom is nothing like a campaign trail," Meredith interjected. "Bad analogy, Dad. Gordon Hewitt comes highly recommended and he's my guy."

"Fine, but don't shut your family out. We've been here all along and this guy barely knows you."

"I promise I won't."

Stevie watched the exchange, impressed with the deft manner in which Meredith handled her father's domineering ways, which couldn't be easy. He'd been a powerful governor and was the chief executive of the nonprofit that bore his name. After Emily told her that the Mitchell Foundation was a client of Folsom Enterprises, Stevie had done a little digging. Stevie hadn't found anything that connected the foundation to the information Barkley had leaked to the press, but she now knew quite a bit about the nonprofit. James Mitchell had set up the foundation soon after he retired from politics to focus on economic development and civil rights around the world. The foundation employed dozens, but James Mitchell was the primary fundraiser and he set the direction for its agenda. Clearly, he was used to running the show, which she'd expected, but she was completely unprepared for his next question.

"And what about you two? What are you going to tell people when they ask what kind of relationship you have?"

Stevie looked at Meredith who was shaking her head. Jen hid a smirk behind her napkin, and Michael looked down at his plate.

"Dad, drop it," Meredith said.

"Your father has a point," Anna Mitchell chimed in for the first time since she'd asked if anyone wanted another slice of cake. "Stevie needs to know what she's in for if she's going to be by your side over the course of the next year."

Stevie could feel Meredith's tension start to bubble over, and she was feeling stress of her own. She'd been worried about questions from the media, but she'd never expected an interrogation from Meredith's parents over Christmas dinner. How naive. Of course, the Mitchell family would have strong opinions about who stood by their daughter's side on her quest to carry on their political dynasty. But even more surprising was the whole "over the course of the next year part." Since when had their casual dating morphed into her serving as an escort on the campaign trial? She scrambled to come up with an appropriate response, but Meredith spoke first.

"Mom, Dad, I love you both, but today is a campaign-free zone. Thanks for dinner. It was delicious, but we're going to duck out and have a private holiday celebration of our own." Without waiting for an answer, Meredith stood and extended a hand to Stevie.

Stevie felt like she should say something before they left. Some polite rejoinder or snappy comeback to what Anna Mitchell had said, but words left her. She took Meredith's hand and followed her to the garage.

"Erica took the town car from my parents and left it with the valet at the Hay Adams," Meredith said. She jangled a set of keys in the air. "We'll be returning to the city in my dad's sedan, and I know a secret way out of here."

"Sounds like you thought of everything." Stevie wanted to dial back the slight sarcasm in her tone, but Meredith hadn't seemed to notice, so she let it go. They made small talk in the car, and were back in the city before Meredith broached the subject.

"I'm sorry about what happened back there."

"You mean the part where your mother cast me in the role of campaign escort?"

Meredith laughed. "Is there such a thing? I had no idea."

"Seriously, Meredith. You know exactly what she was implying."

"True. I'm sorry she made you feel uncomfortable."

Stevie waited for her to say more, but Meredith seemed content to let it drop. She spent the silence examining her own feelings about what Anna Mitchell had said. It wasn't so much her words as the expectation that if she was going to date Meredith she'd be expected to accompany her on the campaign trail, presumably to stand in the background and give the appearance of coupledom, stability. In the field of people jockeying for their party's nomination, Meredith was the only single candidate. In Stevie's view, Meredith's bachelor status made her more qualified to take on the all-consuming job of president, but she knew the general population didn't see it that way. Was Meredith looking for someone to fill the role of First Lady-in-Waiting or at a minimum give good optics?

Meredith turned the car into a garage and parked. "Looks like I remembered how to drive after all," she said as she stepped out of the car and led the way to the bank of elevators.

"How long has Erica worked for you?"

Meredith tilted her head back like she was counting numbers in the air. "I'm going to go with forever, but it was probably really just since I was elected councilwoman in New York." The elevator dinged, and they exited and walked down a long hallway before stopping in front of a nondescript door. Meredith opened the door to her apartment and waved Stevie in. "Ready for the tour?"

Stevie stepped inside and gasped. "It's so tiny." She clapped a hand to her mouth. She wasn't sure exactly what she'd been expecting, but the small studio apartment with everything centered two steps from the living room wasn't it. "My turn to be sorry. That was pretty rude."

"Not at all. It is small, but it's private and close to work, which were the primary selling points." Meredith stepped into the miniature kitchen and pulled a bottle of champagne out of the fridge. "And here's another one. You're only ever two steps from your next drink. After today, I could use one. How about you?"

"Yes, please." Stevie watched Meredith ease off the cork on the bottle of Dom, and deftly pour them each a glass. The juxtaposition of the expensive champagne with the scaled down digs made her smile. Meredith was full of surprises.

"What are you smiling about?" Meredith asked as she handed her a glass.

"This." Stevie nodded at the glass. "And this," she said, gesturing at the apartment. "I love it, but after the estate we just left, I expected something different."

"Yes, well, this is one case where the apple fell far from the tree. I love my parents' house, but I'm more of an economy of space kind of gal. My apartment in New York is much bigger than this, but you could still fit it several times over into my parents' house." She looked around the room as if she were seeing it for the first time. "This place does look a little like a stopover and not a home."

Stevie had been thinking the same thing. It made sense, really, that Meredith wouldn't have nested here since she divided her time between DC and New York, but she'd held out some hope that seeing the place where Meredith lived would give her some more insight into what made her tick. Instead, she saw only a studio that could've been featured on the cover of a magazine, but that displayed no personality. "Well, it's not like you'll be spending much time here anyway."

And then it hit her. As soon as the holidays were over, likely before, Meredith would hit the campaign trail, returning to DC for crucial Senate votes and nothing more. She might not want to be Meredith's election arm candy, but she wasn't quite ready to break the connection they'd started to build. She set her champagne glass down and stepped closer to Meredith, tucking her arm around her waist. "I think I might miss you when you're gone."

A slow smile spread across Meredith's face. "Is that so?" She turned in Stevie's arms. "I think I might miss you too."

They were close. Very close. Stevie inhaled and let the soft lavender scent of Meredith's perfume flood her senses. She leaned in and kissed Meredith's lips, softly at first, playful nips that quickly grew more intense with each pass. Meredith opened her mouth, and Stevie eased her tongue inside with slow, gentle strokes, taking her time, enjoying the slow build of arousal between them.

The kiss lasted a long time, long enough to signal she was undeniably attracted to Meredith, and incredibly lucky to see the not entirely put together, somewhat vulnerable side of her the rest of the world didn't get to see. The question was whether she could hang on to these moments when the political machine took over, turning this soft, tender woman into the perfectly packaged candidate who would belong to the country and not her.

Chapter Ten

New Hampshire Primary

Meredith paced the hotel room, trying desperately to ignore the conversations happening all around her. Last week's caucuses in Iowa had her in a dead heat with the governor of Alabama, Jed Lankin, who'd fully expected to slide into first place once Connie Armstrong dropped out of the race. Tonight's results from New Hampshire could tip the scales. The polls had closed an hour ago, and everyone in the room and on TV was busy with predictions, none of which meant anything until the votes were counted.

"Exit polls are showing a higher than usual turnout today for the Democratic primary," the anchor said. "What do you make of that, Linda?"

The brunette by the white board wrote the word WOMEN in big bold black letters. She tapped on the board with a pointer for emphasis. "Women are turning out in droves to be a part of history. Senator Mitchell is the first viable candidate we've seen in years, and everyone wants to tell their children they cast a vote for the first female president."

"That's what I'm talking about," said Jen, pumping a fist in the air.

"No celebrating until the returns are in," Gordon replied with a stern look.

Meredith paused in her loop around the room to watch the two of them stare each other down, but she didn't jump in the middle. The last seven weeks had been a challenge, not just the outward facing part of the campaign, but the internal drain of watching two people she respected stand off when they should be working together. The conflict was taking its toll on the entire team. If the tension escalated, she was going to have to take action, but right now all she really wanted was to slip into her pj's, order a cheeseburger and fries from room service, and curl up in bed to watch the rest of the returns. Only one more thing would make her night complete—if Stevie was here to share it with her.

"I sent her the ticket like you asked."

Meredith looked up to see Jen standing next to her. "It's not that easy for her to get away. It's a Tuesday, and she has a job." When Jen shook her head, Meredith pushed on. "An important job. She can't just up and tell a federal judge that she can't make it to court because her…" She choked on the word girlfriend. "Because I'm going crazy waiting for election results."

"Not just any election results." Jen grabbed her by the shoulders. "It's a presidential primary. This is the beginning of history." She cast a look at Gordon who was standing across the room talking to one of the campaign volunteers, and lowered her voice. "You are going to sweep this thing. Lankin is shaking in his shoes."

"Don't you even." Meredith waved her hands in the air to ward off the bad juju. "Gordon's not the only one who's superstitious. I'm as excited as anyone else in this room, but the votes are still being counted. Get a grip because we might be in for a long night."

No sooner had she spoken than a roar went up from the room, and Meredith whirled to face the TV. It was early yet, but CNN had already made the call, and the entire room was celebrating. Jen pulled her into a hug and held tight. She felt something wet running down her face, but it took a moment for her to realize she was weeping tears of joy. The polls and pundits had predicted her win, but the reality was beyond her wildest expectations. She barely had time to process her feelings before she was swept around the room, being congratulated and offering heartfelt thanks in return for each of these people who'd dropped their lives to become part of hers.

She'd barely made it halfway through the crowd before Gordon was tapping her on the shoulder. "Let's go ahead and head downstairs. If you make your speech now, we can make the late news."

He was right. She had a pretty big war chest, but the more free PR they could grab in the form of replayed sound bites, the more money they'd have to spend in the general election. She appreciated Gordon always thinking ten steps ahead, but after weeks shaking hands and kissing babies, it was hard to leave this bubble of comfort. She looked around the room as if she could divine some reason to stall, and like magic, her gaze fell on Stevie, framed in the doorway with a huge smile on her face.

❖

Stevie stood up at counsel table and motioned to the prosecutor, Emily Watkins. "Your Honor, the government has provided me with discovery, but it's too heavily redacted to be helpful, and some of it's missing entirely. I can't possibly prepare for trial if I don't have access to the exact same material the government has reviewed."

She'd expected more from Emily, but when she'd confronted her, Emily had thrown up her hands and said she had no control over the decision to redact the documents. When Stevie protested, Emily spouted the government's usual line about not sharing the full contents of the classified documents with anyone who didn't have the proper clearance. Stevie was used to this in terrorism cases, but this wasn't that. In fact, nothing she'd been able to glean so far pointed to her client, Barkley, having shared any issues of national security, only embarrassing bumbling in the way the FBI had handled the reports of foreign hacking. It would help if Barkley would talk to her and tell her what was in the documents, but while he'd started to indulge her attempts at small talk, when it came to the case, he was still in his I can't talk about it because everyone's listening mode, which left her no choice but to file the pending motion to compel the government to disclose the full contents of the documents.

Judge Solomon turned to Emily. "Ms. Watkins, what's your response?"

Emily cast her a woeful look and rose to address the judge. "It's the government's response that we cannot share the redacted portions with anyone who doesn't possess the requisite clearance to view them. These documents have been classified as top secret. As for the omitted documents, we're still in the process of decrypting some of the files that were seized from Ms. Palmer's client. She's welcome to ask him to assist us, which could speed the process along."

Stevie shook her head. "And let you use his assistance as an admission of guilt? I don't think so. If they are truly government documents and they are supposed to bolster the government claims against my client, then you should be able to hand them over in a format that I can read. How will the jury assess the veracity of the documents if they can't read them either?"

Solomon nodded. "She has a point, Ms. Watkins. I'm inclined to view the contents of the documents you do have *in camera* in order to make an informed ruling." He looked down his nose. "Unless you're going to contend that I don't have the right to view them?"

Stevie watched while Emily squirmed, knowing that Emily's bosses probably did expect her to withhold the information from everyone, no exceptions, but she had the good sense not to tank her case by denying the judge.

"Of course, Your Honor. We will have them delivered to you this afternoon. As for the files that are being decrypted, I'm going to need a bit more time."

Stevie considered protesting, but decided against it for now. If Solomon reviewed the documents and then denied her access, she'd file a motion to get him to reconsider and work her way up the chain, but for now, she'd bide her time.

"Very well then," Solomon said. "Let's postpone this portion of the hearing until…" He paused to consult with his courtroom deputy. "Tomorrow at two. You'll have the rest of the documents decrypted and delivered to me no later than three weeks from today."

Stevie took a moment with her client in the holdover before she left. "Did you get all that?"

"You're good. She didn't want to give you anything. The judge seems fair."

"I am good, but there's only so much I can do if you won't talk to me."

"What's the point?"

"You tell me," she said, hoping he would take her up on it. She read into his comment that he was resigned to his fate because there was really no dispute that he'd shared the documents in violation of his clearance, but she was still willing to fight for him and make the government prove their case if that's what he wanted. "If you want to end this whole process and take a plea, you can, but the prosecutor is not going to offer a deal unless you agree to meet with the FBI and answer questions they have about other security issues at Folsom."

He shook his head. "If I don't leave soon, I'll miss lunch."

"You still have time to change your mind," she said, wondering why she cared so much when clearly he did not. "You have my number."

Stevie was back at the office by one. The place was virtually empty except for Hannah who was munching on a sandwich at her desk, reminding Stevie she'd forgotten to eat breakfast. "I'll give you twenty dollars for half of that sandwich."

Hannah held out the untouched half. "No charge. Dave makes the biggest sandwiches in all the land."

Stevie munched a bite of the roast beef on sourdough and groaned at the tang of horseradish. "Oh my God, that's amazing."

"I know." Hannah pushed a bag of chips her way. "Try it with these and you'll fall in love."

"Where is everyone?"

"Lunch off campus. It's Leon's last day."

"And you didn't go?"

"I volunteered to stick around and watch the phones. Besides, between you and me, Leon isn't my favorite. Not super sorry to see him go."

"He's not anyone's favorite." Stevie crunched some chips. Leon, one of the attorneys in the office, had never been one of them, always talking about how he was using this job as a stepping-stone to "real" legal work. "I'm thinking everyone else was just angling to get out of the office for a while."

Hannah pointed at the clock on the wall. "You're back early. I thought your hearing was going to run late."

"It was, but the government threw a wrench in the mix by refusing to give me documents I could actually read. Judge Solomon continued us until tomorrow afternoon so he can review the unredacted documents and hopefully decide we're entitled to them. So, now I can handle the Fuentes hearing in the morning."

Hannah tapped her finger against her forehead. "You could. Or, you know, you could do something else."

Stevie knew where she was headed and cut her off. "I'm not going to New Hampshire."

Hannah reached in her desk drawer and pulled out an envelope. "Here's the plane ticket. It's open-ended. You can leave now for the airport, and I can book your flight while you're en route. If you go right this minute, you might make it before the polls close."

Stevie shook her head. "It's her big day. She'll be surrounded by family, friends, campaign workers."

"And apparently, she'd like to be surrounded by you too since her office sent you a plane ticket and has a hotel room reserved."

"I have the hearing tomorrow."

"What time is your hearing?"

Stevie didn't immediately respond, unsure about telling Hannah her real hesitation. It would be tight, but she could make it back in time. The question wasn't whether she could, it was more like whether she should. If Meredith won the primary in New Hampshire tonight, which everyone was predicting she would, the moment would be historic, and like all historic moments, would be the focal point of the entire nation. It was one thing to sneak around, dodging press in between campaign stops, but it would be quite another for her to slip into Meredith's campaign hotel unnoticed on such a big night. "I'll give it some thought." She tossed off the comment and strode back to her office.

She unpacked her briefcase and turned her phone back on, watching while it fired off news alerts, many of which had to do with exit polling for today's primary, but then a text message with Meredith's name appeared in the scroll, and she punched the screen.

Wish me luck. Miss you.

Simple, sweet, and a total gut punch. Stevie sank into her chair. She missed Meredith too, even if she thought it was a tad irrational to miss someone she hadn't known that long. She picked up the phone and stared at the screen, starting and stopping several replies. Good luck sounded so trite and impersonal. Miss you too seemed inadequate. She wanted to say a lot of things, but not in a flat text with no affect.

There's still time to say what you want in person. The internal voice tempting her to travel to New Hampshire was instantly countered with another, more practical voice that told her to use her now free afternoon for additional hearing prep. In the past, the practical voice always won, but she'd never dated someone like Meredith before where catching moments together was so difficult. And she desperately wanted more moments with Meredith.

She stared hard at the files on her desk, their contents full of facts about real people whose freedom hung in the balance. She spent all her time focused on their lives, but she had a right to have a life too, didn't she?

Dammit. She pushed aside the files on her desk, grabbed her briefcase and phone, and strode back to Hannah's desk. She held out her hand. "Give me the envelope before I change my mind."

Hannah didn't hesitate, shoving it into her hand. "I'll call the airline and book you on the next flight." She flapped her hands. "Go, now."

Traffic was snarled and the cab ride was slow. Stevie tapped her foot and fought the voices in her head telling her all the reasons this was a bad idea. She hadn't packed a bag. How was she going to dodge the press? The flights were probably all full since she'd waited until the last minute. Meredith wasn't expecting her. What if Meredith had made plans to celebrate that didn't include her, or more importantly, included someone else? They'd hadn't talked about being exclusive, and Stevie was certain there were tons of adoring women who'd love the chance to stand by Meredith's side, cameras or no cameras.

She fished her phone back out of her bag, and reread Meredith's text, and with a sudden burst of clarity knew exactly what to say in reply. *You don't need luck. You got this. Miss you more than you know.*

She hit send before she could rethink her words and prayed her presence would be welcome.

❖

"You're here." Meredith pulled Stevie into her arms and whispered in her ear. "I didn't think you'd come."

Stevie leaned back and met her eyes. "My hearing got continued at the last minute. I came as soon as I could. Didn't even pack a bag." She ducked her head and lowered her voice. "Is it really okay that I showed up? You've got a lot going on."

Meredith followed her gaze around the room. "Exactly why I need a calming force. Someone who's not part of all this to help me escape." Gordon and Jen chose that moment to appear at her side.

"They're ready for you downstairs. Let's go," Gordon said.

Meredith held her ground. "Gordon, I'd like you to meet Stevie Palmer. Stevie, this is Gordon Hewitt, my campaign manager. He's super pushy, but takes good care of me." She watched as Stevie extended a hand, and Gordon perked up at the mention of Stevie's name. Before he could say anything, she plunged ahead. "Stevie, I have to go downstairs and say a few words to my supporters. Will you come with me? Jen will make sure you have a place to sit near the stage." She saw Jen and Gordon exchange curious looks and hoped Stevie hadn't noticed. There would be a conversation at some point about how to spin Stevie Palmer, she just knew it, but she wasn't having it now.

Jen extended a hand. "Absolutely. Stevie, come with me. I'll get you settled."

Meredith wistfully watched them walk away.

"She's pretty," Gordon said.

"She's gorgeous, but why do I feel like you're looking at her from a casting kind of view?"

"Maybe I am. You know if you start appearing together in public, everyone is going to start imagining her as a First Lady."

"Don't even. We are so far from that."

"You and her or you and the presidency? Because I can tell you the latter isn't true, and by the way you two look at each other, neither is the former."

"I'm having way too good of a night to try to unpack that sentence," Meredith said with an exasperated sigh. "How about we let it go for the night? I'll go say a few words, rally the troops, and then take the rest of the night off and enjoy at least a few hours of privacy."

He looked like he wanted to argue, but he didn't. "The car to the airport leaves at four thirty a.m., and you have a meeting scheduled with Unite Here as soon as we land, and a full day's schedule after that." He wagged a finger at her. "Whatever you do, make sure you're fresh-faced and ready to talk pro union like it's all you ever think about."

"On it." She edged away before she could say anything else, signaling to her speechwriter, Tim Akins, to follow her to the elevator. On the way downstairs, she told him her ideas about freshening up the stump speech, and asked him to write them up and run them by Gordon's team in the morning. She'd planned to talk to Gordon about her ideas later, but this way she could focus on Stevie the rest of the night without interruption. How she wished she could go to her now, strip off this stiff suit, and…

She hadn't thought that far. They'd kissed sure, and their kisses had been amazing, but she'd felt Stevie ease back a bit every time they'd come close to something more. She'd gotten Stevie her own room, but that was when having her here was a hopeful expectation, not a done deal. Now that they were in the same city again, would Stevie want to take their relationship to the next level? Did she?

Yes, she did. From the moment Stevie appeared in the hotel suite, Meredith had been consumed with the thought of making love to her, and if circumstances had been different, she would have dragged her away from the crowd and they'd both be naked right now. She prayed Stevie showing up meant she wanted the same thing.

The elevator doors opened into the ballroom on the first floor, and Meredith put on her game face and strode into the room, shaking hands and smiling at all the supporters who'd gathered to cheer her on. She took the podium and locked eyes with Stevie for just a second before she scanned the rest of the crowd. Acutely conscious and incredibly aroused that Stevie was watching her every move, Meredith gave the speech she'd practiced a dozen times in the shower. After she'd thanked all the right people and given the media the requisite number of sound bites to play and replay over the next week, she stepped down and leaned close to Jen.

"Tell her I'll come to her room. Fifteen minutes."

Jen nodded, and Meredith walked back through the crowd, making time to press flesh with everyone in her path. She hoped no one could tell her responses were rote and her mind was elsewhere. In a few minutes, these moments would all be behind her, and tomorrow she'd start all over again in Nevada and then South Carolina, state by state, until she'd secured enough votes to win the nomination, but for tonight, all she wanted, all she cared about, was having Stevie all to herself.

CHAPTER ELEVEN

Stevie stood in the middle of the hotel room, strangely anxious. She wrote it off to the fact she'd epically failed to pack a single thing for this last-minute trip, but she knew there was way more to her roller coaster of feelings than that.

Jen had escorted her to the room, which seemed a bit like overkill, but when she'd asked her about it, Jen's response had been terse. "Mere said to keep you from the media, and she asked me to see to it personally. All the professionals on staff are busy tonight, and a lot of the volunteers are college kids angling for jobs in the administration—big on enthusiasm and political smarts, but not very savvy when it comes to working the press."

Stevie noted a slight tone when Jen mentioned how the "professionals" were busy, and she wondered if Jen resented having to escort her to this room rather than hang out with the rest of the movers and shakers in Meredith's campaign. She cast about for something to say that would dissolve the tension. "It must mean a lot to Meredith to have you here with her. Have you worked on all of her campaigns?"

"Hers, our dad's, and our brother James Jr. My brother Michael and I are the cogs in the Mitchell political machine."

"She's lucky to have you."

Jen scrunched her face, like she was thinking really hard. "I guess. We work well together, but she's got a whole team for this race."

Stevie detected an undercurrent of resentment in Jen's words, but merely replied, "Teams are good."

"Sure, yeah. Well, if you need anything, let me know." Jen handed her a card and pointed out her cell number at the bottom. "The place is crawling with the press corps, but the registration for this room is not under the campaign block, so no one should bother you, but if you decide to wander the halls or order room service, you do so at your own risk. And Meredith's."

Jen's parting words sounded ominous, and now that Jen had left her alone in the room, Stevie grasped the reality of her situation. She was in a hotel with the entire campaign team for what was expected to be the next Democratic nominee for president. There really wasn't a bigger fishbowl. She was still wearing her suit from court, and she didn't have a change of clothes or even a toothbrush and she hadn't eaten since the half sandwich she'd stolen from Hannah hours earlier and some pretzels on the plane. She also had absolutely no idea when Meredith was going to show up. She'd said fifteen minutes, but that had been thirty minutes ago, and judging by the size of the crowd downstairs, she'd likely only made it through half of them by now.

Stevie paced the room and took in her surroundings. It was more than a room; it was a full suite, complete with a sitting area, a full-sized desk, an oversized bathtub, and a king-sized bed with two robes stretched out across the duvet. She sat on the edge of the bed and fingered the sleeve of one of the robes while her mind processed the implication. She'd spent the time on the plane finishing up prep for tomorrow's hearing, and hadn't allowed her thoughts to wander to what would happen once she showed up at Meredith's hotel, but just being here was a promise of sorts. Was she ready to make good on it?

A knock on the door roused her from her musings. She checked the door viewer before answering and yanked the door open the minute she saw it was Meredith on the other side.

"Did someone call for room service?" Meredith said.

Stevie tugged her into the room and shut the door. Meredith had changed into jeans, loafers, and a sweater. She liked this version of her. "I would've called a lot sooner had I known the wait staff was so cute."

"Cute, huh?"

"Pretty, gorgeous, beautiful—any one of those works."

"You want to know what I'd like better than a compliment?"

"I have a decent idea." Stevie pulled Meredith closer and framed her face with her hands. "I don't think I realized how much I've missed you until this very moment." Without waiting for a reply, she leaned in and took Meredith's lips between her own, slowly savoring their reconnection. "You are the best kisser," she murmured as they broke for breath.

"Sure it's not just a matter of absence makes the heart grow fonder?"

The look in Meredith's eyes betrayed a hint of insecurity that Stevie was anxious to dispel. "Not even." She took Meredith's hand and led her into the suite, bypassing the entrance to the bedroom and settling on the couch. For now. She pointed at the bag in Meredith's hand. "If there's a sandwich in here, I'll be indebted to you for always. I didn't get a chance to eat before I caught the plane, and a miniature bag of pretzels is all that's between me and taking down a pizza joint."

"That would be very bad. I have a vested interest in keeping your energy up." Meredith pulled out her phone and sent a quick text. "There will be food in a few minutes. I promise. In the meantime, I brought other provisions." She handed over the bag.

Stevie filed away the comment about keeping her energy up and rummaged through the bag. She found a pair of plaid pajama pants, a Jefferson Law School sweatshirt, socks, and a toothbrush and toothpaste. And a bottle of champagne. "You're quite the welcome wagon."

"You said you didn't have time to pack anything, and I wanted you to be comfortable."

Touched by the gesture, Stevie kissed Meredith again. "You're so thoughtful, especially considering you had some other things on your mind tonight."

"I did have a few." Meredith reached for the bottle of champagne. "And there's no one I'd rather celebrate with. I have to be up before the crack of dawn, but I want to raise a glass. Are you in?"

The question was so broad. Stevie knew Meredith was referring to the champagne, but there was an electricity in the air buzzing with promise. She was absolutely in for a glass, but what happened after, and was she up for that? To cover her hesitation, she rose and walked to the wet bar to retrieve a couple of glasses. When she returned, she set them down in front of Meredith and watched while she poured. This intelligent, successful, beautiful woman had left an adoring crowd to come to her hotel room and hang out with her. Why was she even hesitating to go all in?

Because this wasn't real life. It was a night in a hotel on the road. And Meredith was riding a high. Stevie sighed. They both had to be up in a few hours and be on—her for her client and court, and Meredith for the crowds and camera. If they slept together tonight and went their separate ways in the dark before dawn, what was the next step? Would there even be a next step?

A knock on the door interrupted her internal rambling. She glanced at Meredith, who nodded her okay. Stevie eased the door open, and a guy who looked like he was still in high school smiled and handed her a white paper bag. He asked if she needed anything else.

"No, thank you," she said, thinking she should probably give him a tip, but he was gone before she could act on her impulse. She shut the door and carried the bag back to where Meredith was sitting on the couch. Meredith reached in the bag and pulled out two cheeseburgers.

"Sean always knows where to find food. Anytime day or night." She handed one of the burgers to Stevie.

"Does he work for the campaign, because he looks like he's all of sixteen."

Meredith motioned for her to go ahead and eat. "He's barely eighteen. Just started college and he's part of the Mitchell for President group on campus. He interned for us at the local office. If it wasn't for volunteers like him, I don't know how we would make this work. Gordon has opened offices all over the country in preparation for the primaries. I thought a Senate campaign was complicated, but this is an enormous machine."

"Can he be counted on to be discreet?"

"Who, Gordon?"

"No, Sean." She raised her burger. "Who, by the way, gets an A for late night food gathering. But earlier, when your sister escorted me to this room she said she didn't trust any of the volunteers to be discreet."

"Ugh." Meredith frowned but didn't say more.

Stevie finished the last bite of her food and reached for Meredith's hand. "Everything okay?"

"You didn't come all this way to talk shop with me."

"Maybe this is a good time to talk about why I am here."

"I'd hoped it was because you want to see me."

"I do." Stevie scooted closer and kissed Meredith lightly on the neck. "Very much. And this room...It's very nice. Inviting."

"I hear a 'but' coming."

Stevie paused before answering, not wanting to kill the mood, but certain if she didn't say what was on her mind, she'd regret it later. "It's not like that. I just can't help but feel a bit like this is a campaign trail booty call." Meredith started to protest, but Stevie raised a hand to stop her. "Let me finish. And under other circumstances there would be nothing wrong with that."

"Under other circumstances?"

"Circumstances like I didn't want to get to know you better. Not just naked in bed you, but you—the woman behind the candidate. Don't get me wrong, I want to know the other one, but I don't want to fall in bed and wake up in a few hours feeling like we shared something very intimate, but weren't very intimate, if that makes any sense at all."

"Actually, it does. You'd like a little time with the unofficial version of Meredith Mitchell. But fully clothed."

Stevie smiled. "Maybe not *fully* clothed."

Meredith mock pushed her away. "Don't even start down the road, because I can't promise to turn back. I mean, have you seen yourself?"

Stevie hadn't looked in a mirror since she'd arrived, but she imagined if she did she'd see a very tired, mussed from travel version of the put together lawyer who'd started her day very early that morning, and she was amazed that Meredith could be attracted to her right now. "Are you disappointed?"

Meredith scrunched her brow. "When I looked up to see you framed in the doorway, I was so excited to see you. Did I want to jump your bones? Absolutely. But I also wanted to get you alone and talk and cuddle and share a meal, and all the other things that two people do when they're dating. Two regular people that aren't in separate cities or beholden to insanely busy schedules." She pulled Stevie closer until their foreheads were touching. "So, no, I'm not disappointed. I'm just happy you're here."

A warm flush coursed through Stevie. "Thank you."

Meredith motioned to the bag she'd brought. "Now go change out of that skirt and into the very unsexy pajamas I brought you."

Stevie walked into the bedroom and pulled the door almost shut. As she peeled off her suit, she experienced a bit of a thrill knowing Meredith was in the next room, and for a moment she considered abandoning her resolve and calling out to Meredith to join her.

"I'm glad we'll have a chance to talk," Meredith called out.

"Me too." Stevie shook her head, part relieved the decision had been made for her and part disappointed in the missed opportunity. She changed and took a moment to shake out and brush her hair and splash some water on her face. She did look tired, but there was a glow there too. No matter what happened tonight, this trip had been a good idea, and she was glad she'd let Hannah talk her into it. There would be other opportunities to be alone with Meredith. She had to believe it.

❖

When Stevie emerged from the bedroom, Meredith let out a low whistle. "You look good in my college colors."

"You're sweet to say so. I've been going since early this morning, but I have a feeling you have me beat in the how much I had to do today department."

Meredith used the back of her hand to stifle a yawn. "It was a long day, but worth it apparently."

"Apparently." Stevie reached for the still half full champagne glasses, and handed one to her. "Too much of this will put me to sleep after such a long day, but we should toast your victory. How does it feel to be another step closer?"

"Ask me in a month." Meredith's mind started darting in a million directions as she mentally scrolled through her calendar. "Make that less than a month. The first Super Tuesday is right around the corner."

"You tensed up just now."

Stevie shifted so she was sitting behind her on the couch and started rubbing her shoulders. Slow, lingering circles of amazing relief. "Your hands are magic." Meredith groaned. "That feels amazing." She turned to look back over her shoulder. "Magic." She wished she could see Stevie's face to tell if she'd gone too far with the innuendo.

"I'll put that on my résumé. It'll go good with zealous advocacy and vigorous defense."

"Definitely. You could massage the jurors and all the not guiltys would be yours."

"Filing that idea away for future use. If that fails, I could take this talent on the road and soothe weary presidential candidates."

"Candidates plural? Think again." Meredith reached a hand up and pressed it into Stevie's. "I'm not sharing this with anyone." There she went again with the innuendo, but she didn't care. She was determined to enjoy this moment, this night, and not let thoughts about what would happen tomorrow or next week or next month get in her head and spoil the little time she had to share with Stevie.

"So, how is the campaign going?" Stevie asked. "Earlier it looked like you wanted to say something. If you want to talk, I'm happy to be a sounding board, and I'm known to be very good at keeping secrets."

Meredith tussled with how to respond, not wanting to talk shop, but figuring it might be safer than other topics. Besides, she really could use a sounding board. "Okay, here goes. I'm sure you know this already, but my family believes that public office is a calling and many are called, but not everyone gets chosen."

She watched Stevie nod, clearly interested in what she had to say, but sharing her feelings this way was a big step. When it came to family business, the Mitchells had an unspoken *omertà*, and if what she was about to say got out, it would be fodder for the media, and could drive a wedge in her relationship with her family.

"I meant what I said about keeping secrets," Stevie said. "I'm not fishing here. You don't have to tell me what's going on, but you should find someone you can talk to. Outside the bubble of Team Meredith."

"Are you telling me you're not on Team Meredith?"

"Oh, I'm head cheerleader, but I'm not working for you and that's a big difference." Stevie's fingers stroked hers as she spoke. "I'm sure you have people you can talk to."

Meredith ran through the list. The only other person she could think of that she trusted to vent to was Addison, but Addison wasn't here, sitting next to her, giving her a glorious massage. Stevie was, and if she was going to take their relationship to the next level, she needed to be able to trust her. Right? She took the plunge.

"Jen is four years older than me. She's run for public office a couple of times. Nothing big, just some local races in New York." She scanned Stevie's face for signs she already knew this information, and was pleasantly surprised to see no sign that she was sharing old news. It was a casualty of being born into a famous family—never quite being sure if everyone you met already knew everything about you.

"I assume she either didn't win her campaigns or she decided elected office wasn't for her."

"She won a seat on a town council, but when she launched her bid for statewide office, it came out that she'd been having an affair with the husband of one of her fellow Junior Leaguers—a very influential member—and her career was instantly tanked. No amount of Mitchell political magic could resurrect her aspirations after that, and she settled for a support role in little sister's political future."

"That's rough. Did you always want to be involved in politics?"

Meredith noted that Stevie always turned the conversation back to her, which had a way of making her feel special. "That's a good question. For a long time, I'm not sure I knew there was anything else to be involved in. When we were kids, we'd ride around with my parents, canvassing neighborhoods and attending town meetings. I'm sure some of that was for show, but Dad also wanted us to see how important community involvement was. James Jr. and I took to it right away, but Jen always felt like she was being forced to join in, and that she was missing out on all the fun stuff in the process."

"What about your brother Michael?"

"Dad was smart enough to realize from early on that Michael's talents were better used in the background. He's a brilliant statistician, but not so great with hiding how he really feels. He'll tell a supporter to their face that he thinks their ideas are stupid. I love him dearly, and he's helped me tremendously, but he has no filter, which is why he's not on the road with me, although I talk to him daily."

"How did Jen come to work for you?"

"It was a mutual decision, but it was her idea. I never would've asked her after her very public dust-up. Not that I didn't believe she was capable or worthy, but I figured she'd be done with politics for good. Yet, she came to me and offered to work my Senate campaign. At first in a background support role, but increasingly I came to rely on her more and more. She's managed to overcome her past and garners a lot of respect in political circles. At this point, I don't know what I would do without her, which is why it's been somewhat tense on the road. She and Gordon tend to clash."

"Legitimate clashes or power struggles?"

Meredith smiled, pleased at the way Stevie could get to the crux of the matter. "Probably some of both, but likely more power struggle than anything else. Jen's not alone. You got a glimpse of it at Christmas. The rest of my family doesn't understand why I felt the need to hire an 'outsider' to run the campaign, but as successful as most of them are, none of them have national experience, and I need someone completely objective to keep me balanced."

"Makes sense."

Stevie nodded but looked off in the distance like she was thinking things through. "What are you thinking?" Meredith asked.

"It's really not my place."

Meredith leaned back into Stevie's arms. "We're snuggled on the couch, and you just gave me the best massage I've ever had. In a minute, I plan to kiss you silly. There's no such thing as 'place' here. Just you and me, and I welcome any advice or insights you care to share."

Stevie shifted slightly so they were face-to-face. "Here's my question. Have you made it clear who's in charge? Because maybe it's a matter of the roles not being clearly defined. If Jen is used to running the show, it had to be awkward having Gordon and his team step in and take over while she's still involved. Where does his responsibility begin and hers end?"

As Stevie spoke, Meredith realized she'd once again drilled down to the core issue. She'd never set a clear demarcation of Jen's and Gordon's roles, but only assumed that they would work together to get things done. She could see how her failure had caused the rifts that had occurred so far. First thing tomorrow, she was going to set things straight.

That was tomorrow. Now all she wanted to do was engage in some of the silly kissing she'd mentioned earlier.

❖

Stevie swiped at her ear, wishing whatever was disturbing her smoking hot dream would go away and leave her alone.

"Hey, babe. I know it's early, but I've got to leave in about fifteen minutes, and you've got a flight to catch."

The words floated on the edges of her conscious, and Stevie tried so hard to integrate them into the action scene that was tugging her in the other direction. The one where Meredith stood over her, naked, arching her body over hers in an achingly slow caress. But now someone was shaking her, gently sure, but if they didn't stop, Meredith was going to be scared away because they couldn't get caught together. "Go away," she mumbled, pushing her hands out to ward off the distraction.

"That must be one hell of a dream."

Stevie shot upright in bed, suddenly very aware of whose voice she was hearing. "Morning," she mumbled. "I didn't mean to push you. I was—"

"Busy. Clearly," Meredith said with a sly smile. "I can only hope I was a virtual part of that little action sequence."

"Now I'm kind of mortified." Stevie rubbed her eyes, wondering exactly how much of her dream she'd vocalized. "You're all dressed up." Meredith was standing in front her dressed in a crisp navy suit, complete with a flag pin on the lapel. Even through her haze, Stevie could tell she was looking very presidential, but also very ready to leave. "Holy shit, I overslept."

"A little."

Stevie patted the covers, and Meredith sat next to her. "I had this image of us sharing coffee and, I don't know, pancakes together before we each flew off in different directions."

"Pancakes, huh?"

"Or omelets. Or French toast." Stevie squeezed Meredith's hand. "I think you're missing the point here."

Meredith grinned. "I promise I'm not. Plus, I'm sure you worked up a good appetite in your sleep."

"Stop."

"It's hard." Meredith leaned forward and kissed her. "You're pretty adorable."

"I'm not entirely sure that's a compliment."

"Rest assured, it is." Meredith stood. "Rain check on the pancakes?"

Stevie searched for something, anything, to say to prolong the contact without sounding like the desperate one being left behind. "You know it's not about the pancakes, don't you?"

Meredith sat back down. "I was hoping that was the case." She glanced at the door, wistfully, like she was being pulled in two equally important directions. "I'm so glad you came up last night. I really needed to see you. More than I realized. I'm going to miss you."

Her voice dropped low on the last words, and Stevie felt the effect throughout her body. It helped to know she wasn't the only one feeling bereft at the idea of separation so soon after their connection had grown stronger. Strong enough for her to feel compelled to say, "Maybe we should make a plan." She breathed deep and pressed on. "I know your schedule is going to be insane over the next few weeks, but maybe we could have a date, even if it's not in person."

"Drinks via FaceTime?"

"Something like that. You could vent, and I could tell you which judges are abusing me so when you're president, you can exact punishment."

"Everybody wants a favor," Meredith said.

Stevie kissed Meredith's hand. "If you're handing out favors, I can think of more interesting ones."

"Is that so?"

"Yes. Now, go get through Super Tuesday and rack up the delegate count."

Stevie steeled her emotions against an emotional good-bye. This was a lot harder than she'd anticipated. Something had shifted in their relationship, and she was starting to regret her decision not to have sex with Meredith the night before, if for no other reason than she'd have that memory to hold on to over the next few weeks. She pulled Meredith close and kissed her again, a long and lingering kiss, not caring if either one of them missed their plane. Most unlike her. When they finally broke for breath, Meredith stood, but she appeared a little woozy.

"Are you okay?" Stevie asked.

"If you call being lightheaded from all the kissing okay, yes, I'm great. That's going to be hard to do on FaceTime."

"Definitely."

"I have to go," Meredith announced in a quiet voice.

"I know."

"This is harder than I expected."

"I know."

"I should probably just do it."

Stevie watched to see what she would do, her heart sinking as Meredith slowly turned and walked toward the door. Five steps and her hand was on the door. Another second to turn the knob, one to open the door, and just like that she'd be gone and it would be like this whole episode had been a dream. But Meredith turned around.

"Will you come to New York for Super Tuesday? I'll be watching the returns there that night, and I know there will be a crowd of people, but then we can go back to my place, and I promise we'll be alone and I may not be able to take the next day off, but at least I won't have to leave at—"

"Yes."

"What?"

"I said yes. Of course I will. I'd love to see your place, but mostly I'd just want to see you." Stevie waved her toward the door. "Now, get out of here so I can miss you the appropriate amount to make our reunion that much better."

Meredith grinned, kissed her again, and practically skipped out of the room. When the door shut behind her, Stevie raised her arms above her head and stretched like a cat on a sunny day, basking in the glow of the promise they'd just made. All her concerns—the press, the pressure, the politics fell away at the idea of seeing Meredith again, and now instead of holding on to the memory of last night, she had the anticipation of next time. And she had big plans for next time, none of which involved sleeping in.

CHAPTER TWELVE

"Where are we again?" Meredith asked as the plane touched down. She laughed when Gordon shook his head. It was the third time she'd asked the question, but she was only half kidding about not being able to keep track of the hectic schedule. It was six p.m., and this was their fourth stop today as they zigged around the country, making appearances in key battleground states. The pace was exhausting, but she couldn't afford to let up. While she'd handily won the primary in Nevada, South Carolina had been another close call, and next Tuesday's primary races included a lot of Southern states where Jed Lankin, with his Southern drawl and pro-gun stance, had a slight lead in the polls. Rural mid-American and Southern Democrats weren't nearly as progressive as their East and West Coast counterparts, but she hoped to gain ground with them on her more moderate positions on the economy and law enforcement if she could get them to overlook the fact she was not only a woman, but a lesbian to boot.

The plane rolled to a stop in Dallas, and as they made their way through the Jetway, Jen walked beside her. "Before we leave the airport, I've got a couple of VIPs coming on board the bus to meet with you. No more than ten minutes each, and we'll still get to the dinner in plenty of time."

Dinner, right. She'd been asked to make a few remarks at a benefit for the North Texas Food Bank. The events were starting to morph into one another. Meredith slipped a mint in her mouth and smoothed her skirt. "Who's up first?"

"Lily Gantry. Gantry Oil and Renewables. She's an industry leader in renewable resources and has worked hard to bring her family's business away from oil production and into other energy sources. She worked with the speech team on some of your position papers."

"Hold up."

Meredith and Jen both turned to face Gordon who wore a frown. "Gantry Oil was recently the focus of a federal investigation here in Dallas and you're going to give her exclusive access?"

"Lily Gantry hasn't been the focus of anything other than awards for her work in the field of energy development," Jen said with a snarl. "And she happens to be married to the criminal bureau chief of the US attorney's office, Peyton Davis. She's heavily involved in charitable causes, and connected eight ways to Sunday. Meredith has everything to gain from having a sit-down with her, and if she declines it would look bad. Do you really think I'd put my own sister in a position that would be harmful to her?"

Gordon held his hands up in surrender. "I'm not saying there isn't a good reason to meet with Lily Gantry, but I need to be in on the discussion about things like this or I'm not doing my job." He stared pointedly at Meredith. "You understand what I'm saying, right?"

Meredith did. Gordon's contract gave him veto power over any other staff member, including Jen, and Meredith could sense his growing aggravation at the way Jen tried to circle around him. His statement about not doing his job was code for Jen wasn't letting him do his job, and Meredith knew it was only a matter of time before he bowed out. It was becoming more and more of a problem, and she was going to have to deal with it. Soon. "I understand. I'm going to take this meeting, but, Jen, while I'm talking to Lily, give the other names on your list to Gordon, and let his team do an initial vetting before we meet. Thanks."

The bus was parked near the tarmac, and a team was loading their luggage into the storage compartment. They'd stay in Dallas overnight and head downstate to Austin in the morning, followed by a trip to Houston in the afternoon. Meredith walked up the steps of the bus and headed toward her private room in the back with Jen on her heels. When she reached the door, Meredith kept her hand on the handle and faced her. "We need to talk about what just happened."

"What?"

Meredith wasn't falling for the "what in the world are you talking about" tone. "I need everyone on the team to work together."

"You should be telling that to him. Gordon may have a lot of insider contacts, but we need influencers. People like Lily Gantry have powerful friends, and their influence spreads wide. It'll be the best ten minutes you spend on this junket. Way more productive than a few remarks at a dinner full of stuffed shirts."

Meredith shut her eyes and squeezed the bridge of her nose to ward off the headache that was crawling its way up her neck. "I will talk to Gordon, but he's got a strategy. It's carefully thought out, and I signed off on it. I'm happy to incorporate your ideas, but it's hard if you're going to spring them on me at the last minute. A little notice would be nice. That's all I'm saying." For now. They'd hash this out in more detail later, but Meredith wanted five minutes alone before she had to make nice to strangers. Again.

Jen nodded. "Okay. I hear you." She glanced back toward the front of the bus. "Are you ready?"

"I need to make a phone call. Give me five."

"Do you want me to get someone on the line?"

Meredith couldn't tell if Jen was being nosy or just didn't think she was capable of doing simple things on her own anymore. If she won in November, there were lots of little things she'd no longer be able to do for herself, but she wasn't ready to surrender all her independence quite yet. "I've got this. If I'm not out in five, feel free to knock." Without waiting for a response, Meredith ducked into her room and sank onto the bed. The tiny space was her sanctuary for the few minutes she was able to rest during these road trips in between the plane flights, but right now she needed something more important than rest.

Stevie answered on the first ring. "I was hoping you'd call. Aren't you due at a dinner in just a bit?"

Meredith laughed, happy beyond belief at the sound of Stevie's voice. "Maybe I should hire you to go on the road with me since you seem to have such a good handle on my schedule. I can barely keep up with what city I'm in."

"How's Dallas?"

"From what I can see out my bus window, it looks like pretty much everywhere else I've been today."

"You just need some barbecue or a big juicy steak. Some meaty, Western thing, and you'll be just fine."

"I miss you." The words spilled out of Meredith's mouth before she could stop them, and once they were out there, she wasn't sure why she'd held back.

"I miss you too. This is harder than I thought it would be."

"Just a few more days and I'll be back in New York."

"I can't wait to see you."

"Me too, you." Meredith fished around for something else to say. Something that didn't remind them both of the distance between them. "Talk to me about your day. I need to hear about the days of normal people. People who don't try to navigate the circumference of the earth in twenty-four hours."

"Okay, but I'm not sure it was normal. I talked to the prosecutor in the Barkley case today. She released more discovery, but not all of it, yet she continues to pressure me to get him to give up a bigger fish in exchange for a plea deal. The good news is I may have come up with an idea to get Barkley to communicate with me."

"Sounds promising."

"I hope so, because my initial review of the evidence only left me more confused than ever, and I think our only shot is for him to start helping me sift through it. The prosecutor's been dangling the promise of a sweet plea offer, but I can't tell if it's decent until I have a better idea of the case against him."

"Anything you can tell me?"

"No, but even if I could, would you really want me to?"

"Sorry, no. And I know you can't talk. I suppose I'm so desperate to have a conversation that doesn't have anything to do with this damn election."

"We can talk in New York if you want, but I had other thoughts about what we could do while I'm there."

"Is that so?"

"It is indeed."

"I'm very interested in these other thoughts."

"Would you like me to share a few of them now?"

A loud knock on the door startled Meredith, and she stood and cleared her throat. "Be right there," she yelled at the door and then to Stevie, she whispered. "I hate this, but I have to go."

"I get it. Totally. Just a few days and we'll see each other in person. Be forewarned, you're going to need to set aside a few hours with a Do Not Disturb sign on your door and your phone powered off. Got it?"

"Got it."

"You're going to knock 'em dead at that dinner."

"Thanks." Meredith knew this was when she should say good-bye, but she suddenly felt like a drama-filled teenager on the phone with her first girlfriend, worried that by hanging up the phone all would be lost. Funny since she'd never been like that when she actually was a teenager.

"Meredith?"

"Yes?"

"You got this."

A few minutes later when Meredith was listening to the captivating Lily Gantry, her mind kept drifting back to her conversation with Stevie and lingering on what she might have planned for their date in New York, and she vowed to make the most of what little time they had and figure out a way to carve out more.

❖

Stevie walked into the jail, shifted the box she was carrying onto one hip, and prepared to do battle. She slid the slip of paper with Barkley's information on it to the guard. "I'm going to need to see him in a contact room with electrical outlets."

Wrinkles formed on his forehead, and he shoved the slip back at her. "Window seat only today."

She gripped the paper in her hand and shoved it back across the counter. "I called ahead."

He shrugged. "Sorry."

He wasn't, and they both knew it. She set the box on the floor and rummaged through her bag for the ammunition she'd hoped she wouldn't have to use. She finally located it and handed him a one-page document. "That's an order from Judge Solomon. Are you going to comply?"

"It doesn't say you have to see him today. Maybe the room will be available tomorrow."

"Would you like me to call the judge?" She watched while he weighed the fun he got from giving her a hard time against the trouble he was likely to get in if his boss found out a federal judge was on his back.

She heard the large buzz of the gate lock disengaging, and he waved her through. "Room at the end on the left," he said through the intercom. She picked up her box and walked the short distance, taking time to set up her files before Barkley showed up.

Barkley glanced back at the guard who escorted him, and Stevie tried to read his expression. It wasn't fear. Anxiety maybe? Stevie waited until the guard shut the door and his footfalls no longer sounded in the hallway. "How have you been treated here?"

"Fine."

The one word, though more than he usually said, was delivered with flat affect, telling her nothing. "You can tell me if someone is hurting you or threatening you. I can do something about it."

"You have an exaggerated sense of your own power."

"Someone's chatty today. What's the occasion?" She kept her tone light, hoping a bit of levity might spark him to say more.

"Why did you decide to take my case?"

"Somebody has to."

"Not true. I could represent myself."

She nodded like she was considering the idea. "True. You could. But why would you want to when you could have a seasoned professional like me?" She swore she detected a hint of a grin. "I brought you something."

He didn't ask any questions but watched intently as she used the hard edge of a file folder to puncture the packing tape on the box. After digging through the packing material, she pulled out a laptop and plugged it in. "This is an air-gapped computer. I assume you know what that means."

He cocked his head and nodded in approval. "It's never been connected to the internet."

"Yep." She reached into her briefcase and pulled out a flash drive. "This is a flash drive that I purchased yesterday. I took it to the FBI field office and watched them copy the discovery for your case on it, you know, the documents that Judge Solomon told them they had to unredact."

"He issued his ruling?"

"Oh, so you have been paying attention." She smiled to soften her sarcasm, pleased that something had penetrated the walls he'd thrown up between them. "He did issue an order. The government still has time to try to locate the encrypted documents, but they had to provide us with copies of the originals for the documents they already provided to us. I brought a copy of Solomon's order if you want to see it, but the highlights are as follows: we cannot make copies of the documents and you will not be able to keep them in any form with you here at the jail. I did get him to agree to let you use a computer during our visits, but we can only view the documents on a computer that has not ever been nor during the course of this trial will be connected to the internet. The bonus to you is that you can be sure there is nothing installed on this laptop that could capture our conversations and send information about our activity out into the world." She reached into her bag and pulled out a pad of Post-its, peeled one off, and placed it over the pinhole for the camera. "See, I planned for everything."

"You think I'm paranoid."

"Maybe I just think you're really cautious. Let me guess, you've seen plenty of violations of privacy in your time at Folsom."

He nodded so slightly she would've missed it had she not been paying careful attention.

"I'm going to go out on a limb and say that some of those violations were committed by government officials."

Again with the almost imperceptible nod.

She pointed at the laptop. "Let's make a deal. For now, you don't have to say anything about the documents, simply mark anything of note for me to look at later. We'll figure out what to do next if you unearth any smoking guns."

"Who paid for the computer?"

Stevie paused for a moment, struck by his focus on extraneous details, but sensing he has some important reason for wanting to know. "I did. I plan to try to expense it, but you don't need to worry about that. There's no cost to you."

She detected relief in the way his shoulders relaxed and the concern in his eyes dissipated slightly. She imagined that whatever he'd been thinking when he chose to send classified documents out into the world was nothing compared to the reality of sitting in a jail cell, not knowing who you could trust. She wanted to ask him if he had friends or family to be a support system while he was going through this mess, but she shoved her questions aside. Considering how little he spoke at all, she couldn't waste her time with him on things that didn't directly pertain to the case. "You ready to start looking at documents?" she asked, hoping her plan to involve him in this document review would get him to open up more.

His only answer was to fire up the laptop and reach for the drive. He studied it for a moment and then plugged it into the USB port. She watched, fascinated, as his hands sped over the keys and the screen in front of them turned into a giant bunch of unintelligible letters and numbers. Screens whizzed by faster than she could read them, but she suspected it wouldn't have mattered anyway since what little she did see was nonsense. After a few minutes of this, he minimized all the open windows on the screen and turned the laptop so that it was situated directly between them.

"Do you want to drive?" he asked.

"I think you should," she said, earning another look of approval.

"There's an index, but it's not very helpful. Probably designed to bury important information." His fingers flew as he spoke. "We should come up with a list of keywords if we want to find anything specific, but aside from that, we'll have to page through all of these if you want to know the scope."

"How many documents are there?"

He opened the utilities on the computer and clicked on the drive. "This drive has a capacity of two hundred and fifty gigabytes, and it's about fifty percent full. Each gigabyte can comprise anywhere from two thousand to five thousand documents, assuming they are only documents and not videos or large-scale images." He tapped his fingers on the desk and furrowed his brow. "I'd say anywhere from fifty thousand to a hundred thousand pdf documents."

She held in a groan. This wasn't the first time she'd worked on document heavy cases, but they weren't that common in the PD's office, since the kind of cases that usually generated that kind of paper tended to be the kind with big money on the defense side. "Well, either I'm going to have to move in here with you, or we're going to have to figure a way to plow through these documents in time for a July trial date."

They could probably push the trial date off, but she hated to do that with him in custody since it only delayed his chance at freedom. It might be time to start trying this case in the court of public opinion. She'd held off on speaking to the press for all the usual reasons, but maybe it was time to make them work for her instead of the other way around. Emily hadn't asked for a gag order, probably because she knew who she was dealing with, and Solomon's protective order about the discovery only pertained to revealing the contents of the documents she'd been provided, but was silent on whether she could talk about the case in general. Generating sympathy for her client in the media might bring Emily around to a better plea offer that didn't involve Barkley flipping on someone else since she didn't hold out much hope the scant conversation they'd shared today was going to suddenly morph into him running his mouth.

She filed the idea away, resolving to speak to Joe and get his advice, and turned her attention back to the computer screen. Despite her determination to focus, the words started to blur and her thoughts wandered. In just a few days, Meredith would be back on her side of the country. The polls had her neck and neck with Lankin with Meredith a lock on both coasts and Lankin still with a slight lead in the South, but Stevie didn't give a damn about polls. All she cared about was that she was about to see Meredith again, and this time she was going to make the most of what little time they would have together. Meredith had already sent her a plane ticket and instructions for the car service that would drive her to Meredith's apartment building, undetected. At least Stevie liked to think that Meredith had been involved in the planning, but it was more likely the arrangements had been made by Jen or one of the interns working on the campaign. She didn't care how it happened as long as it happened.

She shook off the distraction and focused her attention back on the computer screen. *Just get through this work, and you'll get your reward.* Believing the promise, she spent the rest of the next hour letting Barkley explain the documents they were viewing. A lot of it was fluff, designed to slow down her ability to review everything, which, based on her experience, meant there was something exculpatory contained on the drive. They just had to find it.

CHAPTER THIRTEEN

W hat do you mean the plane is grounded?" The minute the words left her mouth, Meredith regretted the shrill delivery, but the idea that she would be stuck in Atlanta watching the election results while Stevie was in New York at her apartment, was bitter icing on the shit cake of a day she'd just had.

"We're working on it," Gordon said, "But worst-case scenario, we switch up the schedule and stay here tonight. I've already got someone checking on a room block downtown."

"That's definitely a worst-case scenario. Gordon, I need a night at home. In my apartment surrounded by my things. I need to sleep in my own bed."

"Someone's grouchy again today. This wouldn't have anything to do with meeting up with a certain someone would it?"

She scanned his face for clues about his reaction to what he apparently already knew and decided it was pointless to try to hide how she felt from him. "It might. How did you know?"

"It's my business to know. Besides, one of my people overheard Jen making the arrangements."

Meredith raised her hands in surrender. "Is it wrong that I want to have a little personal time with someone who has nothing to do with this campaign? Because I'm telling you right now that if I don't get this, I'm not going to make it for the long haul."

Gordon pursed his lips and studied her like he was trying to figure out how to deliver unpleasant news. She poked him in the arm and said, "Out with it."

"Fine. It's not wrong for you to want some private time. Key word private. But just how on the down low do you think you're going to be able to keep this? If I found out, someone else will too."

"Trust me, we'll be careful. The last thing Stevie wants is to be caught in the eye of a media hurricane."

"And that's the last thing I want for you too."

His statement was emphatic and stoked a fire of rebellion in Meredith. "You object to me dating someone?"

"No, I object to the candidate dating someone while trying to land the highest office in the land. It's not just about you anymore." He pointed toward the crowd of campaign workers waiting on the other side of the room. "All these people, and thousands more across the country, are giving their time and money to do whatever they can to help get you elected. You owe them a duty to stay focused on the prize, and the prize right now is getting elected." He lowered his voice. "Not getting laid."

"It's not like that," Meredith hissed, ready to punch him in the mouth. "She's—"

"Amazing? Wonderful? I know, I know. She may be all of those things, and you can indulge in all of her wonders. After you're elected."

Meredith started to fire off a response, but she knew in her heart she owed it to him to at least consider his advice or why else have him lead her campaign in the first place? Was he right? Did her growing feelings for Stevie affect her focus? She reflected over the past few days. She'd been at times excited and grumpy and out of sorts. The excited part had nothing to do with the campaign and everything to do with the knowledge that if she could just hang in there for a bit longer, she could escape it all with a beautiful woman and a few blessed hours of privacy. If thinking about what she was missing was affecting her this much so early in the campaign, what did the next seven months have in store?

She couldn't think about it right now. Not while she was standing in the airport watching the plane with her name emblazoned across the side be put out of commission. Not while she waited for the results of today's primaries to roll in. Eleven states were up in the air, and Lankin was nipping at her heels. She was already so on edge, what would happen if she didn't see Stevie tonight?

Nothing, because not seeing Stevie tonight wasn't an option. Maybe Gordon had a point, and if she survived tonight's delegate count, she could reevaluate, refocus, and put things on hold while she finished out the campaign, but tonight she wasn't going to move the goal. She'd counted on this reward for getting through the last month of nonstop travel and appearances, and she damn well deserved it. Tonight, whether she was victorious in the polls or not, she was going to have a win.

❖

Hannah poked her head in Stevie's office. "We're headed to happy hour after work. Are you coming with?"

"No thanks. I've got plans." Stevie barely looked up from the work on her desk, not because she was focused, but to avoid Hannah's natural lie detector. She did have plans, just not ones she could tell Hannah or anyone else about because she was determined to keep her trip to New York as clandestine as possible.

"Plans, huh?" Hannah walked into her office and plopped down in one of the chairs across from her desk. "Let's see. You can't possibly have plans with the hot chick who's running for president because she's going to be pretty busy tonight."

"What? Oh, yeah, I guess that's right."

Hannah narrowed her eyes. "Wait. You do have plans with her, don't you? But how? She's in Atlanta and you're here. Are you going to have phone sex with the next president of the United States? I could totally sell this story to the *National Enquirer* and retire to that beach house I've been dreaming about."

Stevie stifled her visceral reaction to the *Enquirer* reference because she knew Hannah was kidding. She knew Hannah pretty damn well, and it felt weird not to share her plans. "Shut the door."

Hannah leaned over and pushed the door shut. "Spill."

"This is top secret, like if you tell anyone I'll rip your tongue out top secret. Got it?"

Hannah mimed locking her mouth shut and throwing away the key. "Mmm-mmm."

"You're a goof. I'm flying to New York this afternoon and staying the night at Meredith's place in the city." She watched Hannah's face for some reflection of her own excitement, but she got nothing but a puzzled expression. "What?"

"Does Meredith know you're coming?"

"You're hilarious."

"No, really. CNN says her plane was grounded in Atlanta and her campaign coordinator there is looking at hotel space for her entire team and a ballroom where they can watch the returns."

Stevie's stomach pitched, and she inched a hand toward her phone, but she'd checked it just seconds ago and there'd been no message from Meredith or anyone else about a change of plans.

"You didn't know."

"No, but I'm sure there's a good reason."

"Of course there is. I'm sure she's planning to let you know."

Hannah's voice was full of soothing tones, but it did nothing to shut out the disappointment Stevie felt at the idea she wouldn't see Meredith tonight. If tonight didn't happen, who knew when they would see each other? It could be weeks, months. Her brain was already scrambling for solutions, thinking of ways she could catch up with Meredith on the campaign trail again. The next Super Tuesday was over two weeks away. Would Meredith come home to watch returns again, or set up shop in one of the big states that was sure to swing her way?

Her internal voice shut down the spiral. *You have a job, and a caseload, and trials, and hearings, and clients. You can't shut your entire life down for a night with a woman whose life is headed into complete insanity.* There was barely room for her to be in Meredith's life now. The general election and, if she won, the presidency were going to be all-consuming for Meredith. There would be no time for a personal life, which made Stevie question why she was investing so much energy in a future that would never be. "It's for the best." She murmured the words and willed herself to believe them.

A loud ring pierced through her thoughts, and she looked down to see her phone flashing an unknown number.

"Are you going to answer it?"

Stevie looked up at Hannah and back at the phone. She didn't feel like talking to anyone right now. "It can go to voice mail. Not in a headspace to talk to anyone."

"What if it's her?"

What if it was? Two competing factions warred in her head—one that urged her to go with the flow and the other warning her to resist the rising tide of chaos that could consume her, make her want things she'd never have with Meredith. Another ring and another. Time was running out, and she snatched the phone and punched the answer button. "Hello?"

"Thank God you answered. It's been a hell of a day."

And just like that, Stevie curled into the warm curve of Meredith's clear pleasure at being with her, even if it was only on the phone. "I'm sorry. I heard your plane was grounded."

"Key word 'was.' I'm pleased to report that we're boarding now, and I'll be in New York soon. I'll tell you all about it when I see you. What time does your flight leave?"

Hannah stood, made a heart out of her fingers, and headed for the door. Now was the perfect time to bow out, but it seemed chickenshit to do it on the phone. They did need to have a talk, but not tonight, another big night in Meredith's campaign.

"You're still coming, aren't you?"

Meredith's voice carried a trace of worry, a hint of insecurity, not emotions Stevie usually associated with her. "If you want me to."

"Knowing that I was going to see you tonight is the only thing that's gotten me through the last week."

It was a big admission, a vulnerable one, and one that deserved something better than a "not sure I want to be caught up in your crazy life" response. Stevie's mind drifted to the plane ticket saved on her phone and the packed bag under her desk. A few hours ago, she would've agreed that knowing she was about to see Meredith was the one thing that had gotten her through this week too. Nothing had changed really, and now, hearing Meredith's voice on the phone, her determination to let go wavered. One night. They deserved at least one full night together before they went their separate ways.

"I'll be waiting at your apartment."

CHAPTER FOURTEEN

Tuesday evening, Meredith paced the hallway outside her suite at the Peninsula Hotel, waiting for the next round of returns. Inside, the rooms were crackling with energy and packed with the key players in her campaign, but she couldn't help but feel like something very important was missing. Make that someone. Everyone here had a vested interest in a victory, but they were all rooting for what was best for their party, their political interests, and their country. Even her family, all of whom had decided to make the trip, were more interested in her professional future than how winning would affect her personal life or whatever personal life she could fit between the obligations of her candidacy.

Any resolve she'd formed to reevaluate her relationship with Stevie was fading fast. What she had with Stevie, however infrequently they saw each other, was a connection to a life she hadn't known she wanted until now. A life with something outside the job and public service. A life with someone to share it with, and even if that person wasn't ultimately Stevie, she wanted to make the most of this opportunity to be with her and navigate what it meant to have a portion of her life that didn't belong to her constituents.

Gordon poked his head out the door. "They're about to call Texas, Oklahoma, and Minnesota."

She glanced down the hallway toward the door marked Exit. "Guess it's too late to make a break for it." She tacked on a smile so he would think she was kidding, but a tiny part of her was serious. When had her life's dream become a liability? "I'll be right there."

He ducked back into the suite, and she took a few deep breaths and focused on getting her head right. All the people in that room and thousands more across the country were working hard to get her elected. It wasn't just about her dreams anymore, if it ever had been. She'd made a decision early on to dedicate her life to public service, and that meant personal sacrifice. She brushed her hands down her skirt and straightened her jacket. With her armor in place, she was ready to face whatever fate the ballot box had to offer. She took a step toward the suite but stopped when she spotted Jen coming down the hall toward her.

Things had been rocky between them, but family meant you were in it for the long haul, no matter what road bumps you encountered along the way. She embraced her sister. "Where have you been?"

"Checking on a few details downstairs," Jen said. "Congrats on Georgia. That's a big get."

"They're about to call three more big ones." Meredith nodded toward the door. "Come in and hold my hand?"

"Absolutely. And speaking of holding hands," Jen lowered her voice to a whisper. "She's here. Well, not here, but at your place. Erica made sure she's squared away."

Meredith glanced wistfully at the exit door again, wishing there was some way she could sneak off and watch the rest of the returns with Stevie by her side. "We should go in."

"I promise I'll get you out of here as soon as I can. Erica's waiting downstairs, and she'll be ready to take you home, right after your victory speech."

"Stop it. You're going to jinx the results. We have no idea how the rest of the night is going to go."

A loud roar accompanied by applause sounded from inside the room. Jen pointed at the door. "Sounds like it's going spectacularly well." She grabbed Meredith's hand and tugged her into the room where they were both enveloped by the cheering crowd.

Gordon walked over and grabbed her by the shoulders, his face lit up with an uncharacteristically positive smile. "You took Texas, Oklahoma, and Minnesota. The rest of the night will be frosting on the cake."

"Don't let people hear you talk like that or they'll think you've grown a sunny disposition."

"I know I have a tendency to downplay things, but this is a big deal. We still have a lot of work to do, but tonight you should celebrate." He pulled her into a hug.

Meredith embraced him back, feeling a tad bit guilty that her celebration plans involved a secret rendezvous with Stevie on the Upper East Side instead of an all night blowout with the staff. "We're still taking tomorrow off, yes?"

"You are. I'll be flying to California to work with the office there. Your strong showing in the Southwest means we need to beef up our staff out West so we can be ready for the general election. You lay low and do something you enjoy, because in a few days we'll be hitting the road again."

She fully intended to take his advice.

❖

Stevie scanned the crowd of drivers holding placards, searching for the name she'd been given for the evening. When she finally spotted it, she was pleased to see a familiar face. "Erica, what are you doing here?"

"I'm here for the day since you know who is in town. Plus, she thought it might be more comfortable for you if a familiar face was waiting."

Stevie melted at Meredith's thoughtfulness, touched she'd taken time from her busy schedule to consider her feelings. Who thought about details like that when they were in the middle of a presidential campaign? "I'm glad you're here."

"Did you check a bag?"

"No. I'm all set." Stevie started to protest when Erica reached for her small carry-on but decided it wasn't worth the battle. The bag was light, and she smiled when she remembered Meredith's suggestion that she not bother packing any clothes at all because she wasn't going to be wearing them for long. Of course, that had been a conversation from last week. Today when she'd spoken with her, Meredith had been stressed about the logistics snafu, and no doubt she was on edge right now waiting on the night's results to come in. All their sexual tension ramp-up might be for nothing. She should've packed tights and a hoodie just in case.

As Erica whipped through the crowded Manhattan streets, Stevie tried to get her bearings. She loved the city but hadn't spent much time here and wasn't familiar with the different neighborhoods. "You seem to know your way around."

"I've worked for the senator for a long time, since she was a councilwoman here in Manhattan. I learned to drive on these streets, and in my opinion it's much easier than getting around DC."

"DC is supposed to be easy to get around because of the mathematical way it's laid out, but I agree it can be a pain to navigate if you're not used to it." Stevie pointed out the window. "Is that Saint Patrick's Cathedral?"

"Yes, it is. And the hotel where the campaign is based tonight is that building, just up ahead."

Stevie gazed at the Peninsula Hotel as they drove by, her mind flashing back to the hotel in New Hampshire. Maybe she should've suggested they stay at the hotel tonight. Going to Meredith's apartment was so much more personal than a hotel room. *You're just nervous, wondering which direction tonight will go—stay up too late talking like old friends or ripping each other's clothes off at first sight, like long-separated lovers.*

A few minutes later, they pulled up to an apartment building on the Upper East Side. Erica left the car with the valet and escorted her upstairs via a private elevator to the penthouse of the twenty-story building. Stevie stood by as Erica unlocked the door, wondering if Erica usually had a key or if this was another thing Meredith had asked her to handle personally. When they walked into the apartment, Stevie sucked in a breath. When Meredith said this place was slightly bigger than her home in DC, she'd obviously underplayed her description.

"There should be plenty of food in the kitchen. Help yourself. I have your number, and I'll text you when I'm on the way back with Meredith. Do you need anything else before I leave?"

For some reason, it hadn't occurred to Stevie that Erica would leave her here alone, but of course, she'd be going back to meet Meredith, and bring her here when her night was done, whenever that might be. In the meantime, Stevie would wait here, and the fact that she was all alone amplified how out of place she felt. Everyone important in Meredith's life was sitting in a hotel suite with her, cheering her on or comforting her as the results rolled in, but she was here instead. What did that mean?

"I'm good," she told Erica. She wasn't, but she'd figure out a way to get there before Meredith got home.

❖

Meredith looked down at her phone and smiled at the simple text from Erica. *She's here.* Stevie was in the city and either on her way to her apartment or there right now. Dear Colorado, can you please count your votes faster?

"Looks like they're getting ready to call the rest," Gordon said, appearing at her shoulder like a fortune-teller. "The ballroom downstairs is already full. Are you about ready to go down?"

"Shouldn't we wait until the results actually come in?"

"You do realize you're going to need to make a speech either way?" He cocked his head. "Do you have somewhere else you need to be?"

She laughed to deflect his inquiring gaze. She'd managed to keep Stevie's visit a secret from everyone except Jen and Erica, and there was no sense blowing it now. "Just anxious, I guess."

"No need to be. You've got this. I'm so sure, I already had them load the teleprompter with the victory speech. I expect we'll get a call from Lankin in a few minutes. The rest of the field will clear out after today, and he won't be long behind. He was counting on Georgia and Texas to get him through to the convention."

Meredith spent the trip to the ballroom trying not to feel guilty that she was feeling more excited about seeing Stevie than she was about tonight's landslide. She took the call from Lankin, gave her speech, and shook the hands of all her big donors, but every movement was rote, born of years of practice. What she had no practice for was the building anticipation she felt as she counted the minutes until she saw Stevie. She'd never felt this way, and it both excited and terrified her. When she finally was able to make her escape and slid into the back seat of her car, all she could think about was that just a short while ago, Stevie had been sitting here too. What was she thinking right now? Had her hesitation dissipated, or was she ready to take the next step, whatever that may be?

When Meredith finally reached her apartment door, she took a calming breath and vowed that whatever the night held, she'd be grateful Stevie was here and expect nothing more than the opportunity to spend some uninterrupted time with her. She walked through the door to find Stevie asleep on the couch. She tiptoed her way toward the bedroom, intent on changing clothes, but halfway there, Stevie shot upright.

"Oh my God, I fell asleep," Stevie said.

"It appears you did."

Stevie rubbed her eyes. "I'm so sorry. I was sitting here, and I was going to read for a bit, and then the next thing I knew I was dreaming and now you're here and I'm…rambling. That's what I'm doing."

Meredith sank into the space next to her and reached a hand up to her face. "You might also be drooling. You know, sleep drool. It's cute."

Stevie pulled away, a look of mock horror on her face. "And that, folks, is how you start the perfect date."

"Oh, you had a perfect date planned did you?"

"Planning might be an overstatement, but isn't a celebration in order? Before I so sexily drifted off to sleep, I heard the news. I should've thought to get some champagne."

"A celebration is definitely in order, but I don't need any champagne." Meredith breathed in the woodsy citrus of Stevie's cologne. "I've been thinking about you all day." She leaned closer and nipped at the corner of Stevie's mouth. Stevie's lips parted, but Meredith sensed a trace of hesitation. "Is this okay?"

"It's incredible."

Stevie drew in a breath and Meredith could tell there was more. "But?"

"Should we talk for a minute? Before you got here, I was thinking we should talk for a minute."

Meredith kissed her again. "And now?"

Stevie turned in her arms and whispered in her ear. "And now I'm thinking talking is overrated."

Meredith didn't wait for more. All her apprehension about how Stevie would or could fit into her life faded into a hazy cloud of desire where logistics were a distraction to be ignored. In this moment, she knew exactly what she wanted, and this moment was the only thing that mattered. She stood, held out her hand, and prayed Stevie would come with her.

CHAPTER FIFTEEN

Stevie held tight to Meredith's hand and followed her past several rooms, no longer bothered by the fact her entire house would fit into a corner of this space, or wondering how her quiet existence would fit into the circus Meredith's life had become.

Meredith paused in a doorway and turned to face her, the hint of a question in her eyes.

"Are you worried I'm going to judge you if there are clothes on the floor?" Stevie asked with a smile.

"Maybe," Meredith said with a grin. "I haven't been here in a while."

"I can't judge you if you don't let me in." Stevie stood on her toes to peer over Meredith's shoulder, and Meredith rose to meet her. A second later, they were locked in a kiss. Stevie moaned as Meredith's lips pressed down softly at first and then harder as her tongue traced the line between them, urging her way in, melting away her doubts. "You are an amazing kisser," Stevie said when they broke for air.

"You are."

"Let's call this one a tie." Stevie circled her arms around Meredith's waist, pulled her closer, and took a leap. "I want to do more than kiss you." She tugged Meredith's blouse from her skirt and eased her hands under the cloth and along her soft skin. Meredith shuddered in her arms. "More than this." She used one hand to slowly unbutton Meredith's blouse while tracing circles on her skin with the other, and when the shirt was open, she dropped her head to Meredith's cleavage and nipped a trail of kisses along her lacy black bra.

"You're making me crazy," Meredith groaned.

"Is that a bad thing?"

"Only if you stop."

"I have no intention of stopping." Stevie pointed at the perfectly appointed four-poster bed. "Can you actually use that thing or is it a display piece?"

"Let's find out."

This time Meredith led the way, and when they were at the edge of the bed, she pushed Stevie onto the mattress. Stevie sat back on her elbows watching while Meredith eased her blouse off her shoulders and let it slip to the ground. Next she reached around and unfastened her bra and tossed it aside. Stevie licked her lips at the sight of Meredith's beautiful, swollen pink nipples.

"You like?" Meredith asked.

"I like very much." Stevie crooked a finger. "I'd like better if you were closer."

"Me too. I'll be there in a minute."

She took a step back and lowered her skirt. Heat flamed through Stevie at the sight of her sexy black swatch of cloth underneath. "Very presidential."

Meredith made a show of looking down. "Are you sure? I was thinking maybe I should go with navy blue."

Stevie leaned forward and held out a hand. "If you don't get over here right now, your candidacy will be in jeopardy."

Meredith, wearing only her tiny black thong, climbed onto the bed and slid between Stevie's legs. "I feel like I'm working really hard for your vote, counselor." She cupped Stevie's crotch, and traced the seam of her jeans with her thumb. "But I really want it."

"I can tell," Stevie gasped, her body arching to meet Meredith's hand. Her clothes felt too tight, oppressive. She sat forward and pulled her sweater over her head and tossed it aside and fumbled with her bra while Meredith continued to stroke, applying increasing pressure. When she was finally free on top, Meredith's hand stilled. "Please don't stop."

Meredith sat up. "I'm not. I promise."

Stevie felt Meredith's hand in the waist of her jeans and the gentle pull of her fingers as she unfastened the button. Eager for the feel of her skin against Meredith's, she raised her hips as Meredith pulled the jeans along with her underwear in agonizing slow motion down her legs and off of the bed. And then nothing. No words, no touching. Just still silence. She looked up to see Meredith sitting over her, seemingly in a haze. "What's wrong?"

Meredith's eyes flicked up to meet hers. "Wrong?" She stroked the inside of Stevie's thigh, eliciting a groan of pleasure. "There is absolutely nothing wrong." She leaned forward, stretching her body across Stevie's, skin on skin, the wet, hot heat unmistakable. "This could not be more right."

Stevie nodded, but she couldn't find words before Meredith's lips closed on hers again, this time claiming her rather than seeking permission. She surrendered to the touch, craving more, craving everything Meredith had to offer. She arched from the bed as Meredith stroked her breasts, teasing her nipples with light pinches punctuated by wet hot circles with her tongue. She'd imagined sex with Meredith would be amazing, but the reality was so much more than the buildup, with even the lightest touches sending shockwaves of pleasure through her entire body. She was soaking wet and aching for release but desperate to prolong the ecstasy until she couldn't take it anymore.

The first stroke between her legs was delicious, but the second was electric. She rose off the bed, pressing into the contact, no longer able to count, no longer caring about anything but the push and pull of nerve endings lit up with desire. Meredith's fingers were soft, firm, tender, and fierce. She was everywhere—her tongue lapping at Stevie's breasts, then drawing a path down to her center while she slipped first one, then another finger inside to begin a steady rhythm of thrusts that had Stevie thrashing across the bed. When Meredith's mouth closed on her clit, and her tongue slid the length of it, Stevie stiffened and cried out, and then rode the waves of her orgasm until she was spent.

Meredith kept her hand on her thigh and curled around her side, holding her close. Stevie relaxed into the feel of her skin, the warmth of her touch, and wondered if she'd ever felt this fulfilled.

"Are you okay?"

Stevie heard the slight undercurrent of uncertainty, and she turned in Meredith's arms. "Okay is not quite the word I'd use to describe how I feel." She tucked Meredith into the crook of her arm. "Incredible, wonderful, sated—all much better words."

Meredith shifted to look at her and raised an eyebrow. "Sated? Really?"

Stevie grinned. "For now." She reached down and trailed her fingers along Meredith's naked thigh, enjoying the soft moan her touch elicited. "And how about you? How are you?"

Meredith reached for Stevie's hand and guided Stevie between her legs. "You tell me." As Stevie gently stroked her wet folds, Meredith grabbed the sheets with her fists and held on tight. She was more aroused than she'd ever been, and making love to Stevie had almost taken her over the edge. She teetered there now, torn between prolonging the ecstasy and giving in to the pull of pleasure from Stevie's touch.

"You're so wet."

"You. Make. Me." Slow then fast. Stevie kept a steady pace as she inched her way down until she was between Meredith's legs. Meredith watched as Stevie bowed her head. She knew what was about to happen, but when Stevie's tongue traced the first stroke through her center, she lost her mind. Stevie eased her hands behind Meredith's ass and cupped her closer, alternating gentle nips with long, lingering strokes that pulled her closer and closer to orgasm. She surrendered to the sensations, letting the slow build rise higher and higher until she no longer remembered anything outside of this space, these feelings, this woman. Stevie with her silky touch and her gentle heart was the only thing that mattered, and she called out her name as she came in a rush of rapture.

❖

Meredith rolled over and looked at the clock. They'd been making love for the last three hours, and she'd lost track of how many orgasms had occurred in that span of time. Stevie, who'd just had the last one, was tucked up next to her and already exploring again. "I have something to tell you."

Stevie's hand stilled. She looked up, concern in her eyes. "What is it?"

"I can no longer do this…" Meredith paused for effect. "Without food. I can't remember when I ate last, and I need sustenance to continue to do all the things I want to do to you." She kissed Stevie. "With you."

Stevie rolled over on top of her and started tickling her sides. "You need to work on your delivery, missy." She grinned. "Hey, you're really ticklish."

Meredith squirmed to escape. "You've discovered my secret."

"I think I've discovered several secrets about you tonight." Stevie's voice dropped to a whisper, and she dipped her hands lower, lightly grazing Meredith's thighs. "You know, I'm hungry too. How about we grab a snack and get back to the main course?"

Meredith pulled on a Jefferson T-shirt and handed her favorite, super worn, super soft one to Stevie, and then led the way to the kitchen. She missed this apartment. Her place in DC was small and furnished with only the basics, but here she had a few more creature comforts including a large kitchen. She opened the fridge and peered inside. "We have lots of choices. I can make us an omelet or a grilled cheese or—"

Stevie peered over her shoulder. "You sure do have a lot of food in there for someone who doesn't actually live here."

"Erica stocked it for me." Meredith started pulling ingredients out and setting them on the counter. "I make a mean omelet."

"Erica is pretty all-purpose for a driver."

Meredith heard a question beneath the statement, and she stopped what she was doing. "This was a special favor. I figured the fewer people who knew you were here, the better." She studied Stevie's face. "Something's bothering you."

"It's nothing."

But it wasn't nothing, and Meredith could feel her withdraw. Desperate to recapture the easy intimacy they'd enjoyed all evening, she took Stevie's hand and led her to the kitchen table. "Have a seat and tell me what's on your mind."

"I feel a little silly since I'm the one who made a big deal about not wanting to be included in the vortex of attention that surrounds you, but I guess I'm wondering how I fit in your life. I know I should just enjoy the moments we have and not try to make it more than it is." She hung her head. "I'm sorry. I don't want to spoil tonight."

Meredith's heart ached at the sight of Stevie looking out of sorts. She tilted Stevie's chin up. "Don't be sorry. This is an important conversation, and I'm sorry I haven't made time for it." Stevie started to speak, but Meredith rushed ahead. "My life is absolute chaos right now, and I wouldn't blame you if you didn't want to be a part of it. But I want you to know that despite my days being booked down to the minute, not an hour goes by that I'm not thinking about you and wishing I could see you, talk to you." She stroked Stevie's arm. "Touch you." She locked eyes with Stevie imploring her to get the full thrust of what she was about to say. "I've never felt this way about anyone, and I don't know what that means beyond tonight, but I do know that I'm not ready to let you go."

"I'm not ready to let you go either."

"Then all we have to do is work out the logistics. I'd be proud to have you by my side anywhere, anytime." Meredith pushed away the replay of Gordon's voice telling her to tread carefully, especially when it came to optics. If Stevie started appearing with her at events, people would naturally start to speculate on the details of their relationship. Were they dating? Was it long-term? She didn't care for the fact her personal life was never off limits, but not having one at all wasn't any kind of life. Besides, what kind of leader would she be if she didn't have a personal life?

"I want you in my life in whatever capacity you feel comfortable. If that means staying out of the limelight, I get it. If you want to join me on the trail when you can, I'd love to have you. I don't ever want you to think I'm keeping you a secret for any reason other than for your comfort. I'm not trying to hide anything from the public about who I am, and I have no problem with potential voters seeing me cast as a woman who has a personal life." She laughed. "Hell, Lankin makes such a big deal about how he has a family, and I'm just some single woman who can't relate to the average American family. Seriously though, I promise I won't share anything about you to the press that you don't want me to."

"I'm not quite sure what I'm up for yet, but I feel better knowing where things stand between us. Thanks for indulging me."

Meredith walked around behind Stevie's chair and wrapped her arms around her. "Indulging you is easy. Whatever you want, whenever you're ready." She nibbled on Stevie's ear. "But right now, I have a special request of my own."

"Let's hear it."

"Can there be omelets and sex?"

Stevie leaned her head back and captured Meredith's lips in a kiss. "Does it have to be in that order?"

Chapter Sixteen

Stevie heard a whispered voice in her ear, but she couldn't quite climb out of the deep slumber induced by a full night of sex.

"Babe, I hate to do this."

Meredith's voice. She'd heard the voice in her ear all night, coaxing her to orgasm, but this was different. There was an urgency that had nothing to do with arousal. She rolled over and squinted into the light to see Meredith dressed in a suit standing at the edge of the bed. "What's happening?"

"I'm sorry, babe, but I have to go. The majority leader called a vote on the gun control bill, and he needs all hands on deck to get it to pass. I think he's hoping the Republicans won't be able to cobble together an opposition this quickly. I'm taking a charter back to DC in less than an hour."

Stevie pushed up from the bed, still struggling to wake up. "I should go too."

"Nonsense. It's six a.m. You stay here and sleep. Erica can pick you up when you're ready. I left her number on the kitchen counter. Call me when you're back in DC. I told Gordon I'm taking tonight off since the schedule's on the rails anyway. I should be free by five at the latest." Meredith leaned down and kissed her. "Besides, you'll need some rest for what I have planned later."

Stevie slipped her hands around Meredith's waist and returned the kiss. She should get up, get dressed, and head home, but the offer to stay in bed for just a bit longer and nest in sheets that smelled of their lovemaking was too tempting to resist. "Okay, but you're going to need a nap, so see if you can fit that in."

"Will do." Meredith straightened up, but she seemed hesitant to leave.

"What's the matter?"

"Nothing." She smiled. "I guess I just like this look. Sleepy, tousled Stevie tangled in my bedsheets. I could get used to this."

Stevie sighed, content to bask in Meredith's glowing gaze. Her doubts had subsided, and she was ready to figure out how to make this—whatever this was between them—work.

Sometime later, she rolled over in bed and checked the alarm clock. It was nine a.m. Holy shit, she didn't remember the last time she'd slept so late. Of course, she couldn't remember the last time she'd stayed up so late for anything other than poring over case files. This morning-after sex hazy feeling was much better than that. She swung her legs out of bed and fished Meredith's Jefferson T-shirt from the floor where she'd tossed it the night before. She pulled it on and made her way to the kitchen. Beside the note with Erica's number was another message.

Bagels in the bread box on the counter and veggie cream cheese and fresh OJ in the fridge. The coffee's ready to go—just hit the button. Wish I were sharing breakfast with you. Rain check? Soon?—M

Stevie held the note against her chest. Sweet, thoughtful, kind. Meredith was doing all the right things to win her over, and she was loving every minute. She took her time eating breakfast, not eager to dive back into the reality that waited outside the doors of this sanctuary. She'd taken the day off work, but tomorrow she'd be back in court, and Meredith would be back on the road. Today she'd have to make enough memories to hold until they could see each other again.

When she finished eating, she took a shower, relaxing in the enormous bathroom. Meredith's luxurious lifestyle was foreign to her, but that didn't mean she couldn't enjoy it. After she finished in the shower, she dressed in the clothes she'd worn the day before, but instead of the sweater she'd worn on the trip from DC, she put on Meredith's T-shirt, savoring the scent of her against her skin. She rang Erica who told her she would be downstairs in fifteen minutes.

Stevie idly wondered if Erica was always within spitting distance of Meredith or Meredith's escorts.

She shook her head, pushing away thoughts of other women. Last night she'd been the sole focus of Meredith's attention, and she was ready to give a relationship with her a real try. She resolved to make sure Meredith didn't have any energy left over for other women while she was on the road.

When the elevator doors opened, the lobby was crowded with security. She ducked to the side, wondering what in the hell was going on, but it didn't take long to register the horde of reporters crowding the sidewalk, pressing their faces against the panes of glass. Several uniformed guards were blocking the doors. Instead of approaching the crowd, she approached the concierge desk.

"May I help you, ma'am?" the harried gentleman asked her.

"What's going on?"

"I'm not sure. We've sent someone out to check. Is there something I can help you with?"

"I have a car picking me up, but I'm not too keen on plowing through that crowd. Is there another exit?"

He glanced around, looking as if he'd like to make a break for it. Before he could answer, Stevie felt a tap on her shoulder and whirled around to see Erica standing behind her. "Thank God it's you. I hope you didn't park out front."

Erica shook her head, her usual easygoing manner laced with an anxious edge. "I saw the crowd, and I came around to the service entrance. Follow me."

Stevie walked behind her, keeping up with her brisk pace. "Do you know what's going on?"

Either Erica didn't hear her or she ignored the question, but when they finally burst through the door to the service garage, it didn't matter because the noise level drowned out any chance they could have a conversation. Through the constant flashes of light, Stevie was able to make out another crowd of reporters, almost as big as the one out front. She reached for Erica who turned back toward her, arms extended. "What's going on?"

Erica nudged her back toward the door. "I don't know, but I don't like the look of it. Let's get back inside." She motioned for Stevie to walk in front of her this time and shielded her with her jacket, but the shouts of the reporters made it clear why they were here.

"Ms. Palmer, how long have you and Senator Mitchell been dating?"

"Are you going on the road with the campaign?"

"Are you living with the senator now?"

The questions were like gunshots, fired rapidly and delivering piercing blows. Stevie paused right before they reached the door, her indignation building. What right did anyone have to know what was going on between her and Meredith? Certainly not any of these people who were only looking for juicy tidbits to entice their audience to stay tuned until the next bit of gossip came along. She started to turn, to tell them her personal life, and Meredith's for that matter, was none of their business, but she felt the firm press of Erica's hand on her arm.

"Not a good idea," Erica said.

Erica was right, of course, which just made her madder. They pushed through the doors and crossed the lobby, back to the concierge desk where Erica took charge.

"Someone needs to clear those reporters out of the garage now," she told the concierge. "We have a matter of urgent importance, and if I have to drive my car through a crowd, you'll be responsible for the fallout, and I'll make sure Senator Mitchell knows how her guest was treated here today."

The man nodded effusively. "Yes, ma'am. I have more security on the way. It'll just be a moment. I promise."

Stevie watched the exchange, feeling strangely distant. Was all this attention really because of her, because she'd spent the night at Meredith's apartment? Or did Meredith attract this kind of attention on a daily basis?

No, they'd been calling out her name, and since her presence was supposed to be a secret, this media blitz was unique. "Who told them?"

"What?" Erica asked.

Stevie thought she'd whispered the words to herself, but now that she'd voiced the question, she needed to know the answer. "Someone must've tipped the press off that I would be here." She watched Erica's face morph from genuine concern to anxious. "We need to warn her.

Maybe we can catch her before she goes into session." She pulled her phone out of her pocket, but her call went straight to voice mail.

"You're not going to reach her. She's already at the Capitol."

"I'll text her."

Erica placed her hand on the phone. "Careful. You don't want to leave a trail. If someone gets hold of your texts, well…"

Stevie nodded as if she comprehended, but she couldn't quite wrap her head around the implication that everything in her life, even her private text messages might be fodder for gossip columns. "How do you know so much about this?"

"I've worked for the Mitchell family for years. Every one of them has survived close scrutiny, and it's because they and the people close to them know how to handle themselves."

Stevie's gut clenched. Did she have the wherewithal to "handle" herself in these circumstances? What did that even mean? She could face down hostile prosecution witnesses, hardened criminals, and doubting juries, but this was different. It was personal. No matter how intimate things had gotten with Meredith last night, she hadn't been prepared to parade what they shared in front of the strangers waiting outside, not to mention, the millions more the reporters could reach with their salacious headlines and innuendos. "What am I going to do?" she whispered.

"I've got this." Erica's voice was calm and confident, and she directed her attention back to the concierge. "You have a housekeeping staff—are they here now?"

He raised his eyebrows. "Excuse me?"

Erica looked around and lowered her voice. She gestured toward Stevie. "This woman is an attorney and a guest of the senator. Someone tipped off the press so they could sit outside and ambush her. We need a maid's uniform and a way out of this building or she'll file a lawsuit that'll tie your employers up in court for the next decade. You have five minutes to get us what we need."

He picked up the phone and started dialing while she paced in front of the desk. Stevie stared at them both, confused about what was happening, and within moments, a maid appeared carrying a uniform identical to the one she was wearing. Erica stepped toward the woman whose name tag read Marcela and reached for the uniform, looking it up and down. She turned to Stevie. "I think it will fit. How about you?"

Realization dawned, and Stevie nodded. She made a note of how the maid wore her hair pulled back and pinned up. "Where can I change?"

Marcela ushered her to a restroom, and Stevie began her transformation from happy, satisfied girlfriend of a senator to morning-after mess, dressed like a maid. When she emerged from the restroom with her own clothes stuffed in her carryon, Erica was standing right outside. "What's next?"

"The concierge says there's a door outside the storage room where all the cleaning supplies are kept. Marcela can take you there. It's in an alley, and if you turn left when you exit, you'll be within a few steps of the back of the building. From there walk down to the next block, and I'll pick you up." Erica looked at her watch. "I'll take your bag. They should have the garage clear in about two minutes. You ready?"

"As I'll ever be, but how do I know there's not another crowd at the airport waiting to ambush me there?"

"I couldn't get in touch with the senator, but while you were in the bathroom, I reached her secretary, and she's going to arrange a private charter for you out of Teterboro. The Mitchells have a plane there."

Of course they did. Stevie sighed. She didn't see any other way, although she was reluctant at this point to cede so much control, since giving up control was what had gotten her in the mess to begin with. She had a sneaking suspicion the mass press arrival wasn't the result of some reporter accidentally stumbling across her presence in the city. Someone had tipped them off. If she'd made her own plans, showed up on her own terms, no one else would've had her schedule and been able to leak it. Whoever it was definitely didn't have her best interests in mind, but this wasn't the time to sort out who she could trust. She had to go with her gut and get the hell out of here.

Fifteen minutes later, she bid farewell to Marcela and stepped into the back of the town car, out of the watchful eye of the media frenzy back at Meredith's apartment building. She leaned back against the seat and unclenched her fists, noting the half moon marks on the inside of her palms from the force of her grip.

"Are you okay?"

She looked in the rearview mirror and noted Erica's concerned expression. "I think so."

"We'll be at Teterboro in less than thirty minutes. Would you like me to call Senator Mitchell's office and leave her a message to call you when she breaks free?"

Hearing Meredith's name spoken so formally felt like a sign. Meredith would never be just a citizen living her life. Senator, president, former president—the title didn't matter, but the baggage that came with it did, and today was Stevie's first real opportunity to find out if she was willing to sacrifice her privacy to help carry the load. Earlier, she'd been concerned about Meredith and how the news about her leaving Meredith's apartment in a way that made it obvious they'd spent the night would affect her, but now that she was out of the immediacy of the situation, Stevie knew there was much more to it than that. Could she handle this kind of pressure and the affect it would have on her own life?

If it meant having more nights with Meredith like the one they'd shared last night, she was willing to try.

❖

Meredith walked into Majority Leader Chip Serno's office at the Capitol Building, and greeted several of her colleagues. After several rounds of grandstanding on the Senate floor, Serno had called a brief recess so the majority whip could work on a couple of senators who were still on the fence. He and the whip were in his office now, likely making all kinds of political promises to the holdouts.

After a few minutes of waiting, she started to pace.

"What's the matter, Mitchell?" Sandra Dixon, the senior senator from California, asked. "You've looked at your watch a half dozen times in the last five minutes. Got a hot date?"

Meredith felt the burn of a blush rising up the back of her neck, but she did her best to keep smiling. "You try running for president someday and see how much free time you have." She touched her fingertip to her thumb and shook her head. "Gordon gave me a rare day off, yet here I am."

Dixon clapped her on the shoulder. "Great job yesterday. You've got this."

"I hope so, but there's still a lot of delegates in play."

"Hardly any in contention. Quit being modest." Dixon cleared her throat. "Have you started thinking about a running mate? Because I have some ideas."

Meredith kept a smile plastered on her face, but inwardly, she groaned. These kind of conversations were only just starting, but they were likely to become more commonplace as they got closer and closer to the convention. Everyone wanted to cozy up to the front-runner to start carving out their personal piece of the presidential pie. "I'd love to hear your ideas," she lied. "I'm headed out of town again tomorrow, but call my office and set up a meeting for the next time I'm back in town." Dixon didn't need to know that she had no plans to be back in town until the convention, and by then it would be too late to incorporate any last-minute choices. She already had a few names in mind, and the decision wasn't going to be the result of groupthink.

What bothered her more than everyone offering their unsolicited advice was the fact this was her last day in town for the foreseeable future, and this vote was eating up the time she should be spending with Stevie. She glanced around, looking for Serno to ask him what the holdup was and saw him standing with a few of her other colleagues in front of the bank of televisions that lined the wall of his outer office, one for each network, including cable. Everyone's eyes were glued to the screens, but she couldn't make out what they were watching. She walked over and listened in to MSNBC, the only channel with the volume turned up.

"Press gathered en masse this morning outside of Senator Meredith Mitchell's Manhattan apartment," the anchor said, "hoping for a glimpse at the senator's girlfriend, but she either slipped away unnoticed or hunkered down for the long haul."

Meredith gasped when a photo of Stevie appeared on the screen.

"Stevie Palmer works as a public defender in the District of Columbia, but apparently, she's been tagging along with the senator on the campaign trail. We've assembled a panel of experts to talk about how this news, that the formerly single senator has a new girlfriend, might affect her election bid. With me this morning are…"

He kept talking, but all Meredith heard was a dull roar.

Dixon grasped her arm and whispered, "Are you okay? You're white as a sheet."

This was horrible. Where was Stevie? *Please, God, don't let her walk out into that horde of hungry journalists.* Stevie's voice telling her about the gossip columnists reporting about her after the wedding echoed in Meredith's head. She'd written that off as idle nuisance, but that was also before she'd been running for president. Judging by the size of the press presence outside her apartment building right now, this was another level entirely. She edged away from the crowd around the television. "I need to make a phone call."

Serno chose that moment to emerge from his inner office. "We've got the votes. Everyone get to the floor pronto. I want this wrapped up in the next hour."

Meredith felt her phone in her jacket pocket. She could talk on the run. She shot out of Serno's office and dialed as she walked, but the call went directly to voice mail. Damn. She hoped no reporters had managed to get Stevie's cell phone number, or she'd be smothered with calls. Meredith slowed her pace while she composed a text, but there simply wasn't time to say all she wanted to say, and caution told her to be careful what she put in writing now that her dating life was splattered all over the network news. She settled on a few simple words and hoped they would Band-Aid the wound until she could see Stevie in person. *I heard. I want to see you. It's going to be okay.*

She pressed send before she could rethink the words that weren't completely impersonal, but weren't nearly as personal as she wanted them to be.

CHAPTER SEVENTEEN

Stevie walked off the plane, and Erica led her to the waiting car where she held the door open. Stevie glanced inside at the total stranger behind the wheel and looked back at Erica. "You're not driving?" She felt foolish. After everything Erica had done for her today, for her to assume Erica was going to chauffeur her around all day was selfish, but she was genuinely apprehensive about being carted around by a stranger. Silly, really, when she considered how many times in her life she'd stepped into a taxi. *But you weren't being pursued by paparazzi at the time.* "I'm sorry," she said. "It's just…"

Erica smiled. "I'm sorry too, but I need to get to the Capitol and be ready when Senator Mitchell's done there. I don't even know if she's aware of what's going on, but I don't want to leave her in someone else's hands if there's a crowd waiting for her. I'd take you along, but…"

"I get it. If I'm in the car, it's just more fuel for the fire."

Erica pointed at the guy in the driver's seat. "This is George. He works for Rook Daniels—I believe you met Rook at Addison and Julia's wedding. You can trust him to be discreet."

Stevie decided she was being ridiculous. "I'll be fine. I won't leave my house until I hear from Meredith."

"About that."

Stevie held her breath while Erica drummed her fingers on the door. "Yes?"

"I've arranged for you to check into a hotel. Your house is surrounded."

"What?"

"Just until the furor dies down. George will handle all the details and get you whatever you need, but trust me, it's best this way."

Stevie wanted to protest. Her home was her safe place and she'd been looking forward to being tucked away in its comforts since she snuck out of Meredith's building. Other than the maid's uniform that she'd changed out of on the plane, and the sexy underwear she'd packed for her visit to Meredith's the night before, she didn't have any clothes. But she knew Erica was right. If her house was indeed surrounded, she wouldn't get any rest there anyway, and Meredith certainly wouldn't be able to come over. A hotel rendezvous was much more likely under the current circumstances.

An hour later, she was tucked away in a suite at the Hay Adams. She had no idea who was paying for the room since George had made all the arrangements from the car and warned her not to use her own credit cards to pay for any charges. Whoever was paying, it wasn't cheap. The prices on the minibar were off the charts, but raiding it was her only chance for any kind of lunch. She stripped off her clothes, wrapped up in a fluffy robe, and grabbed a tin of cashews and an Amstel Light. Hunkered down in bed, she channel surfed her way to a B movie about a serial killer hijacking a plane, taking small comfort in watching someone's life being more difficult than her own.

The more she watched the movie, the more normal she felt. In the scheme of things, nothing had really happened to her. Sure, her privacy had been violated, but it wasn't anyone's fault. If she was going to date Meredith, she would have to get used to some level of exposure of her private life. She just thought she'd have more time to prepare for the onslaught of attention, and she hadn't expected an explosion of it so soon after she and Meredith had been intimate for the first time.

That's what she should be dwelling on—their night together, not the craziness that followed. She reached a hand underneath her robe, not at all surprised to find she was wet just thinking about Meredith touching her. Every detail of their night together came flooding back, and she prayed Meredith would be able to finish up at the Capitol and find a way to sneak over here as soon as possible.

❖

Meredith walked through the tunnels from the Capitol Building to her office. She vowed to spend no more than fifteen minutes there, wrapping up anything necessary, and then she'd find Stevie. She burst through the doors, and her secretary Kate sprang from her chair.

"Have you seen the news?" She pointed at the TV on the wall. "The cable channels have spent all morning on this."

Meredith kept walking. "News? That's not news they're airing. It's gossip. Where's Jen?"

"She's in your office making some phone calls." Kate handed her a sheet of paper. "Here's a list of everyone who's called for you this morning, not including reporters. I listed them in order of who I figured you'd care about."

Meredith glanced at the list, noting Erica's name listed first with three stars next to it. She'd call her first. She walked into her private office and shut the door behind her, but instead of finding solitude, she saw Jen sitting at her desk, talking on the phone. Jen held up a hand before saying to whoever was on the line, "I've got to go, but I'll call you back with more details in just a bit. Thanks." She hung up. "How did the vote go?"

Meredith suppressed a frustrated scream. "The vote? I don't care about the vote. Have you seen the news? The press is all over Stevie. Have you heard from her? What's going on?" She paced as she talked, but no amount of physical exertion quelled the mounting anxiety she felt.

"Hey, calm down. Everything's okay."

"Everything is not okay." Meredith waved her hands for emphasis. "The press surrounded my apartment building in Manhattan this morning, shouting her name. We were so careful. How did they even know she was there? If I find out one of the employees there leaked info to the media, I'm going to—"

"Meredith!"

She looked up to see Jen staring at her, and she realized she'd been rambling. "What?"

"Sit down and let's talk about this."

Meredith sat on the sofa in her office but stayed on the edge of her seat, ready for action. "We need a plan."

"I'm way ahead of you."

Meredith sighed with relief. Despite the fact they'd been at odds over election strategy the past couple of months, it was nice to know she could count on Jen to step up when her personal life was taking a bad turn. "I've been trying to get in touch with Stevie. I can't even imagine how she must be feeling right now."

"She'll be fine. Once she realizes she's right in the middle of her moment of fame, she'll be glad she was able to help you out."

"What?" Meredith struggled to process Jen's words. "Help me out how?"

"Now hear me out before you get mad."

"No one on the receiving end of those words ever stays calm. If you have something to say, spit it out."

"Gordon thinks your personal life shouldn't be the centerpiece of your campaign, but he's looking at it from a guy's perspective. Your votes are going to come primarily from women, both now and in the general. Female voters want to connect with their chosen candidate, and that means letting them see into your personal life. Of course, that means you have to have a personal life. Stevie may not have been who I picked for the role, but since you did, we can work with it."

Jen paused and Meredith jumped on her words. "'Work with it?' What does that even mean? And I don't appreciate you judging who I choose to have a relationship with."

"Oh, I'm over the judging part. I've moved on to the leveraging part. Now that the secret is out, Stevie can play a more active role. Nothing too out front, but she can appear at your side at events, maybe a few photo ops of the two of you at charitable events. You know, personal glimpses of the candidate. The press will eat it up, and I guarantee it'll buy you more votes in the female demographic."

"Stop talking." Meredith was out of her seat, her mind racing toward the only logical conclusion it could find. "Was it you?"

"Excuse me?"

Jen narrowed her eyes at Meredith's accusatory tone, but Meredith wasn't fooled at the feigned indignation. "I think you know exactly what I'm talking about. Are you the one who tipped off the press that Stevie was at my place? Please tell me it wasn't you."

She stared hard at Jen, willing her to deny the accusation, but Jen only held out her hands as if in supplication. "Hear me out. I know you're mad at me now, but I promise you, this is for the best. This way we can control the narrative."

"Narrative?" Meredith's voice rose. "There is no narrative. There's only me and a woman I care about, and for you to think you can make decisions about how and when we make that public is beyond my understanding." She grabbed her purse and started walking toward the door.

"Where are you going?" Jen called out. "We have a lot more to talk about."

"Not right now we don't." Meredith didn't look back, but she did indulge her anger by slamming the door behind her as she left the room. She ignored Kate's frantic waving and left the office, dialing Erica on her cell as she walked.

"I need help," she said into the phone as soon as Erica answered.

"I know where she is. I'm downstairs with the car."

"Thank God. Can you get me to her?"

Several decoy stops later, Meredith walked down the hallway of the Hay Adams Hotel, scanning the doors for the room number Erica had given her. She paused when she found the one. She had a key, but felt like using it would be just another violation of Stevie's privacy. She knocked lightly on the door and hoped the noise wouldn't draw any of the other hotel guests to look out into the hall. When the door swung open, she was unprepared for the sight of Stevie in a fluffy white robe, and despite everything that had transpired since she'd left her that morning, it took her breath away.

"Can I come in?"

Stevie pulled her into the room, wrapping her up in her arms, and shutting the door with her foot. "I'm so glad to see you. Are you okay? Did you get mobbed on the way over here? I'm so sorry I wasn't able to avoid them completely, but they were everywhere."

Meredith's head spun at the whirlwind of Stevie's comments, and she reached to steady herself. "Do you mind if we sit down?"

"Of course not." Stevie led her to the sofa, and once they were seated, pointed out the minibar. "Can I get you a drink?"

Meredith pointed at the empty Amstel Light bottle on the coffee table. "I'll have one of those if there's another." When Stevie handed her the beer, she took a long draught as fortification. "Are you okay?"

Stevie nodded. "I don't know what I would've done if Erica hadn't been there. She's great under pressure, but all in all, I guess it was bound to happen sometime. It wasn't anyone's fault."

Meredith heard the echo of Jen's words in Stevie's pronouncement, and for a second she considered abandoning her quest to come clean. Maybe exposing their relationship was bound to happen, and at least now it was behind them. She could have Gordon's team draft some talking points, and they could develop a strategy to make this whole revelation work for them instead of the other way around.

But if she was going to have a relationship with Stevie, it needed to be based on trust, not on expediency, and that had to start by dispelling the notion that what had happened this morning wasn't anyone's fault. "I need to tell you something."

Stevie placed a hand on her thigh. "Can it wait? Now that I know you're okay, I just want to forget this ever happened."

Meredith desperately wanted to say yes, but she knew she wouldn't be able to truly relax into Stevie's embrace until she told her the truth. She placed a hand over Stevie's and eased gently away. "I wish it could wait, but it's important."

Stevie gazed into her eyes for a moment. "Okay." She straightened her robe and crossed her arms. "What's up?"

"It was Jen," Meredith blurted out the words quickly before she changed her mind. She plowed ahead. "Jen told the press you'd be at my apartment and exactly when they could find you." She looked into Stevie's eyes, trying to read a reaction, but she got nothing, but a flat stare. "Please say something so I know you're not mad."

The silence was deafening, but she resisted the urge to talk through it, merely watching while Stevie stood and walked across the room. Stevie paced for a few moments, and Meredith could tell her mind was churning, but she didn't have a read on her emotions until Stevie finally spoke.

"I brushed it off for your sake, because I didn't want you to think I couldn't handle the stress of constant scrutiny that I know you experience every single day since you've started your campaign."

"And I appreciate that—" Meredith started to say, but Stevie raised a hand to cut her off, and she immediately shut up.

"So I brushed it off," Stevie repeated. "But it was pretty horrifying, not just to have to sneak out of your building in a maid's uniform, but to see my name plastered all over the internet, not for some accomplishment I achieved, but as fodder for all of the gossips who want to know who's sleeping with the future president." She paced some more. "I could get past all that. Eventually."

Meredith heart beat quicker at the idea of getting past this, but she could tell there was more. "What would it take?"

"To be honest, I don't know." Stevie shook her head. "You're saying Jen did this?"

"Yes. She just told me and I came straight here. It was her way of trying to humanize me for the voters—show them I have a personal side. I guess she thought since Gordon was against me making our relationship public, the only way to accomplish what she had in mind was to just get it out there. If anyone else had done this, I'd fire them on the spot. Although I'm sorry it happened this way, but I have to say there's a part of me that's relieved that we don't have to sneak around anymore. Like you said, it was bound to happen."

"Do you hear yourself?"

Meredith did a mental replay. "I promise I'm not trying to minimize what you went through, but don't you want this too?"

"'This' being a good solider for the campaign?" Stevie's tone was incredulous.

"No, of course that's not what I meant." Meredith waved a hand between them. "I mean this, us. We'll have to navigate this carefully, but now that things are out in the open, we can actually go to a restaurant or a movie without having to worry about what people will think." She saw Stevie start to frown. "That's not what I meant. It's just—"

"It's just that there's no room in your life for anything that isn't carefully crafted to garner more votes. I get it. Running for president is your life's mission, but I want to be with someone who I can build a life with, not fit into someone else's preordained plan. Right now, I'd just like you to go."

Meredith stood, unable to believe how fast things had spiraled out of control. Less than twelve hours ago, she scored a major campaign victory, she and Stevie had made love. She'd believed anything was possible—a relationship, the presidency, everything. Now, the news had completely shifted away from her big win and onto her personal life which was crashing down around her. She searched Stevie's face for any sign they could get past this, but for now anyway, Stevie was completely closed off, and she didn't know how in the world she was going to win her back.

❖

Stevie watched the door shut behind Meredith and held on for several minutes before bursting into tears. The stress that had been growing since she'd walked into the lobby of Meredith's apartment building that morning bubbled up inside her. Not usually prone to tears, she gave in to the raw pain of finding out the Meredith she thought she knew was as chameleon-like as any other politician, and she let it wrack her with sobs until she was finally spent.

An hour later, she washed her face, got dressed, and stood in the middle of the hotel room, ready to go. The question was, where? Going home meant fighting through a crowd of reporters, but staying here on Meredith's dime was out of the question. She pulled out her phone and turned it on, half expecting to see a text from Meredith, half hoping she hadn't given up so easily, but the only notifications were from Hannah—three missed calls and a chain of texts escalating from "are you okay?" to "CALL ME, 911." No longer caring if anyone was tracking her calls, she called Hannah and waited impatiently for her to answer.

"Thank God. I've been trying to reach you for hours," Hannah said. "Where are you?"

Stevie started to tell her, then stopped. "I'd rather not say, but I can't stay where I am. What's the office like?" she asked, hoping Hannah would get the hint.

"There was a crowd earlier, but Joe shooed them all away, telling them you weren't working today. I saw a couple hanging around though when I went out for lunch. MSNBC says there's still a bunch at your house, so you definitely shouldn't go there."

"Damn."

"I know a place you can stay. One of the proprietors makes a mean roast beef sandwich with horseradish."

Stevie breathed a sigh of relief, but she hesitated to accept Hannah's generous offer. "Are you sure?"

"Absolutely. If you can get to our favorite spot, I'll pick you up there."

"On it. I can be there within the hour."

"There's one more thing."

Stevie braced for more bad news. "Yes?"

"Emily Watkins came by with discovery on that case you're working with her. She wouldn't leave it though, and she insisted she has to talk to you today. I told her you weren't at the office, and she'd have to be blind and deaf not to know what's going on, but she made me promise to try to reach you. I have her cell phone number."

Stevie racked her brain for what could be so important on the Barkley case but came up empty. "Okay, I'll get her number when I see you. And, Hannah?"

"Yes?"

"Thanks."

Stevie hung up the phone, grateful to have a plan that didn't involve being dependent on one of Meredith's inner circle. She'd stay at Hannah's until the heat died down and occupy her time by working on Barkley's case and all the others that had probably suffered from her lack of attention since she'd met Meredith Mitchell. Getting involved had been a mistake, and once she made it out of here and back to the cocoon of her uneventful life, she and Meredith were done no matter how much it wounded her to break their connection.

CHAPTER EIGHTEEN

Stevie sat at Hannah's kitchen table and struggled to process what Emily was telling her, but after everything that had happened that day, her brain was sluggish. "You came all the way over here, at eight o'clock at night, just to tell me your agents have finally decrypted the files you seized from William Barkley's computer?"

Emily cast a look over her shoulder. "Who else is here?"

"For crying out loud, quit acting like a spy on a mission. Hannah is here, but she works in the PD's office, so there's nothing you can say to me that you can't say in front of her. Her husband Dave is out of town, and no one else lives here. Now, I've had a really shitty day, and I'm not in the mood to play games, so tell me what's on your mind, and let's get this over with."

"Are you really dating her? Meredith Mitchell?" Emily asked. "I mean, I know you went to Justice Riley's wedding with her, but this seems more serious. Is it true?"

Stevie stood. "Did you come here to gossip? Because if you did, you can leave right now. My personal life is off limits for conversation. Understood?"

Emily nodded. "I hear you, but what if your personal life creates a conflict for you on a case?"

"What?"

"I'm sorry, I didn't approach this very well, but we need to talk, so can you please sit down?"

Stevie sank into her seat, unable to process where this conversation might be going. "I'm sitting, now spill."

"It's about the files. They were on your client's hard drive, but they didn't originate on his computer, so we're not sure if he's the original source."

"Did you bring them to me?"

Emily ducked her gaze. "I have them with me."

"Way to dodge the question. Can I have the files?"

"If you're dating Meredith Mitchell, you may have an insurmountable conflict of interest."

Stevie's gut churned at the ominous tone in Emily's voice. "What are you talking about?"

Emily faced her square on. "I have a ton of respect for you as a lawyer and a person, but I have a duty to make sure that any prosecution of your client isn't going to get tossed out because his attorney has a conflict of interest that might impair his defense. I need you to answer the question."

The answer should be easy, but Stevie had struggled on and off all day about whether she'd done the right thing by sending Meredith away. Had she overreacted to the way Meredith brushed off Jen's leak like it was all part of the game? Maybe she had, a little, but that didn't change the fact that when it came to politics, she might never be certain Meredith would choose her feelings over expediency. She'd sent Meredith away, but a part of her held out hope Meredith might make some grand gesture to demonstrate the intimacy they'd shared and the fledging relationship they'd begun were at least as important as publicity that might buy her votes. Silly, really. Meredith's goal to be president was a lifelong dream, and Stevie knew she was nothing more than a stop along the road to Meredith's goal.

"No, we're not dating. We're not in a relationship. We're not really even friends." Stevie crossed her hands. "Now, tell me what you've got."

Emily studied her for a moment, and then seemed satisfied with her answer. "I told you before that the Mitchell Foundation is one of the clients of Barkley's employer, Folsom Enterprises."

"I remember."

"The decrypted files show a direct connection between the Mitchell Foundation and the Russian hackers that your client was trying to expose."

A dull roar flooded Stevie's eardrums, and she gripped the table. "Are you okay?" Emily asked.

Everyone kept asking if she was okay today, like she was some kind of petite flower who couldn't handle a cluster of reporters or a bombshell piece of evidence in a case. She'd always been able to hold her own against anything life tossed her way; when had everyone started thinking she was so weak? Was it when she started being cast in the role of the senator, soon to be president's, girlfriend? Well, it was time to reclaim who she was and do what she did best—advocate for her clients. "I'm fine. Lay it out for me."

Emily pulled out a piece of paper and started drawing a flow chart. She pointed to the boxes. "Here's what we know. The Mitchell Foundation hired Folsom Enterprises several years ago to handle its IT work, as you know. Folsom also does IT work for several government agencies, which is how your client got the information he released about the ongoing FBI investigation of Russian operatives hacking social media accounts."

"You say 'ongoing,' but I say 'prematurely closed' investigation," Stevie said. "The FBI dropped the ball on that case, and my client was merely exposing their shoddy work and waste of taxpayer dollars."

Emily looked around. "There's no jury here, so quit grandstanding. The upshot is that your client leaked classified information, and we think someone was trying to get him to leak more."

"I don't follow."

"When your client was arrested, his computer was seized, but there were emails in the pipeline to him, on the Folsom server, that he hadn't downloaded yet. Folsom gave us the runaround when we served them with a subpoena, claiming they couldn't release all of Barkley's incoming emails because they contained information that pertained to their government clients and might contain classified material. We fought them on this, *ex parte*."

"Why did you feel the need to go around my back?"

Emily had the good sense to look slightly embarrassed. "It just seemed easier. If we found something that pertained to your client, we would've shared it with you, but if what we found was truly unrelated and also classified, then it was best if you were never exposed to it."

The reasoning made sense in the abstract, but Stevie was still confused about how this all tied together. "Fine, we can argue the finer points later. Tell me what happened next."

Emily nodded. "Someone sent a bunch of encrypted files to your client within days of him releasing documents to the press about the aborted FBI investigation."

"And these are the files that supposedly tie the Mitchell Foundation to these Russian hackers?"

"Yes. Of course we just found that out. The files weren't easy to decrypt, but apparently whoever sent them to your client thought he could handle it. They probably weren't counting on him getting arrested before he even had a chance to download them and, they hoped, release them to the press."

"So what do you want from me?"

"I want to talk to Barkley and find out everything he knows. Bottom line, I want to know if the Mitchell Foundation is trying to influence this election."

"Whoa, that's a big leap. Even if the foundation hired these hackers, you don't know if it has anything to do with the election. Meredith hadn't even put her name in the ring when Barkley was arrested."

"Don't be naive, Stevie. This entire town was talking about the possibility of her getting into the race weeks before Connie Armstrong tanked."

Stevie scrambled for a response, but she had to admit Emily was right about the timing. For all either of them knew, Connie's leaked emails could've been the result of a hacker too, since no one had come forward yet to claim credit. Could the same people be responsible? Was the Mitchell Foundation behind it?

She shook her head, unable to conceive that the Meredith she knew would've had anything to do with a scheme to influence the election. Stevie thought back to Christmas Day at Meredith's parents' house. Clearly, Meredith's entire family was vested in her success, and Jen's actions to try to get her sister elected were over-the-top. Maybe Meredith wouldn't do anything nefarious to win, but her family might do it for her.

Suddenly, she was overcome with the desire to reach out to Meredith, share this information, and gauge her response. She was convinced Meredith would tell her she wasn't involved, and she was confident she'd be able to tell if Meredith was telling the truth.

But going to Meredith wasn't an option. The information Emily had given her was classified, and Emily had only shared it with her because she'd given her word there was no relationship between her and Meredith. Her only obligation right now was to her client and the truth, whatever that might be. "Let's set up a meeting with Barkley, but you better come prepared with a really juicy offer if you want me to persuade him to talk."

They agreed to meet at the jail in the morning, and Emily promised she'd make it worth Barkley's while. As they shook hands to seal the deal, Stevie couldn't help but feel like she'd just sold Meredith out, even as she vowed to do whatever she could to protect her.

❖

Meredith rolled over in bed and reached for her phone on the nightstand. It was six a.m. She checked the local Miami weather and saw there was a chance of thunderstorms, which seemed like a perfect reflection of her current mood. It had been three days since she left Stevie at the Hay Adams in DC, and every moment since had been a struggle between putting on a face for the crowd and curling up in bed in a fit of self-pity.

She'd stopped calling and sending texts to Stevie after a full day of no response, but she hadn't stopped thinking about her. Gordon, who thankfully hadn't said he'd told her so, had commented that she was distracted, but she hadn't given in to his attempt to fish more information from her about what was really wrong. Jen was the only one she'd talked to and that conversation had been short.

"We need to put out a statement or you'll never get the press to cover any of your talking points," Jen said. "Is girlfriend too strong a word or would you prefer something more vague like 'Stevie Palmer and Senator Mitchell have been dating'?"

"I need you to explain to me what the hell you were thinking? You knew I wanted to keep my relationship with Stevie under wraps, but you tipped off the press?"

"Come on, Mere. It was inevitable they would find out. Don't you think it's best that we control the narrative?"

"Except there is no narrative to control anymore. You thought you were doing me a favor by showing the public I was relatable because I had a steady girlfriend? Well, ironically, your little trick cost me any kind of relationship with Stevie. She's not returning my calls, and I wouldn't be surprised if I never hear from her again."

"Don't be silly. She'll come around. I mean, who wouldn't want to be involved with the woman who's about to be the most powerful person in the world?"

"I hope to God you don't expect me to answer that question. And there won't be any statement from this office about Stevie. Not a word. Understood?"

Meredith had walked away from the conversation shaking her head. Jen had been immersed in politics too long to realize Stevie had no interest in dating her as a power play. She had more integrity in her little finger than all the members of Congress put together.

Meredith heard a knock on the door and prayed it was the coffee she'd ordered the night before. She put on her robe and padded to the door, annoyed to find both Jen and Gordon standing outside. She fought the urge to ignore their presence and swung open the door. "One of you better have coffee for me."

Gordon barreled into the room and shoved a piece of paper in her hand. "Tell me you weren't keeping this from me."

His angry tone was more effective than caffeine. She scanned the paper, and dread filled her with each word she read.

Mitchell Foundation Implicated in Scheme to Influence Social Media

William Barkley, arrested last fall and charged with violations of the Espionage Act for disseminating classified documents, has provided information to government officials regarding allegations against the Mitchell Foundation in exchange for a plea deal on his original case. A source, who prefers to remain anonymous, stated talks are already underway between the US Attorney's office and public defender Stevie Palmer.

There was more, mostly vague innuendo, but Meredith tossed the paper onto the bed. "At least they didn't say, 'Stevie Palmer, Senator Mitchell's girlfriend.'"

"Very funny," Gordon replied. "CNN is running this story as breaking news in less than an hour, and they'd like a statement from the campaign. You can bet that right after they finish hashing out a possible criminal case against your family, they'll have a roundtable to discuss your relationship with Palmer." He shook his hands in the air. "This is serious."

Meredith motioned for them to sit down. "I know, and I am taking it seriously. This is the first I'm hearing about any of this, and I can assure you I've done nothing wrong. Do you have any suggestions?"

Jen piped up first. "Let's not add fuel to the fire. We've been holding steady with a 'no comment' about Stevie. Let's stick with that on this too. Let them show their cards and then you'll know how to respond."

Meredith turned to Gordon. "Do you agree?"

Gordon shot an apologetic look at Jen and shook his head. "I think we need to get out in front of this. You, on camera, vehemently denying the charges, but you won't answer any follow-up questions, because, as a former prosecutor, you know how important it is to let the process work without interference from the outside. Then we need to examine every scrap of paper, every email you've ever written, sent, or stuffed away to see if there's anything to implicate you if the Foundation winds up getting indicted."

"Next you're going to say she needs an attorney," Jen said.

"Probably not a bad idea," Gordon replied.

Meredith held up a hand to stop the back-and-forth. "We're all on the same team, remember?" She looked down at her hands, formulating a plan. She knew what she had to do, or at least the first step, but she dreaded the fallout. While she ruminated, her thoughts drifted to Stevie, and a thousand questions filled her head. When did Stevie find out her client had information about the Foundation? Meredith understood attorney-client privilege as well as any seasoned lawyer, but if all of this was percolating while they were seeing each other, shouldn't Stevie have given her some indication something was up? Had she held back on giving this information to the government until they broke up? If they hadn't broken up, would she have shared it at all?

The timing was suspect, but none of her thoughts squared with the Stevie she thought she knew. She wanted to call her, ask her what was going on, but her attorney brain said it was a bad idea. A few days ago, she would've ignored the practical voice in her head, but she was already feeling the consequences of not paying attention to the full implications of her actions. She'd hurt Stevie, and she'd caused a major distraction for her campaign. Now that she was faced with a real disaster, it was time to focus and listen to the one voice she could trust. "Jen?"

Jen looked up with a satisfied smile on her face, and Meredith felt a twinge of regret for what she was about to do. "I need to talk to Gordon. Alone."

Jen's smile faded, but she didn't protest. She walked out the door with a respectable display of dignity. When the door shut behind her, Meredith sat down and met Gordon's eyes. "We're going to do this your way from here on out. I'm not going to fire Jen outright because of how it will look, but she is going to recede from the campaign to handle the workload at the Senate office while I'm campaigning."

Gordon nodded. "Do you want to tell her or should I?"

"I'll take care of it later today. Go ahead and prepare my statement, and let me know where you think we should give it."

"Your first appearance this morning is down the street from the Miami-Dade County Courthouse which will look nice framed in the background. We'll park near the courthouse and have you stop and give the statement as you walk down the street. You'll need to have it memorized so it doesn't look like a photo op."

"You're kind of scary good at this."

"I learned from the best." Gordon tapped his fingers against the arm of his chair. "About Stevie…"

"What about her?"

"No need to growl, I just wonder if maybe you should say something to address your relationship. Get it out of the way. There are bound to be questions, more so now that she's tied to the investigation of the Foundation."

"Gordon, I'm going to say this once. You have full rein over every aspect of this campaign, but Ms. Palmer doesn't fall under the category of campaign-related issues. No statement, no questions."

He stared at her for a moment. "Got it." He stood. "I'm going to get to work on the stuff we can talk about. I'll meet you downstairs in half an hour."

Meredith walked him to the door and sagged against it as it closed behind him. She was both relieved and disappointed that the campaign was barreling forward so fast she barely had time to think. Her entire family was going to think she'd lost her mind when she fired Jen from the campaign, but she knew it was the right thing to do. Maybe if she'd done this from the very beginning, Stevie would still be talking to her and they'd have a chance to build on the intimacy they'd shared.

She had no idea, but she did know that if she was going to survive today's news, she would need to put serious distance between her campaign and everything personal in her life, and that included her family and Stevie Palmer.

CHAPTER NINETEEN

Super Tuesday II

"Are you sure you want to watch this?"

Stevie looked up from the TV to see Hannah staring at her with a concerned expression, and, not for the first time, she thought she might have overstayed her welcome. She'd been camped out in Hannah's guest room for the past two weeks, hoping with each passing day that the press would finally get tired of stalking her house. It wasn't much better at the office, but at least Hannah and Dave lived in a gated community, which meant the reporters weren't able to follow her all the way home. Home. As welcoming as Hannah and Dave had been, this wasn't home, and she couldn't hide out here forever. "I should go."

Hannah settled onto the couch beside her. "Nobody said anything about you going anywhere." She pointed at the TV where the primary election returns were starting to come in. "I'm just not sure you want to put yourself through watching this. Predictions are it's not going to go well for her tonight."

Stevie knew Hannah was right. She'd read the headlines on every major news site. Hell, she'd been more obsessed with election news in the days following the allegations against the Mitchell Foundation, than she had been when she was dating one of the candidates. But she couldn't stop. It was as if by consuming all the information she could access, she could keep some connection to Meredith, however tenuous. "I have to see it," she said. "But I can go to my room and stream it on my iPad if you'd rather not."

Hannah shook her head. "Nope. I'm in this with you. Dave had to work late, but he left us sandwiches for dinner. Don't say you're not hungry."

"I won't say it." Stevie managed a smile. She knew Hannah was only trying to help, but she'd lost so much lately—her privacy, her connection to Meredith—that the loss of her appetite seemed like such a small thing. "I might be convinced to eat if there's roast beef and horseradish involved."

"You got it." Hannah stood. "I'll be right back."

"Wait." Stevie pointed to the television where the anchor sat at the desk and the breaking news banner was flashing. "Results are starting to come in." She motioned for Hannah to join her on the couch. "Stay, please?"

Hannah settled back onto the sofa, and Stevie held tight to her hand as the news anchor adjusted his tie, and started reading from the prompter.

"We have the results of the North Carolina and Florida primaries, and, as expected, the tide has turned against Senator Meredith Mitchell, who up until two weeks ago, was favored to win the Democratic primary in both states. We are prepared to announce that Governor Jed Lankin has won the majority of delegates in both states, making a rousing comeback from the first Super Tuesday, earlier this month. Stay tuned because we still have several states in play tonight, and—"

Stevie released Hannah's hand and fumbled for the remote, punching the off button before he could say more. She'd heard enough.

"It's not your fault."

"On some level, I know you're right, but part of me wonders how much of this," she pointed at the now silent television, "is because of the news about the Mitchell Foundation, and how much is fallout from the whole does she, doesn't she have a girlfriend? Maybe it's some of both, and maybe we never should've gotten involved in the first place."

"That's a lot of maybes. Maybe you should hand Barkley off to some other lawyer, and talk to Meredith about what happened. See if you can work things out."

Hannah's idea sounded so simple, but Stevie had played through the various scenarios dozens of times. "If I claim a conflict now, no one in the public defender's office would be able to represent him, and Soloman would have to appoint some random lawyer on the wheel to take over. Emily would throw a fit because I swore I didn't have a conflict, and she could wind up taking it out on Barkley. Besides, Barkley only just started talking to me. I can't take the chance he'll clam up again if he gets assigned to someone new." What she didn't add was that the damage was done. If tonight's primary results were any indication, Meredith's bid to become the Democratic nominee was in serious jeopardy, and directly or not, she was to blame. Meredith might be able to find a way to win the nomination, but when it came to their relationship, it was over. So over.

❖

Meredith sat in her hotel suite in Miami and tried not to focus on the differences between tonight and the first Super Tuesday two weeks earlier, but the contrast was glaring. Jen was back in DC instead of at her side. There was a small bar service, but no champagne on ice. The mood in the room was somber, and although she knew they were trying to hide it, Gordon and the few campaign staffers—a much smaller crowd than usual—were having a whispered conversation about how to tweak her stump speech for tonight in light of the fact it looked like she was about to lose most of the primary elections that had been held today.

All of these things were bad, but when she added in the void left by Stevie's absence, she wanted to quit—the race, the senate, anything to do with public life—and retreat to her apartment in New York.

And then she remembered that wasn't a safe place either.

She hadn't stayed at her apartment since the night she'd spent with Stevie, but the memory of Stevie naked in her bed was still vivid in her mind, tugging at all the thoughts she had about duty and obligation, pulling strings from the tightly woven life she'd sewn together. What would have happened if Jen hadn't tipped off the press about Stevie? What if the majority leader hadn't called a vote that morning? She would've slept in with Stevie, perhaps making love to her again in the light of day, the two of them enjoying precious, uninterrupted time away from the demands of both their careers.

Maybe if they'd had more time together to lay a stronger foundation, Stevie wouldn't have broken things off. And if they were still together, then Stevie would've had to withdraw from William Barkley's case. And if she'd had to withdraw, then... *Then she would've resented you for having to compromise her career on your behalf.*

Meredith sighed. She knew it didn't matter who the defense attorney was on Barkley's case. The news about the connection to the Mitchell Foundation had been bound to come out. Better that someone with Stevie's integrity be involved with the case than a stranger who might have some political motive to take her down. Although it looked like she might be going down no matter what if tonight's results were any indication.

"They're about to call Illinois," one of the interns called out, pointing at the screen.

Meredith froze and stared at the TV, not wanting to look, but scared to shy away. This was the last race tonight, and the state had been heavily favored to go her way. If it didn't, she wasn't sure—

"You won!" yelled a voice from behind her, but she couldn't stop staring at the screen. It wasn't much—one state out of five—but it was better than a big fat zero for the night.

Gordon walked over to her side. "Illinois is a big deal."

"You're just saying that to try to pump me up."

He answered by clapping his hands together, loudly. "Rebecca, I need you to head to the press room." He handed her a sheet of paper. "Here are your talking points. Everyone else, clear out. I need a moment with the senator."

There was some mumbling as they filed out, but Meredith barely paid attention, relieved at the idea of being alone. Or at least somewhat alone. When the last person out shut the door, she collapsed on the couch. "I assume you want to go over the speech?"

He shook his head. "No speeches today. You'll make a brief statement downstairs, but first I have my own set of talking points just for you. Are you ready to hear them?"

"Sure. This night couldn't get much worse."

"Actually, you're wrong. You could've lost Illinois. And you might lose more states in the next few weeks. You still have several really big races ahead of you, including Washington, New York, Maryland, Pennsylvania, Wisconsin, and campaign donations are already under goal. If you lose the majority of these upcoming races, you're toast."

"Way to give a pep talk."

"You don't need a pep talk, what you need is a kick in the butt. Yes, you took a beating tonight, but in light of the recent news cycle, it could've been worse. And it could still get a lot worse unless you're willing to do what it takes to stop the bleeding. Right now."

Meredith sat up straight at the commanding tone in Gordon's voice. He was right, the road ahead was laced with pitfalls, but her life felt so out of control she wasn't sure how to maneuver around the obstacles and finish on top. "I'm listening."

"I have a plan, and it starts with us becoming a leaner and much more efficient operation. You're going to have a different stump speech for every city you visit over the course of the next month if we have to stay up round the clock to get them written. The press will have so many sound bites from you, they may have to add an extra hour to the day to stay current.

"You've been the frontrunner from the start, and there's a good reason for that, but it's time to pull off the gloves and go full force after Lankin's record. Let the voters know that you may have taken a hit in the news, but you're not going down without a fight."

Meredith stood and started pacing the room, energized by Gordon's speech. "Tell me what to do."

"I will, but first you have to answer one question."

"Ask away."

"Do you still want this?"

Meredith froze. The blunt question took her completely by surprise. Did she still want to be president? The abrupt breakup with Stevie, the steady stream of verbal attacks on her family, the inability to walk down the street without being swarmed by press all represented only a small taste of what was to come. If she won, she'd live the next four to eight years of her life surrounded by other people, but completely alone, with any chance at a personal life put on hold. A year ago, she wouldn't have cared, strong in the belief that government service was a calling, and it was her duty to make whatever sacrifices necessary to rise to the task, but that was before she'd gotten a glimpse of what it could be like to have a future with a smart, sexy woman who liked her in spite of her power and influence, not because of it. What would Stevie say right now if she asked her for advice?

The answer was clear, telegraphed in the way Stevie plowed ahead with the Barkley case, while never once giving an interview or otherwise divulging a word about the behind the scenes time they'd shared. Stevie was clearly fully focused on her career, and Meredith should follow her lead, sacrificing the personal life she wanted for the professional one that she was destined to fulfill, but she couldn't help but wonder why she couldn't have both.

CHAPTER TWENTY

July

Stevie adjusted the hard metal chair so she was closer to the computer screen, but she still couldn't tell what Barkley was working on. Emily had arranged for him to get extra time with a computer in the break room at the jail so he could examine the files that had been sent to his email account at Folsom in preparation for his testimony before the grand jury that would hear the case against the Mitchell Foundation. Yesterday, he'd summoned Stevie to the jail to show her what he'd found. So far, it was just a big jumble of nonsense.

"I heard she was your girlfriend," Barkley said.

Stevie cursed the day he'd decided to become talkative with her, and she feigned ignorance. "Who?"

"You know who. The future Madam President. She seems like a nice lady."

Stevie considered the description. Yes, Meredith was definitely nice, but that was not one of the descriptors she'd use. She'd tried to avoid seeing her, but every time she turned around, Meredith was on TV, in the paper, on the radio, and she was as attractive as ever, although slight bags under her eyes and a haggard expression were signs she was beginning to experience exhaustion. Meredith's presence had become even more prevalent this week since the Democratic National Convention was taking place in Baltimore. Some had speculated that Meredith would drop out of the race when the news of the investigation into her family's foundation came out followed by her stunning primary losses, but she'd stayed in and continued to fight for every delegate vote she could get, seemingly energized by her new role as the underdog. Neither she nor Lankin had a clear margin of victory going into this week, and some were predicting a brokered convention. The news outlets were eating it up with 24/7 analysis and predictions. For her part, Stevie was just glad they'd stopped talking about her for a while.

"Did you bring me here to talk about my personal life or did you really want to show me something?"

He motioned to the screen. "I'll walk you through it." He pointed. "See this code right here?"

"Yes."

"Those are the IP designators. When email comes into Folsom's system, it gets tagged with code indicating the time and date and origin of the sender."

"Like geographic location?"

"Kind of. We can backtrace what computer it comes from, using the IP address."

"Okay." Stevie didn't know where this was going, but Barkley seemed intent on explaining it a certain way, and she'd bear with it a bit longer.

"I looked at the source of the encrypted files and compared them to the designation information for the email addresses in the documents I leaked that got me in this mess to begin with." He paused to let that sink in. "There were several matches. Whoever sent me these files was one of the hackers that the government decided not to prosecute."

Stevie let the concepts rock around in her head for a minute. "So, you're saying that these hackers, who were peddling influence on social media with impunity, are the same ones who sent you information that supposedly connects them with the Mitchell Foundation?" When he nodded, she shrugged. "Is that really a revelation? I mean, it sounds like maybe they had it out for the Mitchells."

"Exactly. Why would they have it out for the Mitchells if the Mitchells were paying them to exert influence? It doesn't make any sense. The only motivation I can see for this 'anonymous' source to send me this information is to hope that I would release it and it would do damage to Mitchell's chances at the presidency."

"Well, here's another problem. They sent you this information about Meredith before she even entered the race. Seems like if their goal was to smear her campaign, they didn't do a good job of timing."

"Or did they? I follow the news even though I'm not dating the senator, and there was plenty of talk about Meredith getting into the race in the weeks before Armstrong's campaign went up in smoke. Maybe someone offered these people more money to release this information in the hope it would keep her from running at all. In any event, the revelations are doing damage now, so it was a win for whoever was behind this either way."

Stevie nodded. "Good point. I guess it doesn't really matter. If it's true the Mitchells hired these losers to do their bidding, then they should've been prepared for them to sell out to a higher bidder."

"But here's the thing. I'm not absolutely convinced the revelations are true." He pointed to another section of code that looked like gobbledygook. "I don't have the tools I need on this computer to properly analyze this, but someone should verify that these documents are authentic, because from what I can see, it looks like there are issues with the metadata. It's possible whoever the prosecutor used to do the analysis was in too big a hurry and didn't bother looking deeper when they spotted the info about the possible connection to the Mitchell Foundation."

"Wait a minute," Stevie said. "What do you mean, 'possible connection'?"

"I'm just saying this could fall under the category of fake news, and it's possible someone cooked this up to keep Mitchell out of the race or damage her chances. Like you said, if these hackers were hired by the Mitchells, why would they want to damage her chances unless someone came along willing to bid more money for their services to get a different result?" He shrugged. "Maybe all of it is a lie and the Mitchells didn't hire the hackers to begin with."

Fake news. Stevie hated the term, but she couldn't deny the jolt of excitement she got at the idea the Mitchells might not have done anything wrong, leaving Meredith in the clear. She'd certainly acted like an innocent person. Ever since someone had leaked the news just days after her initial meeting with Emily at Hannah's house, Meredith had fully cooperated with authorities, giving them full access to her personal and official email accounts, and publicly encouraging her family to do the same with the Foundation's records. Stevie couldn't help but notice that Jen seemed to have receded into a background role in Meredith's campaign. More than a few times since Super Tuesday II, she'd considered reaching out to Meredith to ask how she was doing, but this case and the residual pain of the rift between them kept her from reaching for the phone.

Barkley's voice broke through her thoughts. "How is this going to affect my plea deal?"

Legitimate question. This investigation had already netted big headlines, and there were plenty of people who expected Emily to deliver a big conviction of a high profile family, but the truth was the truth, and Barkley had done what was expected of him, no matter how the cards fell. "You let me worry about that. We have a deal and I'll make sure the government keeps their end of the bargain." If the Mitchells hadn't done anything wrong, someone had tried to set them up, and it was up to her to convince Emily to point her resources in a different direction. She told herself she wasn't doing it for Meredith's sake, but she couldn't help but feel relieved to be able to help her, even if Meredith could never know.

❖

Day Four of the Democratic National Convention

Meredith sat across from Jed Lankin in one of the conference rooms at the convention center, neither one of them saying a word. They were each flanked by their campaign managers, and Meredith was grateful for Gordon's calming presence, because she wanted to launch across the table and choke Lankin for all the hateful things he'd let his campaign say about her over the past few weeks.

In a couple of hours, the delegates were set to begin their third round of voting, and there was no indication the breakdown would be any more decisive than the rounds before. The White House had summoned them to this meeting, hoping for some kind of agreement to bring the party together, and they were waiting for someone from President Garrett's office to show up. When Julia Scott, the president's chief of staff, walked through the door, Meredith sighed with relief and shot a look at Gordon who raised his eyebrows.

Julia didn't waste any time. "Are we having fun yet? Because I'm here to tell you this is becoming a spectacle. Neither one of you are gaining anything by continuing to fight it out on national TV. Whoever walks out of this convention with the nomination is going to have to immediately start doing battle against Bosley," she said, referring to the Republican nominee, "and the less wounded you are, the better you'll be able to fight." She paused and looked back and forth between them. "Have you discussed merging your campaigns?"

The question was a nonstarter for Meredith. She and Lankin had way too many ideological differences for her to consider asking Lankin to be her running mate, and she'd rather drop out entirely than run as his VP.

"I'm open to the idea of having Ms. Mitchell on the ticket, but there would have to be certain concessions," Lankin said.

Meredith's temper flared. "Like walk ten steps behind you and never mention that I'm a lesbian?" She turned to Julia. "I know you came here to get us to work something out, but unless it involves Jed dropping out, then it's not going to happen." She pointed to the door. "This vote belongs to the delegates, and it's not up to us to take it out of their hands. Let them keep voting. Eventually, the tide will turn one way or another, but then we can all be sure that the process stayed democratic."

"If you think it's going to turn your way, you're wrong," Lankin spit out the words, no longer even trying to appear congenial. "Any day now there's going to be an indictment against your family's so-called nonprofit, and if you wind up getting the nomination before that happens, then we're all doomed. You should do us all a favor and pull out now."

Meredith seethed and started to fire off an icy retort, but Julia beat her too it.

"Actually, I have some news on that front. The attorney general just spoke with the prosecutor on the case, and it appears there have been some developments in the last couple of days. They've suspended their grand jury hearing and are now focusing their resources on other suspects."

Lankin's jaw dropped, and he engaged in a whispered conversation with his campaign manager. Meredith watched them for a second, and then stood. "It looks like we're headed for another round of voting. I, for one, am really looking forward to the outcome."

During primetime that evening, Meredith stood in the wings with Julia, watching the results of the latest round of voting being broadcast on the JumboTron hanging high above. Earlier, the evening news had run with the story that the federal prosecution against the Mitchell Foundation had been dropped, and the good news was reflected in the climbing delegate counts in her column. Gordon was in the press room, spinning talking points that would form the headlines for all the major news outlets if, as was expected, there was a Mitchell landslide tonight.

Julia leaned over and said, "Addison wishes she could be here with you for this."

"Tell her I said thanks, but I totally get it. Not good form for a supreme court justice to be picking sides."

"I think you know whose side she's on."

"I'm just grateful to still be in this race at all." Meredith watched the chair of the Texas delegation wave a Stetson in the air, and then cast all their votes in the Mitchell column. "Who do you think tried to smear me?"

"I don't know, but they're looking in several directions, including Bosley's campaign. He never wanted to come up against you. Hopefully, he wasn't that stupid, but if it wasn't him, then it might have been one of the PACs that supports him." She gave Meredith a knowing smile. "The AG's office is on this now. I'm confident they'll figure out who was responsible."

"Thank you. And thanks for being here tonight."

"Just supporting the future of our party."

"It's more than that, and you know it."

"True. Addison made me promise you wouldn't be without a friend when the results came in, good or bad, and she figured since I've been through this with other future presidents, I was the next best thing to her being here instead."

Meredith didn't have words to express her gratitude, so she squeezed Julia's hand. There was a sea of people around tonight, but like every race over the past six months, they would all be celebrating the victory for her party, and not her personal accomplishment. She hadn't wanted to be alone tonight. She'd dreaded it so bad, she'd almost texted Stevie several times, hoping against hope that enough time had passed for Stevie to forgive her and join her for this special night. But she'd stopped before sending any message. There was more to it now. She'd not only hurt Stevie, but there was the legal case too, and she knew Stevie well enough to know she wouldn't compromise her client with a conflict.

Like she could read her mind, Julia said, "You know, it was Stevie Palmer's client who unearthed the truth. Guy could've kept his mouth shut and let them indict you, but he dug a little deeper. I've got to think she may have been partly responsible for that."

Julia's words rang true, but Meredith wasn't sure of the implication. Stevie wouldn't have acted on her behalf if it meant a risk to her client, but perhaps the digging deeper was partly about her?

It didn't matter. It was nice to think Stevie cared enough to try to help her, but she would be foolish to make anything more out of Stevie's actions than that. She'd blown her chance, and all she could do was try to make something good come out of the mistake by serving her country as best she could.

CHAPTER TWENTY-ONE

Election Day

Hannah followed Stevie into her office. Where's your sticker?"

"Sticker?"

"You know, your 'I voted' sticker? I thought you were going to go by your polling place on the way into work."

Stevie forced a smile. She should be deliriously happy, like any other liberal in the country that the Democratic candidate had a solid lead in the polls, but she'd woken up today with a deep sense of melancholy. She was pretty sure it had something to do with seeing Meredith everywhere around her, but without any ability to make a connection. Pressing the button next to Meredith's name was the closest she could hope to get. She sat down behind her desk. "Trust me, I voted, but there was a line to get a sticker and I've got a lot to do today."

Hannah sat across from her and crossed her arms. "Right."

"What?"

"You seem a little down lately. We miss having you at the house. You should come over sometime."

Stevie nodded, but she didn't have any intention of inflicting her bad mood on her friends, so she kept her response vague. "Sure, let's plan something."

"I was hoping you'd say that. Dave's boss is a big Democrat donor, but he had to travel out of the country this week, so he gave us his tickets to the watch party at the Ritz. We can celebrate together."

"Yeah, no. I've got a lot of work to do."

"Tonight? The entire world's going to be watching the results of the election. It's history. No way are you going to work right through it. Besides this is the kind of experience you should share with your friends. There'll be lots of rich and famous people there, and did I mention these important two words? Open bar." Hannah slowly nodded her head. "Say yes."

Stevie didn't want to go. Not because she had work to do, but because everything about today felt off somehow. Like she'd had an opportunity to be part of history and she'd let it pass her by. All the reasons she'd broken up with Meredith had been valid at the time, but in hindsight, she wished she'd tried harder to get past her reservations. Meredith had been the one with the future of the Democratic Party on her back, not to mention the pressure to make history, but she'd been willing to try to make it work. Increasingly over the past few months, Stevie wished she'd given their relationship another chance.

But the window had closed on rekindling anything with Meredith. She'd seen Meredith on the news this morning, smiling for the cameras and casting her ballot in Manhattan. No doubt she was spending the day trying to relax while waiting for the polls to close, and likely failing miserably. Did she have her family with her or had she chosen to spend the day alone? None of these things were any of Stevie's business, but she was suddenly desperate to know the details of Meredith's life. She had to figure out a way to shake her malaise and move on with her life. Maybe the best way to do that was to try to get some closure. If she couldn't see Meredith in person, at least she could be on hand to witness her victory with a crowd of like-mind well-wishers. Before she could change her mind, she blurted out what Hannah wanted to hear. "Okay, I'll go."

❖

Meredith stepped into the back of the limo with Gordon close behind her, muttering about the time. "Quit griping at me. We're doing this," she told him. "One hour tops and then you can pull me out of the room and get me on a plane to New York."

That morning, she'd rolled out of her bed in Manhattan after a fitful night full of memories of the last time she'd spent the night there with Stevie by her side. She'd dutifully dressed in a navy blue suit with a flag lapel pin and walked to her polling place, flanked by her Secret Service detail. She cast her vote, smiled for the cameras, and returned home, where there was nothing left to do but wait. She'd called Gordon, who was handling last-minute details at her election office in DC, no less than a dozen times with suggestions and rumination about the campaign before it struck her that her restlessness wasn't only because of the impending results, but a factor of spending the day in her apartment where memories of the night she and Stevie had made love greeted her at every turn.

The only solution she could think of to stave off her melancholy was the tried and true solution of throwing herself into her work. Without giving Gordon any advanced notice, she'd notified her Secret Service detail that she'd be returning to the Capitol for the day, and she surprised the campaign team when she'd strolled into the DC office, asking for something to do. She made some phone calls, preemptively thanking many of her large donors, and she was between calls when one of the interns asked if she was going back to New York for the results or if she was going to join the local Democratic watch party. At first, she'd laughed off the naive question. Of course she'd be going back to her home state in keeping with tradition, but then she cornered Gordon and told him she planned to do both. He'd called the idea crazy at first, but she'd finally managed to persuade him to let her make a quick stop at the Ritz on her way back to Manhattan.

The convoy of cars pulled up to the service entrance at the hotel, and she tapped her foot impatiently while she waited for the agents in front to give the all clear. She sorely missed the days it was just her and Erica driving around town, no advance planning required.

The ballroom was already filling up despite the fact the polls on the East Coast wouldn't close for another hour. The presence of the Secret Service detail was creating a buzz in the room, and when Meredith waded into the crowd, everyone burst into applause and cheers. She wasn't sure what she'd expected, but any idea she'd simply shake a few hands and wander out vanished as the throng of high-dollar supporters started acting like high school students, snapping selfies with abandon. She smiled and posed and soaked up the good will, relieved to feel a kinship with these people who supported her with unabashed enthusiasm, but it wasn't until she looked across the room and locked eyes with the last person she'd expected to see at a Mitchell for President event that she felt truly connected to anyone in the room.

Gordon whispered something in her ear, but she didn't register his words. Her focus was entirely on Stevie, dressed in the vintage Dior suit she'd worn to Addison and Julia's wedding. Stevie raised the glass of champagne in her hand, a distant toast and a truce of sorts, and all the regret Meredith had felt earlier that day came rushing back.

"We better start making our way to the car," Gordon said. "It's going to be hard getting you out of here."

"I need a minute." She started to walk toward Stevie, but Gordon followed her gaze and pulled her back.

"Don't."

"Just a minute. I promise."

"Remember how angry you were when the press mobbed her before? It'll be ten times that if you make a beeline over there. Go to the car and I'll see if I can get her to meet you there, but promise me, you'll make it quick."

He was right. Her selfish desire to find some closure wasn't a good reason to put Stevie's privacy in jeopardy. She'd do as he asked and wait in the car, hoping he could convince Stevie to talk to her, and hoping she could figure out what to say.

❖

Stevie recognized the man staring her way as Meredith's campaign manager, and she looked over her shoulder as he approached, certain it couldn't be her he was coming to see. Meanwhile, Meredith had vanished into the exuberant crowd, and the room was buzzing with excitement that the top of the ticket candidate had stopped by to thank her key supporters.

"Ms. Palmer," the man said when he drew close. "I'm Gordon Hewitt, Ms. Mitchell's campaign manager. I wonder if I might have a word with you." He looked around. "Privately."

Stevie partly wished she'd joined Hannah and Dave at the bar, but her interest was piqued as to what Gordon could want with her. "Yes, but only for a moment. I'm here with friends."

He ushered her out a side door and walked down a long hallway dodging waiters with trays headed into the ballroom. She started to ask him where they were going, but he placed a finger over his lips and kept walking. Curiosity propelled her forward.

A moment later, he pushed open another door, and when they stepped outside, they were standing in a parking garage. Stevie heard a car engine come to life and spotted Meredith's face through the open window of an approaching limousine. She watched, transfixed, as the car drew closer, unable to take her eyes off Meredith, who looked more beautiful than ever. Until this moment, she hadn't truly realized how much she'd missed their connection, and when the car stopped in front of her, she didn't wait for an invitation before walking toward it.

"Come inside?" Meredith asked.

Stevie heard the trepidation in her voice, and she met it with definitive clarity. "Absolutely."

She climbed into the back of the limo and took a seat directly across from Meredith, facing the front of the car. The privacy shield was up, and she pointed toward it, looking for something to break the time and distance barrier between them. "Erica still driving you around?"

"I wish. I'm a hostage to Secret Service procedures. Bulletproof cars, constant surveillance, and only their drivers. She's working for my parents for a while until we find out which direction my life is headed. I didn't realize how much I'd miss her." Meredith gazed at the tinted window. "I didn't realize how much I'd miss you either."

"I miss you too." The words spilled out before Stevie could stop them. She'd had no time to prepare for this encounter, to steel her emotions against the onslaught of hope that things could be different between them. "This is a surprise."

"Seeing me here or missing me?"

Meredith's smile was teasing, playful, and Stevie couldn't help but grin in return. "Both?"

"I was getting antsy in New York. I'm pretty sure I'm not getting off on the right foot with my Secret Service detail by dragging them back and forth, but if I win, it's my last day of freedom for the next four years, and if I lose, well, then they can move on."

"Eight years."

"Excuse me?"

"*When* you win, you'll be on the hook for eight years, because unless you mess things up, you're definitely a two-term president. Count on it."

Meredith reached for her hand, and Stevie held on tight. "I heard it was your digging that unearthed the connection between Bosley and the smear campaign against me and my family."

Stevie shrugged, but she didn't let go. "My client did all the work. He thinks you're a nice lady."

"Well, that's one person who does."

"He's not the only one. Everyone's predicting a landslide tonight."

"I'm not talking about the election."

Stevie leaned forward and took both of Meredith's hands in hers. "You *are* a nice lady. You're a wonderful, kind, generous person who's given her entire life to public service. You deserve all the success you have coming to you, and what you've accomplished over the past year is incredible."

Meredith raised a hand and cupped Stevie's cheek. "Thank you for saying those things, but I have to say that I'm not entirely sure the sacrifice was worth it. It was easier when we were apart. I could tell myself the breakup was for the best. That you would be better off without my chaos in your life, and I'd be able to focus without you around. I don't think that's true anymore."

Stevie took a deep breath. Meredith's words tore at her heart. She wanted to tell her they should give it another shot, but while Meredith might have had an epiphany about how her choices affected Stevie's life, nothing had really changed. If Meredith won tonight, the tumult had only just begun. Stevie tried to imagine how a future would look, dating the president of the United States, but the details were a blur. She couldn't make it out of Senator Mitchell's New York apartment without a clandestine mission; what hoops would she have to jump through to go on a simple date with President Mitchell?

And it wasn't just her. When Meredith won the election, her life would become exponentially more complicated. Her Secret Service detail would triple in size and be with her for the rest of her life, seriously curtailing her privacy. She'd be on call 24/7, having to be ready to handle a world crisis with a moment's notice. She'd have no time for the distractions of dating even if they could find their way past all the complications. "The chaos isn't your fault. It just comes with the job, and—don't take this the wrong way—but you kind of thrive on it, and that's not a bad thing for someone about to be president." Stevie paused, searching for words. She'd argued her cases for her clients dozens of times, zealously advocating for whatever they needed, but in this moment, with her own future in the balance, she didn't have the heart to ask for more from Meredith, knowing it might ultimately tear them apart. "If we'd met another time, under different circumstances—"

Meredith didn't wait for her to finish, pulling her into a kiss. A deep, soul-searching kiss, and Stevie surrendered to it, unable to deny that while circumstances might be against them, their connection was undeniable.

The knocking noise was light at first, the kind you could ignore, but it grew more insistent, and Stevie, realizing someone was at the car window, murmured against Meredith's lips. "Should you get that?"

Meredith groaned and kissed her again, softer, lighter this time, before pressing the button to lower the window. Gordon was standing on the other side, pointing at his watch. "Way past five minutes," he said. Meredith answered him by pushing the button to raise the window.

Stevie watched the exchange, certain it was a microcosm of Meredith's personal life for the next four to eight years, and she knew in her heart it was time for her to go. She placed her hand on the door handle, but Meredith stopped her.

"Wait."

"You need to get to New York."

"I know."

Stevie wanted to kiss her again, one last time, but she wasn't sure she could walk away if she did. She had to stay strong because this could never work, and while she wished she'd known that all along, she didn't regret one moment of her time with Meredith. The kiss they'd just shared would be the memory she'd hold on to. She opened the door. "You're going to be great at this," she said. Not waiting for an answer, she stepped out of the car and walked away, wishing she had as much confidence in her own ability to adjust to a life without Meredith.

CHAPTER TWENTY-TWO

Inauguration Day

"If you keep pacing, you're going to wear out the floor."

Meredith paused and smiled at Addison who'd been standing off to the side, shaking her head. "I seriously doubt it. We're standing on marble." She resumed her pacing. "Are you telling me my nerves aren't justified?"

They were standing in the rotunda at the Capitol, and the inauguration ceremony was about to begin. Her family and friends were seated on the balcony, and people had been lining up in the plaza to get in since the night before to get a good seat or place to stand. Every last moment of this day had been choreographed in fine detail, and the Park Service was reporting a record crowd. All she had to do was place her hand on her leather-bound copy of the Constitution, repeat after Addison, and then she'd officially be the first woman president of the United States. Nothing to it. "Oh, wait, you've done this before. This must be old hat to you."

"Once, and I was the swearer, not the swearee," Addison said. "Or was it the other way around?" She shrugged. "All I know is I have no idea how you're feeling right now, but I can promise you two things."

"Spill."

"First, everyone who has stepped out onto that dais to take the oath is as nervous as you. Trust me, Garrett was jittery as hell, and it was his second time."

"And the second thing?"

"You're going to be the best damn president in our lifetime. I have absolutely no doubt."

Meredith grinned. "Remember that when you think about ruling against my administration on a future case."

Addison returned the grin. "Good presidents know about the balance of power."

"Touché. Not to worry. I wouldn't take advantage of our friendship."

"I know. It's kind of an unusual situation. President and chief justice of the United States as best friends. I anticipate some people will try to manufacture conflict about it."

"True, but we'll work it out," Meredith said, confident in her assessment.

"Speaking of working it out, have you talked to Stevie lately?"

"You're going to need to work on being a little more subtle. I guess Julia told you I put her on the list for today."

"She may have mentioned something about how you asked her to send Stevie an engraved invitation to the inauguration ceremony and the balls."

"Do you guys share everything?"

"Most things. When that balance of power thing isn't in the way."

"And it works?"

"Anything can work if you want it to badly enough. Is it ideal for me to be married to the president's chief of staff? No, but I'm in love with Julia, and when you feel that way about someone, you don't let anything get in the way."

"Erica checked the crowd on the balcony. Stevie didn't show."

"Maybe an engraved invitation to a party attended by a couple million of your closet friends wasn't the best way to let her know you're in love with her."

Addison's words hit her like a strong wind, and Meredith took a step back to assess the change in atmosphere. Was she in love with Stevie? She wasn't sure, but if she was it would explain her unrelenting and inexplicable despondency since election night, and her inability to get Stevie out of her mind. "I've botched this from the get-go. What am I going to do?"

Addison linked arms with her and led her toward the balcony. She swept her hand out across the open space and said, "Today, you're going to walk out there in front of all these people who love and support you, take the oath of office, and become president of the most powerful country in the world. You're going to celebrate with your friends and family. You're going to be the belle of ten, count 'em, ten inaugural balls. And tomorrow, your first order of business is to reach out to Stevie. No subtle gestures, no crowds of people. You'll have the resources of the entire government at your disposal. Surely, you can figure out a way to get a girl alone and tell her how you feel."

Meredith felt the weight of her worry fall away as she took in Addison's advice, and for the first time in her life she thought she actually could have it all. All she had to do was convince Stevie they could have it all together. First thing tomorrow, she would make it her mission to win Stevie back, but right now, she had an oath to take.

"I do solemnly swear that I will faithfully execute the Office of President of the United States…"

❖

"…and will to the best of my ability, preserve, protect and defend the Constitution of the United States."

Stevie applauded with the rest of her coworkers as they watched Meredith take her oath on the balcony of the Capitol. It seemed surreal to think Meredith was less than a mile away. She might as well be in outer space. As Meredith walked to the podium to deliver her inauguration address, Stevie turned away to head back to her office. She'd felt compelled to watch Meredith take the oath—it was a historic moment—but she couldn't handle watching her for an extended length of time without feeling a vast emptiness inside.

Hannah walked alongside her. "You could be there, right now."

"It's too late. Besides, I threw the invitation away."

"No, you didn't." Hannah looked slightly sheepish when Stevie stared her down. "I may have spotted it when I was picking the Brewer file up off your desk earlier." She raised her hands. "Don't be mad. I'm just saying that you could still go if you wanted."

Stevie walked into her office and fished the invitation from underneath the files on her desk. The beautifully engraved card promised her full VIP access to all the Inauguration Day festivities and admission to the balls scheduled for that evening. At the bottom of the card, in flowing fountain pen script were the words, *I'd love to see you. M.* She held up the card. "Did you read it?"

"Maybe." Hannah hung her head. "Okay, I devoured it. She invited you to everything. That pass gets you into all ten inaugural balls. Hasn't it occurred to you that she really wants to see you?"

"It has."

"Do you want to see her?"

Stevie considered the question. "Seeing" Meredith was easy these days. Images of her were everywhere from the television to newspapers to the vendors on the streets hawking T-shirts emblazoned with her picture. "I'm not going to see her if I go. I mean not really. I'd be better off watching her on television."

"Way to avoid the question, counselor. Do you want to see her? In person?" Hannah waved the invite in the air. "Because I'm thinking there aren't a lot of these golden tickets handed out, especially not ones with personal inscriptions, which tells me she'd like to *see* you."

Hannah was crazy, but maybe she was also right. "I can't go alone."

"Yes, you can."

"I don't have anything to wear."

"Are you seriously saying that to me?" Hannah rolled her index finger. "Spin for me."

Stevie narrowed her eyes but obeyed.

"Okay, you can turn back around. I have the perfect outfit for you."

❖

Hours later, Stevie stepped out of the cab and glanced around. She'd chosen the Commander-in-Chief Ball for her grand gesture. It was being held at the National Building Museum where Addison and Julia had gotten married, and Stevie thought a familiar setting would bolster her courage. But now that she was here, she was having second thoughts about coming at all. Everywhere she looked she saw tuxes, ball gowns, and limousines. She looked up the steps that led to the building, and then down at her dress, a borrowed De La Renta, and she felt like Cinderella, faking it for a few hours until her ball gown turned to tatters and she ran off with only one shoe. At least the last time she'd been here, she'd been with Princess Charming. This time Meredith would be surrounded by all her supporters. She'd be celebrating her victory, as she should, and she would have no time to talk, let alone intimately. Stevie cursed Hannah for talking her into this.

I'd love to see you.

Stevie replayed the words in her head, over and over, hoping the message was more than a simple courtesy.

"Stevie?"

She started at the sound of her name and looked up to see Colonel Zoey Granger and Rook Daniels walking toward her. They looked dashing, Zoey in her dress blues and Rook in a sleek black tux with white tie. Of course they'd be at this ball that honored members of the military, and Stevie was relieved to see familiar faces. "Hi," she said. "I was just…" She wasn't sure how to finish the sentence. "Going to run away" didn't seem like something she should say out loud. Thankfully, Zoey took charge.

"Are you here by yourself? Join us." Zoey motioned for her to walk with them.

Relieved to have the decision made for her, Stevie followed them up the steps of the building, but she was completely unprepared for the spectacle inside. The wedding had been large by any scale, but even so, it had not taken up the entire space. Tonight, flags were draped from all the balconies, and the main floor was packed, wall-to-wall with soldiers in uniform raising glasses of champagne and spontaneously cheering. In the front of the room, where Addison and Julia had tied the knot, there was a dance floor, with the Marine Corps Band on one side and an elevated stage on the other. Stevie squinted at the singer on stage. "Is that Janelle Monáe?"

"It is indeed," Rook said. "The president is a big fan."

Stevie felt a jolt at the words, "the president." Even though she knew that's what Meredith was now, hearing one of her friends call her that brought home the reality full force, and she started to lose her nerve. Scrambling to think of a way to duck out, she said, "I'm going to find the rest room."

But before she could step away, the music stopped and the crowd stilled. Out of the silence came a loud voice announcing, "Ladies and gentlemen, presenting the President of the United States," followed by the familiar strains of "Hail to the Chief." Like the rest of the crowd, she stood transfixed as Meredith entered the room, alternately shaking hands and waving to the crowd. She was gorgeous in an off the shoulder red ball gown, and Stevie was paralyzed with desire as she watched Meredith make her way through the throng of admirers.

"She looks great, don't you think?"

Stevie reluctantly pulled her gaze away from Meredith to turn around. Addison was the one who had spoken, and she was standing with her arm around Julia, next to Rook and Zoey. "She is absolutely stunning," Stevie said before she could censor her response into something a bit more reserved. She could feel the smile stretch across her face and she let the happiness of seeing Meredith in person flood her with courage. To hell with it. She wasn't going to duck out. She was going to stand here with Meredith's friends, certain she would stop to greet them, and tell Meredith she'd come here for her, convince her to give them a second chance.

Seconds later, Meredith was standing in front of them, smiling, and her gaze was a laser beam, tracking only her. Stevie stood back as each of Meredith's friends hugged and congratulated her, knowing she would have her turn, and willing to wait for what she now knew without a doubt she wanted. When Meredith stepped close, Stevie pulled her into an embrace.

"I'm so glad you came," Meredith whispered in her ear. "I was afraid you wouldn't."

"I couldn't stay away." Stevie inhaled the scent of her, drinking in the reality of Meredith in her arms and vowing not to let go. "I'm sorry I ever left."

"I had big plans of using my newfound power to find you and convince you to give us another chance. It was going to be my first official action."

"Is that so?"

"A girl's got to do what a girl's got to do."

"And a president probably shouldn't be throwing her weight around to get a girlfriend on her first day in office."

Meredith's smile was broad. "Girlfriend? I like the sound of that."

Stevie returned the smile. "Me too. A lot." She cast a quick look around. "You'd probably better finish making the rounds or people will start to talk."

Meredith held out a hand and motioned to the dance floor. "How about we give them something to talk about?" She quickly added, "No pressure, we can—"

Stevie cut her off. "If you're asking me to dance, the answer's yes. And for the record, Madam President, you can ask me pretty much anything tonight and get that answer."

Stevie followed Meredith to the dance floor where they stood on the big presidential seal and waved to a cheering crowd. When Janelle started singing, the cheers died down, and it was just the two of them, gliding across the floor to the soaring funk ballad, as if there was no one else in the room.

When the song came to an end, Meredith pulled Stevie into her arms. Stevie held her breath, knowing that Meredith would need to leave their bubble, make the rounds, and fulfill her duties, but dreading it all the same. But when Meredith spoke, she said, "I want to dance like that with you for the rest of our lives. I love you, Stevie."

This was it. The time to leap into a life she hadn't expected with a woman she adored, or let the past keep her from the love this amazing woman had to offer. The decision was straightforward, easy, and clear. Eyes wide open, she took the jump. "I love you too. Let's never stop dancing."

THE END

About the Author

Carsen Taite's goal as an author is to spin tales with plot lines as interesting as the cases she encountered in her career as a criminal defense lawyer. She is the award-winning author of numerous novels of romance and romantic intrigue, including the Luca Bennett Bounty Hunter series, the Lone Star Law series, and the upcoming Legal Affairs romances.

Books Available from Bold Strokes Books

A Wish Upon a Star by Jeannie Levig. Erica Cooper has learned to depend on only herself, but when her new neighbor, Leslie Raymond, befriends Erica's special needs daughter, the walls protecting her heart threaten to crumble. (978-1-163555-274-4)

Answering the Call by Ali Vali. Detective Sept Savoie returns to the streets of New Orleans, as do the dead bodies from ritualistic killings, and she does everything in her power to bring them to justice while trying to keep her partner, Keegan Blanchard, safe. (978-1-163555-050-4)

Breaking Down Her Walls by Erin Zak. Could a love worth staying for be the key to breaking down Julia Finch's walls? (978-1-63555-369-7)

Exit Plans for Teenage Freaks by 'Nathan Burgoine. Cole always has a plan—especially for escaping his small-town reputation as "that kid who was kidnapped when he was four"—but when he teleports to a museum, it's time to face facts: it's possible he's a total freak after all. (978-1-163555-098-6)

Flight to the Horizon by Julie Tizard. Airline Captain Kerri Sullivan and flight attendant Janine Case struggle to survive an emergency water landing and overcome dark secrets to give love a chance to fly. (978-1-163555-331-4)

Friends Without Benefits by Dena Blake. When Dex Putman gets the woman she thought she always wanted, she soon wonders if it's really love after all. (978-1-163555-349-9)

Invalid Evidence by Stevie Mikayne. Private Investigator Jil Kidd is called away to investigate a possible killer whale, just when her partner Jess needs her most. (978-1-163555-307-9)

Pursuit of Happiness by Carsen Taite. When attorney Stevie Palmer's client reveals a scandal that could derail Senator Meredith Mitchell's presidential bid, their chance at love may be collateral damage. (978-1-163555-044-3)

Seascape by Karis Walsh. Marine biologist Tess Hansen returns to Washington's isolated northern coast where she struggles to adjust to small-town living while courting an endowment for her orca research center from Brittany James. (978-1-163555-079-5)

Second in Command by VK Powell. Jazz Perry's life is disrupted and her career jeopardized when she becomes personally involved with the case of an abandoned child and the child's competent but strict social worker, Emory Blake. (978-1-163555-185-3)

Taking Chances by Erin McKenzie. When Valerie Cruz and Paige Wellington clash over what's in the best interest of the children in Valerie's care, the children may be the ones who teach them it's worth taking chances for love. (978-1-163555-209-6)

All of Me by Emily Smith. When chief surgical resident Galen Burgess meets her new intern, Rowan Duncan, she may finally discover that doing what you've always done will only give you what you've always had. (978-1-163555-321-5)

As the Crow Flies by Karen F. Williams. Romance seems to be blooming all around, but problems arise when a restless ghost emerges from the ether to roam the dark corners of this haunting tale. (978-1-163555-285-0)

Both Ways by Ileandra Young. SPEAR agent Danika Karson races to protect the city from a supernatural threat and must rely on the woman she's trained to despise: Rayne, an achingly beautiful vampire. (978-1-163555-298-0)

Calendar Girl by Georgia Beers. Forced to work together, Addison Fairchild and Kate Cooper discover that opposites really do attract. (978-1-163555-333-8)

Lovebirds by Lisa Moreau. Two women from different worlds collide in a small California mountain town, each with a mission that doesn't include falling in love. (978-1-163555-213-3)

Media Darling by Fiona Riley. Can Hollywood bad girl Emerson and reluctant celebrity gossip reporter Hayley work together to make each other's dreams come true? Or will Emerson's secrets ruin not one career, but two? (978-1-163555-278-2)

Stroke of Fate by Renee Roman. Can Sean Moore live up to her reputation and save Jade Rivers from the stalker determined to end Jade's career and, ultimately, her life? (978-1-163555-162-4)

The Rise of the Resistance by Jackie D. The soul of America has been lost for almost a century. A few people may be the difference between a phoenix rising to save the masses or permanent destruction. (978-1-163555-259-1)

The Sex Therapist Next Door by Meghan O'Brien. At the intersection of sex and intimacy, anything is possible. Even love. (978-1-163555-296-6)

Unexpected Lightning by Cass Sellars. Lightning strikes once more when Sydney and Parker fight a dangerous stranger who threatens the peace they both desperately want. (978-1-163555-276-8)

Unforgettable by Elle Spencer. When one night changes a lifetime… Two romance novellas from best-selling author Elle Spencer. (978-1-63555-429-8)

Against All Odds by Kris Bryant, Maggie Cummings, M. Ullrich. Peyton and Tory escaped death once, but will they survive when Bradley's determined to make his kill rate one hundred percent? (978-1-163555-193-8)

Autumn's Light by Aurora Rey. Casual hookups aren't supposed to include romantic dinners and meeting the family. Can Mat Pero see beyond the heartbreak that led her to keep her worlds so separate, and will Graham Connor be waiting if she does? (978-1-163555-272-0)

Breaking the Rules by Larkin Rose. When Virginia and Carmen are thrown together by an embarrassing mistake they find out their stubborn determination isn't so heroic after all. (978-1-163555-261-4)

Broad Awakening by Mickey Brent. In the sequel to *Underwater Vibes*, Hélène and Sylvie find ruts in their road to eternal bliss. (978-1-163555-270-6)

Broken Vows by MJ Williamz. Sister Mary Margaret must reconcile her divided heart or risk losing a love that just might be heaven sent. (978-1-163555-022-1)

Flesh and Gold by Ann Aptaker. Havana, 1952, where art thief and smuggler Cantor Gold dodges gangland bullets and mobsters' schemes while she searches Havana' s steamy Red Light district for her kidnapped love. (978-1-163555-153-2)

Isle of Broken Years by Jane Fletcher. Spanish noblewoman Catalina de Valasco is in peril, even before the pirates holding her for ransom sail into seas destined to become known as the Bermuda Triangle. (978-1-163555-175-4)

Love Like This by Melissa Brayden. Hadley Cooper and Spencer Adair set out to take the fashion world by storm. If only they knew their hearts were about to be taken. (978-1-163555-018-4)

Secrets On the Clock by Nicole Disney. Jenna and Danielle love their jobs helping endangered children, but that might not be enough to stop them from breaking the rules by falling in love. (978-1-163555-292-8)

Unexpected Partners by Michelle Larkin. Dr. Chloe Maddox tries desperately to deny her attraction for Detective Dana Blake as they flee from a serial killer who's hunting them both. (978-1-163555-203-4)

A Fighting Chance by T. L. Hayes. Will Lou be able to come to terms with her past to give love a fighting chance? (978-1-163555-257-7)

Chosen by Brey Willows. When the choice is adapt or die, can love save us all? (978-1-163555-110-5)

Death Checks In by David S. Pederson. Despite Heath's promises to Alan to not get involved, Heath can't resist investigating a shopkeeper's murder in Chicago, which dashes their plans for a romantic weekend getaway. (978-1-163555-329-1)

Gnarled Hollow by Charlotte Greene. After they are invited to study a secluded nineteenth-century estate, a former English professor and a group of historians discover that they will have to fight against the unknown if they have any hope of staying alive. (978-1-163555-235-5)

Jacob's Grace by C.P. Rowlands. Captain Tag Becket wants to keep her head down and her past behind her, but her feelings for AJ's second-in-command, Grace Fields, makes keeping secrets next to impossible. (978-1-163555-187-7)

On the Fly by PJ Trebelhorn. Hockey player Courtney Abbott is content with her solitary life until visiting concert violinist Lana Caruso makes her second-guess everything she always thought she wanted. (978-1-163555-255-3)

Passionate Rivals by Radclyffe. Professional rivalry and long-simmering passions create a combustible combination when Emmett McCabe and Sydney Stevens are forced to work together, especially when past attractions won't stay buried. (978-1-163555-231-7)

Proxima Five by Missouri Vaun. When geologist Leah Warren crash-lands on a preindustrial planet and is claimed by its tyrant, Tiago, will clan warrior Keegan's love for Leah give her the strength to defeat him? (978-1-163555-122-8)

Racing Hearts by Dena Blake. When you cross a hot-tempered race car mechanic with a reckless cop, the result can only be spontaneous combustion. (978-1-163555-251-5)

Shadowboxer by Jessica L. Webb. Jordan McAddie is prepared to keep her street kids safe from a dangerous underground protest group, but she isn't prepared for her first love to walk back into her life. (978-1-163555-267-6)

The Tattered Lands by Barbara Ann Wright. As Vandra and Lilani strive to make peace, they slowly fall in love. With mistrust and murder surrounding them, only their faith in each other can keep their plan to save the world from falling apart. (978-1-163555-108-2)

Captive by Donna K. Ford. To escape a human trafficking ring, Greyson Cooper and Olivia Danner become players in a game of deceit and violence. Will their love stand a chance? (978-1-63555-215-7)

Crossing the Line by CF Frizzell. The Mob discovers a nemesis within its ranks, and in the ultimate retaliation, draws Stick McLaughlin from anonymity by threatening everything she holds dear. (978-1-63555-161-7)

Love's Verdict by Carsen Taite. Attorneys Landon Holt and Carly Pachett want the exact same thing: the only open partnership spot at their prestigious criminal defense firm. But will they compromise their careers for love? (978-1-63555-042-9)

Precipice of Doubt by Mardi Alexander & Laurie Eichler. Can Cole Jameson resist her attraction to her boss, veterinarian Jodi Bowman, or will she risk a workplace romance and her heart? (978-1-63555-128-0)

Savage Horizons by CJ Birch. Captain Jordan Kellow's feelings for Lt. Ali Ash have her past and future colliding, setting in motion a series of events that strands her crew in an unknown galaxy thousands of light years from home. (978-1-63555-250-8)

Secrets of the Last Castle by A. Rose Mathieu. When Elizabeth Campbell represents a young man accused of murdering an elderly woman, her investigation leads to an abandoned plantation that reveals many dark Southern secrets. (978-1-63555-240-9)

Take Your Time by VK Powell. A neurotic parrot brings police officer Grace Booker and temporary veterinarian Dr. Dani Wingate together in the tiny town of Pine Cone, but their unexpected attraction keeps the sparks flying. (978-1-63555-130-3)

The Last Seduction by Ronica Black. When you allow true love to elude you once and you desperately regret it, are you brave enough to grab it when it comes around again? (978-1-63555-211-9)

The Shape of You by Georgia Beers. Rebecca McCall doesn't play it safe, but when sexy Spencer Thompson joins her workout class, their non-stop sparring forces her to face her ultimate challenge—a chance at love. (978-1-63555-217-1)